MURDER IN THE MORNING

When the car in front of Charlotte turned off to the side street that the officer was pointing toward, Charlotte was finally able to drive her van closer. She rolled down her window, stopped, then signaled that she wanted to talk to the officer. At first, he resisted and continued motioning for her to move along. But Charlotte could be stubborn, too, and she refused to move, finally forcing the man to walk over to her van.

"Ma'am, you have to keep moving."

"I want to know what's happened."

He firmly shook his head. "This is police business. You have to keep moving," he repeated.

"But Officer, I work for the Dubuissons." She pointed to the house. "Please, can't you tell me what's going on?"

The obstinate man shook his head again. "All I can tell you is there's been a break-in and a murder."

Charlotte gasped as the meaning of the officer's words sank in. A break-in and a murder? At the Dubuissons?

Icy fear twisted around her heart as the faces of Jeanne, Clarice, Anna-Maria, and Jackson flashed through her mind . . .

Books by Barbara Colley

MAID FOR MURDER

DEATH TIDIES UP

Published by Kensington Publishing Corporation

MAID FOR MURDER

BARBARA COLLEY

KENSINGTON BOOKS
Kensington Publishing Corp.
http://www.kensingtonbooks.com

In loving memory of my father, Charles Logan

ACKNOWLEDGMENTS

I would like to express my heartfelt thanks to my agent, Evan Marshall, for his unfailing support, encouragement, and inspiration.

My sincere thanks and appreciation to all who gave me information and advice while I was writing this book: my editor, John Scognamiglio, my wonderful daughter-in-law, Ann-Marie Colley, my good friends and fellow writers Rexanne Becnel, Marie Goodwin, Karen Young, Meagan McKinney, and Jessica Ferguson. Their enthusiasm and encouragement have been priceless.

To O'Neil De Noux, crime writer extraordinaire, and to Officer Haynes Ragas and the Sixth District New Orleans Police Department: thank you for your generosity and for sharing your time as well as your knowledge of police procedures. Any mistakes made or liberties taken in the name of fiction are solely my own.

Last, but never least, a loving thanks to my husband, David, for everything.

Chapter One

"Nadia, it's okay. Just calm down, hon." Charlotte La-
Rue spoke softly into the telephone receiver as she
interrupted the young woman's tearful tirade. "Believe me, I
understand. I really do," she stressed. "Little Davy has to
come first, and you can't help it if he's ill. But Nadia, dear,
just this once, couldn't Ricco take him to the doctor? I know
you need the money, and this will make two days this week
you've had to miss work."

Charlotte drummed her fingers on the desktop while she
listened to Nadia's string of excuses why her unemployed
live-in boyfriend didn't have the time to take his own son to
the doctor or stay with him that day.

With a sigh of frustration, Charlotte glanced at the clock
on the wall. In spite of the clock being a silly cuckoo that
she'd picked up on a whim at a flea market, it kept excellent
time. And according to the time showing, she was going to
be late if she didn't leave soon.

"Hmm, I see," Charlotte finally told Nadia, though she
really didn't understand at all. "Don't cry, now. I'm sure

things will work out. Just take care of that sweet little boy and let me know when you're free to work again."

Charlotte hung up the receiver and made a silent vow to have a real heart-to-heart talk with Nadia about her freeloading boyfriend. Charlotte had met Ricco Martinez on several occasions, and nothing about the man had impressed her. In Charlotte's opinion, the only reason Ricco Martinez stayed around was for the free room and board.

She'd often wondered why Nadia continued to put up with him, but the only conclusion she'd come to was that Nadia had convinced herself she was doing it for Davy's sake. What the younger woman didn't realize, though, and what Charlotte knew from her own personal experience, was if a boy was given enough love and attention, he could grow up just fine without a father, especially a no-account father like Ricco.

Yes, she decided. She definitely needed to have that heart-to-heart talk with the younger woman.

Charlotte flipped through the Rolodex near the phone and finally located the phone number of Janet Davis, one of the three women Charlotte employed on a temporary basis.

Janet answered on the third ring. "This is Charlotte, Janet. I'm so glad I caught you at home. I apologize for such short notice, but I hope you're free to work today."

Janet said she was free, and Charlotte quickly gave her the address of the client's home. "And Janet, Mrs. Dufore likes the ceiling fans dusted each time we clean her house. There's a small ladder in the downstairs storage closet you can use. She's also very particular about the shower in the master bath. Make sure you get rid of all the soap scum, especially around the drain."

Charlotte ended the conversation, grabbed her purse, and fished out the keys to her van. "Thank God it's Friday," she muttered.

Satisfied that yet another crisis had been averted and with

one last glance at the phone as if daring it to ring again, she headed for the front door. "Bye-bye, Sweety Boy," she called over her shoulder. "Be a good little bird today and I'll see you later."

From his cage near the front window, the little parakeet's answer was to burst into a series of chirps and whistles that made Charlotte smile as she pulled the front door firmly shut behind her, then locked it.

The small Victorian shotgun double that Charlotte lived in was located on Milan Street, just blocks away from the exclusive, historic New Orleans Garden District. The hundred-year-old double had been inherited by Charlotte and her younger sister, Madeline, after their parents' untimely deaths, and each half included a living room, a dining room, a kitchen, two bedrooms, and a bath.

Unlike her sister, though, who had long ago sold her half of the double to Charlotte right after her first marriage, Charlotte had never felt the urge or the need to live anywhere else.

To Charlotte, the old Victorian double was more than just the home in which she'd grown up and raised her son. The location was perfect for her thriving, sometimes hectic cleaning service, since all of her clients lived in the Garden District.

Over the years, she'd thought about branching out, expanding her business to other parts of the city, but when it came right down to it, she couldn't imagine working anywhere else.

The old-world ambience of the Garden District, with its many huge, imposing mansions, several well over a century old, was like taking a step back in time. She loved everything about the unique neighborhood—its narrow streets and hundred-year-old moss-draped oaks that shaded them, the brick sidewalks, the formal gardens, lush with ferns, azaleas, palms, and other subtropical vegetation.

Compared to the rest of New Orleans, living near and working in the Garden District was like taking a breath of country air.

Traffic wasn't too bad until Charlotte reached the intersection of Milan and Magazine streets. Turning left onto Magazine was always tricky under the best of circumstances at that time of morning, for there was no traffic light and most of the traffic on the right side was flowing toward downtown. To make matters worse, a large delivery van was parked on the corner, effectively blocking sight of the oncoming vehicles.

When several minutes passed and traffic hadn't budged, Charlotte knew she was in trouble. She glanced around, looking for an alternative route, then groaned. Ordinarily, she could have taken one of the many side streets and avoided the congested area, but the closest one was blocked off by a crew from the Sewerage and Water Board, patching yet another part of the century-old underground drainage system.

In the thirty-plus years since she'd founded Maid-for-a-Day, she'd always prided herself on being thorough and punctual, something that she absolutely insisted on from the two full-time and three part-time women she employed. The one thing customers hated most besides a sloppy cleaning job was having to wait for the maid to show up. Thanks to Nadia, today looked as if it were going to be one of the rare exceptions to her rule.

Charlotte reached for her cell phone and punched out the number of her client, Jeanne Dubuisson. A bit embarrassed, she explained that she was stuck in traffic and would probably be a few minutes late.

By the time Charlotte parked her van on the street that ran alongside the nineteenth-century Greek Revival mansion belonging to the Dubuissons, she noted that even with the last-minute crisis with Nadia and the snarl of work traffic, she was only a few minutes later than normal. Not that Jeanne had any particular place to go. Certainly not to an outside job.

Jeanne St. Martin Dubuisson was wealthy in her own right, having come from an old, established New Orleans family, but Jackson, Jeanne's husband, was also one of the city's most prestigious attorneys. Jeanne could well afford to simply do nothing. If not for her invalid mother, she might have been tempted to join her socially prominent contemporaries who spent their days running from one luncheon to another or heading up notable charitable committees.

Charlotte preferred to use her own cleaning supplies when servicing a customer. From the back of the van, she selected the various cleaners and waxes she would need and placed them in the special carrier she used. She would have to make another trip later for the vacuum cleaner.

After locking the van, she approached the fence that fronted the Dubuissons' house. Made of cast iron and designed in the traditional cornstalk pattern, as opposed to the simpler wrought-iron designs, the fence was typical and almost exclusive to the Garden District. Beside the latch on the double-wide gate was a buzzer that Charlotte pushed. After several minutes, the lock clicked, and she opened the gate.

There were eight steps leading up to the lower gallery that bordered three sides of the old mansion. Charlotte paused on the seventh step.

"Now that's odd," she murmured as she turned her head slowly from one side to the other, her eagle eyes following the trail of debris that had been tracked across the normally fastidiously clean porch. Dried leaves, grass, and dirt left a trail clear across the porch, the same type of debris that she'd swept away on Wednesday, when she'd cleaned.

Oh, well, she thought. Nothing to do but sweep it all up again. Still puzzling about the scattered debris, Charlotte jumped when the front door suddenly swung open.

"Why, Miss Anna," she exclaimed. "What on earth are you doing home?"

Twenty-year-old Anna-Maria Dubuisson was willowy thin, with shoulder-length blond hair and startling green eyes, startling and exotic because of their deep emerald color, fringed by thick, sooty lashes. She was also tall, several inches taller than Charlotte's petite height of five feet three. In the six years that Charlotte had worked for the Dubuissons, she'd watched the gangly teenager grow into one of the most beautiful young women she'd ever met.

Charlotte narrowed her eyes. "I thought there was still another week before spring break."

Anna-Maria flashed her a mischievous smile. "Don't tell Mother," she said softly, "but I skipped out. She thinks I got special permission to leave early." She shrugged in a dismissive gesture. "I just had to come home, though. James's father is giving a small, intimate party tomorrow night for just family and a few select friends. James thinks that's it's a celebration for his sister." She lowered her voice. "It's all hush-hush, but he's pretty sure that Laura has been chosen as one of the maids for Rex next year, maybe even queen." Her eyes widened. "Can you imagine being Queen of Carnival?"

James Doucet was Anna-Maria's fiancé, and it came as no surprise to Charlotte that James's sister might be chosen as a maid or even queen. Since James's father, Vincent Doucet, had reigned as Rex several years back and was prominent in the Krewe of Rex, it was logical that his daughter would be in line for such an honor.

"Since I don't have a thing to wear," Anna-Maria continued, "I came home early to shop." She glanced at her watch. "Oh, shoot, I'm already late. Got to run." She laughed, and with a small flutter of her fingers, she waved as she hurried past Charlotte. "I'm meeting Laura for breakfast; then it's shop till we drop. Oh, and by the way," she called out, "I love your new hairstyle."

Charlotte reached up self-consciously and smoothed back a strand of hair as she watched Anna-Maria skip down the front steps and disappear around the side of the house toward the driveway. Charlotte usually preferred a shorter, no-nonsense style, but it had been a while since she'd had time to get a haircut, and her hair had grown out longer than she normally wore it. Still, if Anna-Maria liked it a bit longer . . . maybe . . .

"Don't be ridiculous," she muttered. She wasn't some silly schoolgirl who had all the time in the world to fool with fixing her hair. Shorter hair was much more practical. Besides, she should just be thankful that she didn't have to bother with getting it colored as well as cut. She considered herself fortunate indeed that what little gray she had still blended with the honey-brown color.

Within moments, Charlotte heard the roar of a car engine come to life. When she turned back toward the door, Jeanne Dubuisson, dressed in a long silk robe and matching slippers, was standing in the doorway.

Unlike Anna-Maria, Jeanne's eyes were blue. Otherwise, in looks, she was simply an older version of her daughter. But in temperament, whereas Anna-Maria was still outgoing and passionate about life, Jeanne possessed a quiet, ageless sophistication that could only be acquired with maturity and time.

"Good morning," she said to Charlotte, sparing her a brief glance and polite smile. At that moment, her daughter's bright red Bimmer Roadster shot out of the driveway and into the street. Jeanne focused a hungry gaze on the retreating sports car. "She thinks I don't know that she's playing hooky, and I guess I should be upset with her. It's just that I miss her so when she's away," she said, her soft voice tinged with sadness. "I worry about her."

Charlotte nodded, fully understanding the emotions Jeanne

was experiencing. "It's hard to let go," Charlotte told her gently. "It's been a while, but I remember well those first two years Hank went off to college. It's almost like a part of you is missing."

The sports car disappeared around the corner, and with a deep sigh, Jeanne turned her attention back to Charlotte. "And how is that son of yours these days? Is he still after you to retire?"

Charlotte grimaced. "Isn't that the most ridiculous thing you've ever heard of? My goodness, I'm only fifty-nine. The way he carries on sometimes, you'd think I was a ninety-year-old invalid."

Jeanne patted Charlotte's arm. "You hang in there, and don't you dare let him talk you into something you're not ready for. Just because he's a doctor doesn't mean he knows everything. Besides, what on earth would I do without you?" Jeanne stood aside and motioned for Charlotte to enter the foyer.

The grand foyer of the old home was a room unto itself, and unlike the mere sixteen-foot ceilings of the other rooms in the house, the foyer soared upward the full two stories. Placed along the walls were several gilded lyre-back chairs and an Empire chaise longue upholstered in red brocade with gold trim. An antique rug, worn thin from decades of wear and all the more valuable because of its condition, covered the wooden floor.

"Today why don't you start upstairs in Mother's room while I serve her breakfast," Jeanne told Charlotte as she pulled the door shut. "She's been so grumpy lately that I thought I would serve it out on the upper gallery so she could get some fresh air and a little sunshine."

Charlotte truly admired Jeanne as well as sympathized with her situation. Jeanne's mother, Clarice St. Martin, had suffered a debilitating stroke just before Charlotte had begun working for the Dubuissons. Clarice could have well afforded the best nurses and round-the-clock care that money could buy, and her condition had somewhat improved over time, but Jeanne had insisted that her mother move in with her so that she could personally care for her.

Charlotte could understand why Jeanne, or any daughter, for that matter, would want to ensure that her mother had the best of care. Even so, the whole situation still seemed a bit strange, especially given their financial means, and she couldn't help wondering if Jeanne had some kind of martyr complex.

"I already have Mother's tray ready in the kitchen," Jeanne said. "I won't be but a moment." She walked past Charlotte toward the entrance to the formal dining room that led back to the kitchen.

"Do you need some help with the tray?" Charlotte called after her.

"My goodness, no," Jeanne answered. "Besides, you've already got enough to carry."

Within moments, Jeanne reappeared with a large wicker tray. On the tray were several covered dishes, but it was the pink rose in a cut-crystal vase that caught Charlotte's eye.

"I see you've already been out to the garden this morning," she said as she followed Jeanne up the sweeping stairway. Though Charlotte knew that Jeanne hired out most of the yard work, one of the few self-indulgent activities she allowed herself was her rose garden.

"Don't I wish I could get out in the mornings," Jeanne answered, her tone wistful. "I really love gardening, and truly the best time is early mornings, before the dew evaporates and before it gets too hot. But lately Mother has taken to waking up so early, and what with Jackson working later, I've had to switch working in the garden to the evenings instead."

The stairway opened to a central hall on the second-story level, a hall similar to the foyer on the first level and wide enough for a claw-foot settee and a pair of pillar-and-scroll mahogany tables. Connected to the central hall were four large bedroom suites, each suite containing its own private bath.

Clarice's bedroom was the closest to the stairs. The old lady was still in bed, her television tuned to QVC, a popular shopping channel. She was dressed in her nightgown, just one of the many soft flannel granny-type gowns that she preferred to sleep in and lounge around in.

"Mother, look who's here." Jeanne set the tray down on the foot of the bed.

Totally ignoring Charlotte, the old lady pointed to the television screen. "Quick, Jeanne, look at that."

Jeanne didn't bother looking, but Charlotte glanced at the screen. A sparkling ruby-and-diamond necklace was being displayed.

"Wouldn't that look stunning on Anna-Maria? And rubies are her birthstone."

With an impatient shake of her head, Jeanne walked around to the side of the bed and pulled back the covers. "I don't know why you insist on watching those shows. Now, come along. I have a special treat for you today."

Though Clarice allowed Jeanne to help her to the side of the bed, her expression grew hard and resentful. "How else is an old crippled woman supposed to shop?"

While Jeanne was busy assisting Clarice into a terry robe, Charlotte opened the French doors leading out onto the upper gallery.

"Besides," Clarice continued, "with July only a couple of months away, I don't have that long to find her a birthday present."

Outside on the gallery, Charlotte quickly wiped the dust off the top of a small glass-topped wicker table. But even from outside, Charlotte could hear Jeanne's exasperated sigh.

"Mother, I've told you that anytime you want to shop, all you have to do is agree to a wheelchair and I'll take you any-where you want to go."

When Charlotte returned for the breakfast tray, Clarice's lower lip was protruding into a pout. "I refuse to be seen in one of those things," she said. "I'm not that crippled."

Charlotte picked up the wicker tray and took it out to the table.

"Come along, then," Charlotte heard Jeanne tell Clarice. "It's such a beautiful day, I thought we could have breakfast out on the gallery."

"I'll get cold out there," the old lady complained.

"No, you won't," Jeanne argued. "Besides, if you don't come outside, you won't get breakfast."

Within moments, Charlotte heard the slide-thump of Clarice's walker, and she quickly slipped back inside before the old lady reached the doorway.

Charlotte retrieved clean sheets and pillowcases for Clarice's bed from the hallway linen closet. As she stripped the bed, she could hear the murmur of Jeanne's and Clarice's voices coming from the gallery. Clarice was complaining again, only this time she was grumbling about having oatmeal for breakfast for the third day in a row.

"I want eggs—fried eggs over easy," she whined. "And bacon—lots of bacon fried nice and crisp. Why can't I ever have bacon?"

"Mother, you know fried foods are bad for your cholesterol."

Once Charlotte had dusted in the bedroom, she began wiping down the sink and countertop in the bathroom. From outside, the murmurs between the two women grew louder.

Charlotte did her best to ignore what was being said. Instead, she concentrated on replacing each item on top of the counter once she'd cleaned beneath it, especially Clarice's numerous prescription bottles. By the time she'd cleaned the toilet and started on the shower stall, the loud murmurs had turned into a shouting match that was hard to ignore.

"He's stealing you blind!"

"Now, Mother, how could you know that?"

"Leopards don't change their spots. That's how I know. You mark my words, missy. He's a no-good scoundrel, and what's worse, he's smart. And if you weren't such a namby-pamby, you'd see him for what he is."

"Mother, stop it!"

"I won't stop it. It's time—past time—you grew a back-bone. If you'd had the guts to refuse to marry him in the first place, your father might still be alive today."

"That's not true, and you know it."

"Don't you walk away from me!"

"I'm not listening to any more of this."

"Jeanne, you come back here!"

Charlotte had just finished scrubbing the scuff marks off the bathroom floor made by Clarice's walker and was mopping the bathroom floor when Jeanne stalked across the bedroom.

At the hallway door, Jeanne hesitated, then turned toward Charlotte. Tears filled her eyes, and her voice shook with emotion. "Would you please make sure that she gets back to bed okay?"

Before Charlotte had time to answer, Jeanne fled through the doorway. Seconds later, Charlotte heard a door farther down the hall slam shut.

"Charlotte!" Clarice called out. "Are you still in there?"

Charlotte set the mop aside and hurried out onto the gallery. There she found the old lady struggling to get out of her chair. "I'm cold," she told Charlotte. "I want to go back inside."

"Here, let me help you." Clarice wasn't much bigger in size than Charlotte, but it was like lifting dead weight. As she struggled to get the old lady to a standing position, she wondered how on earth Jeanne managed day in and day out by herself.

"I swear, I don't know what gets into that daughter of mine," Clarice said as she aimed her walker toward the open

French doors. Then, without so much as a please or thank you, she began her arduous journey back inside.

Charlotte simply shook her head and wondered yet again about the strange relationship between the two women. Why did Jeanne continue to put up with her mother's rudeness, a rudeness that at times bordered on abuse?

By the time that Charlotte cleared off the outside table and set the tray on the floor in the hallway, Clarice was entering the bathroom. Except for vacuuming, Charlotte was finishing cleaning Clarice's suite. Even so, she waited a few minutes before leaving the room just in case Clarice needed more help.

"Be careful, Miss Clarice," she told her. "I just mopped that floor, and it might still be a bit damp."

Clarice stopped, turned her head, and glared at Charlotte. "I'm not going to mess up the floor, Charlotte. I just want to rinse my teeth."

Messing up the floor was the least of Charlotte's concerns, but she figured trying to explain that she only feared Clarice might slip and fall wouldn't do a bit of good. The old lady only heard what she wanted to hear.

Once Clarice was safely back in her bed, Charlotte gathered her supplies and started on the bedroom next to Clarice's. Within the hour, she'd cleaned all of the bedrooms except the master suite. Since the door to that room was still firmly shut and she hadn't heard Jeanne come out, she decided she would wait and clean it later.

After dusting the small tables in the hallway, Charlotte moved to the staircase. The handrail and balusters were fashioned from antique mahogany, but the steps were of oak, sanded and finished to a high gloss.

It was rumored that when the original owners of the Dubuissons' house had built it, they had procured the handrail and balusters from a house that was reputed to have been the temporary headquarters for Andrew Jackson when he had defended New Orleans against the British. Just thinking about the historical significance of the staircase gave Charlotte a lot of pleasure, and she took a great deal of pride in the polishing and upkeep of the old wood.

From her supply carrier, she removed a bottle of lemon oil and a special cloth she used to apply the oil. She also removed a polishing cloth, which she tucked into the waistband of her slacks.

After sprinkling the first cloth with lemon oil, she rubbed it into the handrail, tediously working her way down the staircase. It was when she was working her way back up as she polished the handrail that she noticed the scuff marks on the steps, scuff marks almost identical to the kind made by Clarice's walker.

Impossible, she thought. Even as wide as the steps were, Clarice's walker was wider. Charlotte frowned in thought as she stared at the scuff marks. The only way they could have been made by Clarice's walker was if the walker had been folded and dragged down the stairs, which meant that Clarice would have had to hold on to the banister for support. . . .

"Oh, for pity's sake," she muttered. What on earth was wrong with her, standing there, wasting time obsessing about such a silly thing? Something else or someone's shoes had to have caused the marks. The only time Clarice ventured down the stairs was when she had her monthly doctor's exam. Even then, Jeanne enlisted the help of Max, a part-time chauffeur she'd hired to assist her mother.

It was almost noon by the time that Charlotte had scrubbed away the scuff marks on the stairs and cleaned and vacuumed all but the main parlor and the kitchen downstairs. She was ready to begin dusting in the parlor when she heard the clink of dishes coming from the kitchen.

Jeanne, she decided, had finally come out of her room and was preparing lunch. Once again, she had to admire the younger woman. Jeanne might be hurt or angry with her mother, but she would still take care of her needs.

Charlotte quickly gathered the supplies she needed and climbed the stairs. Now she could finally clean the master suite; then she would take her own lunch break.

By midafternoon, Charlotte was almost finished with everything but one last chore in the kitchen. As she stacked the last of the plates from the dishwasher into the butler's pantry, Jeanne entered the kitchen.

"Charlotte, could we talk for a moment?"

"Of course." Charlotte nodded, then closed and locked the door to the dishwasher.

Jeanne motioned for Charlotte to take a seat at the small breakfast table. But instead of seating herself, Jeanne began to pace the distance between the table and the cabinet. After a moment and a deep, steadying sigh, she finally stopped behind a chair across from where Charlotte sat. Her hands gripped the back of the chair so hard that her knuckles were white.

"I'm—I'm truly sorry about what happened earlier," she told Charlotte in a halting voice. "I want to apologize."

"You don't owe me an apology," Charlotte said gently. "I really understand. Your mother has—er—she has problems."

Jeanne grimaced and sat down hard in the nearest chair. "Oh, Charlotte, what *am* I going to do about her? What Mother has is more than just problems. She's going senile and seems to be getting worse with each passing day."

Charlotte's heart went out to the younger woman. "Sometimes simply talking about a situation helps," she suggested. "At least talking seems to work for me."

Jeanne placed her arms on the tabletop and leaned forward. "You're right, I'm sure. With Anna-Maria off at school and Jackson gone most of the time, I don't have a chance to talk to anyone much."

Charlotte reached over and patted Jeanne's hand. How sad, she thought. She couldn't begin to imagine leading such an insular, lonely life. "Well, I'm here now," Charlotte told her, "and my middle name is discretion, so you just talk all you want to."

Jeanne seemed to hesitate, but only for a moment. "She's always making accusations about someone or something," she blurted out. "Take for instance that stuff she was saying this morning about Jackson. Why, Jackson isn't even home half the time, what with all of the late nights he's been keeping at the office lately. When he is home, he stays holed up in the library. And who could blame him?"

How convenient for him, thought Charlotte. And how totally selfish. Charlotte didn't really know Jackson Dubuisson that well, since most of the time he was at work when she cleaned. But from the different things that Jeanne had let slip over the years, Charlotte's opinion of the man was zero on a scale of one to ten. She had often wondered how such a warm, loving woman like Jeanne could have ever married someone like him.

But if, as Jeanne pointed out, Jackson was never around, why *would* Clarice choose to pick on him? she wondered. *Where there's smoke, there's usually fire.* The old saying played through Charlotte's mind. Over the years, Charlotte had seen the truth in the cliché more than once. "Why do you think your mother is so fixated on maligning your husband?"

Again Jeanne hesitated as a myriad of emotions played across her face. After a moment, she seemed to compose herself. "For one thing, when Jackson and I married, Father made him a full partner in the firm. Ever since, Mother has always claimed Jackson only married me to get control of the firm. She says all he cares about is money, specifically my money. But even worse, she still blames Jackson for Father's death. Never mind that it's been fifteen years since Father was murdered. Mother simply won't stop harping on it."

Murdered. Charlotte's stomach turned queasy. "Oh, goodness, I'd forgotten that your father had been murdered."

Even now, Charlotte only vaguely recalled the incident. At the time, though, she hadn't paid much attention to the story or the gossip. She'd been too caught up in her own tragedy, that of trying to console her son after his wife had purposely aborted their child, her grandchild, a child Hank had wanted badly. "The murder of someone close leaves its mark on the whole family," she murmured, still thinking about the loss she and her son had suffered. "It's a terrible thing."

Jeanne nodded and lowered her gaze to the tabletop. "It was terrible," she whispered. "A burglar broke into the house, robbed the safe, then killed Father."

Charlotte reached out and squeezed Jeanne's arm. "Oh, you poor thing. I'm so sorry."

Jeanne suddenly laughed, but it was a bitter sound filled with irony. "Don't be too sorry. My father would never have won any Father of the Year Awards, and he had a cruel streak." She shrugged. "But my mother loved him just the same, something I never understood."

Charlotte immediately thought about Nadia's situation with Ricco. "I know exactly what you mean," she said, "but I've never understood how a woman could stay with a man who was cruel or abusive. I guess love takes on many forms, but I sometimes think women confuse love with other things, things like security, or they feel trapped or feel there's no other choice." She shrugged. "For whatever reason," she added.

"Yes . . . well, I figure that Mother felt she had no other choice, since my father controlled the money. Even so, she just couldn't accept that he was gone, and she went a little crazy at the time. As if Father being murdered wasn't enough, she made terrible accusations about Jackson to the police. You see, Jackson and Father had argued the night before . . . something about some investments Father had made using the firm's money. But of course Jackson had an alibi the night of the murder. As usual, he was working late on an upcoming court case with his secretary. But not even that seemed to convince Mother he was innocent. Never mind that it completely satisfied the police."

"Was the murderer ever caught?"

Jeanne shook her head. "No—No, he wasn't. And after a while, I think the police gave up."

Jeanne's next words chilled Charlotte to the bone.

"My father's murderer is still out there," she said. "Somewhere . . ."

Chapter
Two

Not even the overhang of the lower gallery was protection against the humid heat of the afternoon sun. Charlotte wiped perspiration from her brow and upper lip, then resumed sweeping away the trail of leaves, grass, and dirt that littered the ten-foot-wide porch. But the one thing she couldn't seem to wipe away or sweep from her thoughts was Jeanne's unsettling statement.

My father's murderer is still out there.

Even now, despite the heat and the sweat soaking the back of her blouse, Charlotte still felt a chill, the kind that went clear to the bone. Though she knew intellectually that it was possible a person could get away with murder, she didn't like to think that it could really happen, at least not in her safe, secure world.

Before long, however, the oppressive heat of the afternoon began to take its toll, and a cool, cleansing shower and a large glass of iced tea were all that Charlotte could think about. She should have swept the gallery earlier, when it was cooler, instead of saving it for last.

"Almost done," she muttered as she turned the corner leading to the side gallery.

The side gallery fronted two rooms of the bottom story of the house—the front parlor and the library. Three sets of double French doors opened out onto the gallery—two sets for the parlor and one set for the library. In the days before air-conditioning, the doors were thrown open to create a draft inside the old house.

Just outside the doors of the library was a white three-piece bistro set, each piece composed of an intricately designed pattern made of cast iron. Though the table and chairs were perfectly situated for an early-morning first cup of coffee, Charlotte knew for a fact that the set was mostly for decoration.

So why had one of the chairs been moved deeper into the shade of the gallery, closer to the French doors?

Charlotte stepped closer, and for several moments she stared at the lone chair sitting sideways. How strange, she thought.

At that moment, the phone inside the library rang, and Charlotte went very still. After only two rings, someone within the house must have picked up one of the extensions, because the phone suddenly was silent again.

Growing more intrigued by the minute, Charlotte couldn't resist the temptation to try out the chair. Once seated, she found herself privy to a perfect view of the library inside through the panes of the French door. She could see in, but she noted that because of the position of the desk inside, if someone were sitting at it, that person wouldn't be able to see her. Not only could a person sitting in the chair hear whatever was going on inside, but that person could also see what was happening there.

What if someone was sneaking around outside on the gallery specifically for that purpose?

"Yeah, right," she muttered, then grimaced. She was doing it again, letting her sometimes overactive imagination get the best of her, but she couldn't seem to help it. She'd always been a sucker for a good mystery and was a huge fan of the genre. Over the years, she'd learned that reading the whodunit novels was the perfect outlet for that imagination.

A sudden loud racket gave Charlotte a start, and she jerked her head around to glare in the direction of the sound.

A lawn mower.

It was just a lousy lawn mower from the house next door. And a noisy one at that.

Of course, she thought, lowering her gaze to the trail of dirt, leaves, and cut grass and feeling a bit foolish. Just like the neighbors and most of the other homeowners in the Garden District, the Dubuissons employed a gardener to maintain their lawn and gardens. The gardener came two days a week, on Tuesdays and Thursdays. Since the trail of debris seemed to end in front of the chair, more than likely the gardener, not some fantasy spy, was the culprit. He'd probably simply needed a place to rest and cool off.

"Big bad mystery solved," she muttered. "The end."

Deciding that the heat was getting to her more than she had thought and that she'd wasted enough time indulging her silly imagination, she stood and firmly repositioned the chair beneath the table, then hurriedly swept away the remaining debris.

Once back inside the house, Charlotte checked her cleaning supplies to make sure she had repacked everything. Since she had already loaded her vacuum into the van, all that remained was finding Jeanne so she could let her know she had finished.

Charlotte found her seated at a small secretary in the back parlor. Her brow creased in concentration, Jeanne was reading a paper on top of a stack of what appeared to be legal documents. Just as Charlotte stepped farther into the room, the phone on the desk rang. Charlotte didn't like to eavesdrop on her clients, but at times, doing so was unavoidable.

From Jeanne's side of the conversation, she learned that the caller was Jackson.

"But Jackson, this makes two nights in a row you've had to work late, and tonight is the Zoo To Do festivities. I thought we were going."

Even from where Charlotte stood, it was hard to miss Jeanne's frown of disapproval.

"Yes . . . yes . . . of course I understand," Jeanne said. "I always do, whether I want to or not, don't I?"

Sarcasm? From Jeanne? How totally out of character, thought Charlotte.

"Of course not," Jeanne continued in a clipped tone. "You know I won't go without you, and yes, I'll leave the gate unlocked . . . again, but don't expect me to keep your supper warm."

After Jeanne hung up the receiver, Charlotte waited several moments before making her presence known. She'd seen Jeanne upset before, seen her hurt, even angry, but she'd never known her to be snide or bitchy.

Finally, Charlotte cleared her throat.

Jeanne glanced up. "Oh, Charlotte, sorry. I didn't see you standing there. Come on in."

"I just wanted to let you know that I'm finished." Charlotte walked over to the desk.

"Oh! Yes, of course. Just a second." Jeanne turned and riffled through another stack of papers on the desk. "I know I put your check here . . . somewhere . . ." She stopped and pursed her lips in thought. Suddenly, she struck her forehead with the heel of her hand. "Now I remember. I put it away in the safe when I made out the bills." She stood. "Wait here. I'll be right back."

While waiting for Jeanne's return, Charlotte took a quick inventory of the room, checking for anything she might have missed while cleaning. Satisfied that all was in order, she glanced down at the stack of papers Jeanne had been concentrating on. The one on top was a mortgage of some type. Curious, Charlotte leaned closer. When she saw that it was a mortgage on a piece of property in a place called Gould, Colorado, and was made out to Jackson, she frowned.

Neither Jackson nor Jeanne skied, and as far as she knew, Jackson didn't go in for hunting. So why would he own property in Colorado? she wondered.

She supposed that Jackson and Jeanne could have decided to take up skiing, but she didn't recognize the town as being near any of the major resorts. More than likely, the property was simply an investment, she decided. Someone with Jackson Dubuisson's means would have various financial investments all over.

From down the hallway, she heard the click of Jeanne's shoes against the wooden floor. With a shrug, Charlotte stepped away from the desk. Why Jackson owned property anywhere was really none of her business.

"Here it is." Jeanne entered the room and handed Charlotte a check. "And I'll see you again on Monday, as usual?"

Charlotte accepted the check and nodded. "On Monday," she confirmed.

Afternoon traffic was heavy, but not nearly as hectic as the early-morning traffic had been. Though Charlotte had worked a bit later than usual at the Dubuissons', she figured she still had plenty of time to rest up a bit before her outing later that night.

When she let herself in the front door, she grinned as she watched Sweety Boy's antics, designed to get her attention. The chirping little bird pranced back and forth along his perch, his wings ruffling and fluttering.

"So you missed me, did you?" she said, locking the front door behind her and setting down her purse in a chair. "Well, it's good to know that somebody misses me when I'm gone."

Charlotte opened the door of the birdcage and offered her forefinger. The parakeet immediately hopped on. "Say 'I missed you, Charlotte,' " she told him in a high-pitched singsong voice. "Come on, Sweety, say it now, say 'I missed you, Charlotte.' "

The little bird cocked his head but said nothing. Charlotte grimaced. The few times she'd given in to a weak moment and envisioned owning a pet, she thought about a cat or a dog, but never a bird. Then, six months ago, the tenants who had been renting the other side of the double skipped out, owing her two months in back rent. Not only had they left the place in a shambles; they'd also left the little parakeet behind.

When she'd discovered him, he was in pitiful shape, half-starved and wheezing, with a discharge coming from his eyes and nostrils.

She'd immediately rushed him to a vet, and with antibiotics, food, and care, she'd nursed him back to health. Only recently had she decided to teach him to talk, but so far, she'd had no luck.

Charlotte repeated the same phrase four more times before finally giving up. "Come on, boy. Enough for today." She withdrew him from the cage. "Exercise time for you."

The moment he was free of the confines of his cage, he flew directly to her shoulder. There he pranced back and forth for several moments, his tiny claws tickling her through her blouse. Finally, he grew tired of the game and flew off toward the cuckoo clock.

The top of the clock was one of the little bird's favorite out-of-cage perches, and Charlotte had a sneaking suspicion that the silly parakeet thought the cuckoo was a real bird. Just thinking about it always made her grin.

She was still grinning when she glanced over at her desk and saw the light on her answering machine blinking rapidly, indicating several messages. Her grin instantly dissolved into a frown, followed by a groan. Still feeling hot and sweaty from sweeping the Dubuissons' gallery, she had hoped to have a nice refreshing shower as soon as she got home.

"Business before pleasure," she muttered as she hit the REPLAY button.

The first message was from her son, reminding her that she'd promised to attend the annual Zoo To Do fund-raiser with him that evening. "As if I could forget," she muttered.

Because Hank was on call at the hospital, he suggested that she meet him at the event instead of his picking her up. Then he gave her specific instructions as to where and what time to meet him.

"And Mother," he added, "you know how dangerous it can be at night for a woman alone, so . . ."

Charlotte rolled her eyes upward toward the ceiling as she listened to her son proceed to give her a short lecture about driving at night and taking the proper safety precautions. Never mind that she'd been driving alone at night since he was in diapers, thought Charlotte.

With a shake of her head, Charlotte let out a weary sigh. Poor Hank. What was she going to do about him? Such a worrywart. And such a pain in the butt at times. First the incessant nagging about retirement and now all these high-falutin social events he insisted she attend.

She hated to admit it, but she was beginning to suspect that her beloved only child was turning into a bit of a snob. He knew better than to come right out and say so, but it was becoming increasingly evident that the great doctor was embarrassed that his mother still worked as a maid.

"How soon we forget," she grumbled when Hank's message ended. "Never mind that it was my maid service that helped put him through medical school."

After Hank's message, there were a couple of inquiries from prospective clients. Charlotte made quick notes of the names and phone numbers so she could return the calls.

The last message was from Cheré Warner, another of Charlotte's full-time employees.

"Charlotte, you've got to call me back just as soon as you get home. Boy, have I got an insider tip for you on a cleaning job up for bid. It's a short-term job for big bucks, Charlotte, so call me."

The excitement vibrating in Cheré's voice was hard to ignore, and after glancing at the cuckoo clock and determining that she still had plenty of time to shower and dress, Charlotte returned the call.

"I'll be right over," the young woman told her when she answered. "Just give me fifteen minutes."

"No hurry." Charlotte laughed. "Take twenty minutes," she suggested. "I need a shower."

It took a precious five minutes to coax Sweety Boy back into his cage before Charlotte finally stepped into the shower. Even though she'd had visions of a luxurious, cool soak in the bathtub, with lots of bath oil, the quick wash she had to settle for was still refreshing.

Charlotte had just dried off from her shower and had slipped into a robe when her doorbell rang. She glanced at the cuckoo on her way to the door. Twenty minutes on the dot.

Cheré Warner was like a breath of fresh air. With her dark, bouncy hair and shining black eyes, she was a bright, energetic young woman who was working her way through college to get a business degree. Cheré was both dependable and reliable, and Charlotte felt fortunate to have her working for her. During the two years she'd been employed by Charlotte, not once had a client ever complained.

"Come in, Cheré." Charlotte motioned for the younger woman to enter. "How about a glass of iced tea?"

Cheré grinned. "Oh, Charlotte, you know I love your iced tea. No one makes it like you do."

A few minutes later, armed with tall glasses of iced tea, both women seated themselves on Charlotte's sofa.

"Okay, now tell me about this insider tip."

Cheré's face lit up with excitement. "You know that old Devillier house on St. Charles Avenue that's being renovated into apartments?"

Charlotte frowned. "That's the house just down from the Pontchartrain Hotel, isn't it?"

Cheré nodded. "Yeah, that's the one. Roussel Construction is doing the job." She took a quick sip of tea. "Well! The construction is just about complete. All they lack are a few finishing touches. And once the city inspectors do their thing, Roussel's will be soliciting bids for the cleanup. In fact"—Cheré was almost squirming with eagerness—"my source says that it will probably be a first-come, first-serve-type thing, that the bidding is mostly a formality, since Roussel's is anxious to be done with this particular job."

"Your source?" Charlotte's right eyebrow rose a fraction, and a grin tugged at her mouth. "And just who is this source of yours, and how reliable is this information? Another one of your boyfriends?"

"Oh, Charlotte, stop teasing. And if you must know, this particular source isn't a boyfriend . . . Well, not exactly—not yet." She giggled. "Of course, if I have my way . . ."

Charlotte simply shook her head. "Cheré, Cheré, Cheré. What am I going to do with you?" But Charlotte couldn't help laughing. Cheré had a personality that just wouldn't quit and seemed to collect boyfriends like some people collected stamps. "So who is this new, soon-to-be boyfriend?"

The younger woman's eyes took on a dreamy glaze. "None other than Mr. Todd Roussel, the son of Roussel Construction. He's taking a semester off from school to learn the business."

"I'd have to say that sounds like a pretty reliable source.

Now, for the big question. What kind of money and time are
we talking about?"

The more Cheré told her about the specifics involved
with the job, the more interested Charlotte grew. Even as she
mentally estimated the extra supplies she would need and
the extra help she would have to hire, the project was still
worth a great deal of money for such a short period of time;
just the type of job that she needed to shore up her flagging
retirement account.

It had been a good six months since she'd been able to
add to the account. Every spare dime had been soaked up by
yet another loan she'd had to make to her sister, Madeline, to
bail her out of her latest financial disaster.

Charlotte instructed Cheré to get the name and phone
number of the contact person at Roussel Construction, and
after thanking the younger woman, she promised her a nice
bonus if the job came through.

Once Cheré left, Charlotte quickly returned the other two
messages she'd received earlier. Both potential clients
sounded like good prospects. She assured the women that
she could fit them in, and she promised to get back to them
once she'd checked her schedule book.

After her conversations, Charlotte pulled out her schedule book. "Hmm, maybe I spoke too soon," she murmured as
she glanced over the present schedule. "At this rate, I might
have to consider hiring another full-time employee."

The Zoo To Do, always held on the first Friday night in
May, was an annual event that benefited the New Orleans
Audubon Zoo and raised thousands upon thousands of dol-
lars.

Charlotte had never attended before, but she knew all
about it from listening to clients who had attended over the
years.

It was a black-tie gala affair held at the zoo. A ticket
could cost anywhere from $155 to $195, depending on

whether the person purchasing it was an Audubon member or nonmember.

For the price of a ticket, the guests could enjoy an evening of music, dining, and dancing, complete with wine, champagne, and a variety of other beverages. Charlotte had heard that the samplings of food were fantastic and were provided by well over a hundred of the finest restaurants in New Orleans. Her mouth watered at even the thought of some of the more popular dishes she'd been told to expect: bananas Foster, shrimp étouffée, turtle soup, grilled alligator sausage . . .

Everybody who was anybody socially attended the event, and they dressed to the hilt—men in tuxedos and women in slinky cocktail dresses.

Charlotte turned her van onto River Road, and as she drew near the intersection of Broadway, she began to grow more apprehensive with each passing minute. She hoped she'd dressed properly, since the last thing she wanted was to embarrass Hank. Nothing in her closet had come close to resembling slinky cocktail attire, and she'd settled for her old, reliable little black dress and pearls.

At the moment, however, what she was wearing was the least of her worries. The cars in front of her had slowed to almost a standstill, and she was stuck in a line of traffic that seemed to crawl forward inch by inch.

Charlotte glanced at the digital clock on her dashboard and grew even more apprehensive. She should have left earlier. Hank would have a fit if she didn't show up on time, and she'd have to listen to him give her yet another lecture.

He'd said he was on call, but did he have his cell phone or his pager with him tonight? she wondered. Just about the time she made up her mind to try his cell phone, the traffic picked up speed, so she decided to take her chances and hope for the best.

By the time Charlotte was able to ease her van into a parking space in the huge, crowded parking lot, she'd had plenty of time to rethink her earlier concerns, and she'd calmed down somewhat. After all, in the grand scheme of things, what she was wearing was nobody's business but her own, and if her son didn't like the way she'd dressed or was embarrassed by it, then that was just tough. She'd never been the pretentious type, anyway, and she was too old to start now.

In the parking lot, she waited by her van for the small transportation bus Hank had told her about that was designated to take guests from their vehicles to the front gate.

The moment she stepped off the bus, she spotted her son striding purposely toward her, a look of relief on his face.

Charlotte caught her breath at the sight of him. There were times, like now, that he reminded her so much of his father that bittersweet whispers of the past tugged at her emotions and almost brought tears to her eyes.

Tall and lean, with sandy-colored hair and piercing blue eyes, he was the spitting image of his father, a man he'd never known except through Charlotte's memories and a few pictures she'd kept.

"I was beginning to get worried," he told her after a brief hug.

Charlotte waved her hand toward the parking lot. "Traffic," she said by way of explanation. "And before you start," she added, "yes, I should have left earlier. But I didn't, and I'm here. So there."

A slow, knowing grin tugged at Hank's lips. "Okay, Mother. No lecture this time. And by the way, you really look lovely."

A warm feeling spread within her, and Charlotte curtsied. "Why, thank you, kind sir. You look pretty spiffy yourself."

Hank gave a crisp little half-bow, then held out his arm. "Now that we've got all of that out of the way . . ."

Charlotte laughed and tucked her arm in his.

Once inside the gate, Hank guided Charlotte toward a small group of people crowded around a nearby bar.

The crowd shifted, and Charlotte immediately recognized one of the women.

"Mother, you remember Carol, don't you?" Hank reached out and captured the hand of the woman Charlotte had recognized.

Carol was a little taller than Charlotte. She was a slim woman with warm brown eyes, and she wore her dark shoulder-length hair in a classic page-boy style.

But it was Carol's dress that really caught Charlotte's eye. The knee-length dress was a deep wine color; it draped softly at the neckline and consisted of layers of iridescent chiffon over a brightly colored purple slip.

"Of course I remember Carol." Charlotte smiled and embraced the younger woman with enthusiasm. "It's good to see you again, dear, and I just love that dress."

"Good to see you, too, Mrs. LaRue, and thanks. I'm so glad that Hank talked you into coming tonight."

Charlotte winced at the "Mrs." but didn't bother correcting the error. "Mrs. LaRue sounds so old," she said instead. "Please call me Charlotte."

"Thanks, I'd like that," Carol told her.

Charlotte had met Carol Jones only on one other occasion, a Christmas party sponsored by Hank and his partners for children confined to the hospital over the holidays. Then, as now, she'd felt immediately drawn to the younger woman. She was relieved and delighted to know that Hank was still dating her. Maybe, just maybe, Hank had finally met the right woman, she thought.

Besides being attractive, Carol had seemed to be a generous, caring woman, and Charlotte had been impressed. Unlike Mindy, Hank's ex-wife, Carol also seemed to have a sensible, practical nature that strongly appealed to Charlotte.

Surely the fact that Hank was still seeing Carol was a good sign, she thought. At least she hoped so. For a long time after he'd divorced Mindy, she'd wondered if he would ever recover from what his ex-wife had done. It had taken him years to get to the point where he was even interested in dating again, and even then, he'd hardly ever asked a woman out more than once or twice.

Hank wasn't getting any younger, and neither was she. If she ever hoped to have grandchildren, he needed to stop fooling around and get down to business.

A granddaughter would be nice, she thought longingly. A little girl she could cuddle and spoil. But a grandson would do just as well.

Then a horrible thought suddenly struck her. Hank's first wife hadn't wanted children. What if Carol felt the same way, too? Surely Hank wouldn't make that same mistake twice.

Only one way to find out, she decided. Charlotte smiled up at her son. "Hank, honey, why don't you get us all a nice glass of wine? Carol and I will wait right over there." She pointed to a bench that was miraculously empty, considering the crowd of people standing around.

Hank firmly shook his head. "Oh, no, you don't, Mother. I'm not letting you get Carol off alone to grill her."

Charlotte feigned a hurt expression but was saved from outright lying about her intentions by Carol.

"What's wrong, darling?" the younger woman crooned to him as she reached up and caressed his jaw. "Afraid I might learn all of your deep, dark secrets?" Then, with a saucy wink, she turned to Charlotte and took her firmly by the arm. "Come along, Charlotte. We can grill each other." With a throaty laugh, she steered Charlotte toward the empty bench.

Two hours later, Charlotte found herself standing alone, just on the edge of the dancing area. After covering yet another yawn with her hand, she glanced at her watch. "Way past my bedtime," she muttered. "Time to go home."

Wondering if she'd stayed long enough to satisfy her son, she glanced around, looking for him. So where was he?

When she finally spotted him, he was among the dancers.

In his arms was the lovely Carol. The band was playing a soft, dreamy song, designed especially for lovers. From the expression on Hank's face, the last thing on his mind was the whereabouts of his mother.

As Charlotte continued watching, once again she felt the familiar tug of the past. From a distance, her son's resemblance to his father was uncanny and more than a bit unsettling.

So why tonight? she wondered. It wasn't as if Hank looked any different tonight than at any other time. Maybe it was the tuxedo. Though a far cry from the army uniform his father had worn, the tuxedo was still a uniform of sorts. And the music . . . the dreamy dance music, what her generation called belly-rubbing music . . .

Charlotte shook her head. "Definitely time to go home," she murmured, pulling her gaze away in an effort to fight the onslaught of past memories, painful ones that seemed determined to intrude on this particular night.

Hank's father, the love of her life, was gone, she firmly told herself, gone forever. And no amount of longing or wishing things were different would change that fact; it was a reality she'd had to learn to cope with the hard way.

"Charlotte? Charlotte LaRue!"

Even with the noise of chatter and music there was no mistaking the squeaky voice calling out to her or the spry, birdlike old lady headed her way.

Charlotte groaned softly. Of all the people she didn't want to get stuck with, Bitsy Duhe headed the list. Bad enough she had to endure the old lady's endless chatter every Tuesday, when she cleaned her house. A shameless gossip, Bitsy seemed to know something about everyone, thanks to the hours she spent on the telephone.

A sudden tug of guilt pulled at Charlotte's conscience, and shame flooded through her for her uncharitable attitude.

Bitsy's husband had once been the mayor of New Orleans, and the couple had led an active social life even after he'd retired. Then he'd died a few years back, leaving her all alone except for their son and two granddaughters. But her son and granddaughters lived in other parts of the country. Bitsy was simply a lonely old lady, so desperate for human contact and companionship that she resorted to phoning around, collecting little tidbits of the latest gossip.

Tuesday, Charlotte told her conscience as she quickly glanced around, seeking the best avenue of escape. *I promise I'll be more charitable on Tuesday, when I clean her house, but please, just not tonight.*

For an elderly lady in her eighties, Bitsy was fast, though, and before Charlotte had taken two steps, Bitsy grabbed hold of her arm.

"Oh, Charlotte, am I glad to see you."

As usual, Bitsy's purple-gray hair was pulled straight back, away from her face, and fashioned into a tight bun at the nape of her neck. She'd once confided to Charlotte that by pulling her hair back, she could smooth out the wrinkles in her forehead. And as usual, Bitsy wore one of her numerous midcalf flowered dresses.

Reminding herself that Bitsy was a client, Charlotte pasted a smile on her face. But before she could return the old lady's greeting, Bitsy was chattering away, nonstop. With Bitsy, one never carried on a conversation. One simply listened.

"I meant to call you today," the old lady told her, "but what with my doctor's appointment and grocery shopping, I never got around to it. I was wondering if you could possibly come in tomorrow to clean instead of next Tuesday."

Charlotte opened her mouth to tell the old lady that, regretfully, she had already made plans, but Bitsy kept right on talking.

"Now, Charlotte, dear, I realize that tomorrow is Saturday, and of course I would pay you extra." She took a deep breath and smiled proudly. "You see, my granddaughter called this morning, and she's coming for a visit—you know, she's the one who lives in New York. And she's flying in to-morrow evening. I really want everything to be nice and tidy for her visit, but I don't have a lot of time."

Again Charlotte opened her mouth to tell Bitsy she couldn't come, but one look at the eager anticipation on the old lady's face, along with the glow of excitement in her faded blue eyes, and she found she couldn't do it.

"What time would you like for me to be there?" she said instead.

"Oh, my, I really hate to ask this of you, but could you possibly be there at seven instead of eight?"

Charlotte groaned inwardly but nodded her agreement.

"Wonderful!" Bitsy gushed. "Now that we've got that set-tled, you must let me buy you a drink."

Charlotte frowned. "Buy? But I thought—"

"Yes, dear." Bitsy snickered. "The drinks are included in the price of the ticket. I was just making a little joke." Bitsy elbowed Charlotte. "Had you going for a second, though, didn't I? My goodness, you've got to learn to lighten up or before you know it, you'll turn into a sour old prune like me." The old lady giggled, and Charlotte couldn't help but laugh along with her.

The last thing Charlotte wanted was to spend more time with Bitsy. What she wanted was to go home. But Bitsy latched on, and Charlotte found herself having a drink with the old lady, after all, as well as enduring another half hour of her endless chatter.

For a while, she was able to ignore most of what Bitsy said as the old lady pointed out first one person, then another one, and proceeded to regale Charlotte with the latest ru-mors circulating about the people she'd singled out.

Then, suddenly, Bitsy threw out a name, and all of Charlotte's senses went on alert.

"Can you believe the nerve of that Jackson Dubuisson? Just look at them." Bitsy shook her head. "And her a married woman. Even more scandalous, she's his partner's wife." As if realizing she finally had Charlotte's full attention, she nudged her and pointed. "Over there, just on this side of the fountain. I tell you, it's one thing to have an affair, but to flaunt it in front of the whole city—well, I never!"

Charlotte followed Bitsy's finger. She couldn't believe her eyes when she spotted the couple. Just as Bitsy had said, Jackson Dubuisson was on the dance floor. Cuddled against him like a satisfied cat who had just found a bowl of cream was Sydney Marriott.

Charlotte had once worked for Sydney and knew that, in fact, Bitsy was right. Not only was Sydney a married woman, but she was married to Tony Marriott, Jackson's law partner.

He'd lied, Charlotte thought. He'd outright lied to Jeanne about working late. While Jeanne was home, tending to her invalid mother, thinking that her husband was working, Jackson was out having a high old time.

Snippets of Jeanne's side of the phone conversation when she'd talked to Jackson earlier began coming back to Charlotte, and she frowned. Had Jeanne suspected that Jackson was lying to her about working late? Did she suspect that he was having an affair? Even as socially insulated as she'd become, someone who was as prominent as Jeanne wasn't totally cut off from the old-girl network. Someone along the way would have let it slip about Jackson.

Yes, Charlotte decided. Jeanne surely had to know. And if she knew, it would go a long way in explaining why she'd been so uncharacteristically sarcastic and short with him over the phone.

Suddenly, Charlotte recalled Clarice's words from earlier that morning.... *he's a no good scoundrel* ... Maybe Clarice wasn't quite as senile as Jeanne thought, after all.

"Oh, poor Jeanne," Charlotte murmured, unable to tear her gaze away from the couple. They were dancing so close that they seemed to blend into one; it was hard to tell where one ended and the other began.

"Humph!" Bitsy scoffed. "Poor Jeanne my foot. You better feel sorry for Sydney. Here comes that husband of hers, and he looks like he could chew nails. I know I wouldn't want to cross him."

Sure enough, Tony Marriott was headed straight for the dancing couple, and the murderous look on his face was enough to give Charlotte the cold shivers.

Chapter
Three

For once, Charlotte had to agree with Bitsy. Even if Tony Marriott's swarthy looks hadn't reminded her of every cliché she'd ever associated with a mafia hit man, his reputation alone would have been enough for Charlotte to steer clear of him.

Charlotte's nephew, Daniel, had once worked as an assistant D.A. before going into private practice. From listening to Daniel talk, Charlotte knew that Tony specialized in representing clients no one else would touch, mostly big-time drug dealers. And more often than not, he always won in court and was paid well for his services.

Bitsy tugged on Charlotte's arm. "Let's get closer. I can't hear what they're saying from here."

Charlotte firmly removed her arm from Bitsy's grasp. "I don't think that's such a good idea." Evidently, neither did the people dancing near Sydney and the two men. All around the men, couples had stopped dancing and were backing away.

Bitsy craned her head. "Oh, Lordy, me. Do you think they're gonna fight?"

Charlotte abhorred violence in any form, and the eager anticipation in Bitsy's voice was more than she could stomach.

"Shame on you," Charlotte told the old lady. "Of course they're not going to fight." At least she hoped not. But if she had to bet on which man would win in a fight, she'd lay odds on Tony. No contest. Jackson was the taller of the two men by several inches, but Tony was more muscular looking and probably outweighed Jackson by at least thirty pounds. And from all accounts, Tony was a lot meaner than Jackson and fought dirty, at least in the courtroom.

Even as the music played on, muting the heated conversation between the two men, Charlotte could feel the tension emanating from them like the vibrations from the strings of a too tightly strung violin.

But the drama was short-lived. Tony's verbal attack abruptly ended when he jerked his wife out of Jackson's arms. Pulling her and half-dragging her along behind him, he stalked off through the crowd. Charlotte followed the couple's exit until they disappeared in the crowd. When she looked back to see Jackson's reaction, he was gone.

"Oh, phooey!" Bitsy grumbled. "I thought for sure we would get to see a fight."

Charlotte took a deep breath, counted to ten, and reminded herself that Bitsy was a client as well as an old lady. Even so, enough was enough for one night.

She motioned vaguely toward a crowd of people huddled around a food table. "I think that's my son signaling to me over there," she lied. "Thanks for the drink, but I've got to run now. See you tomorrow morning, bright and early."

As Charlotte hurried away, she heard Bitsy calling after her, but she ignored her. Now if only she *could* find Hank and Carol . . .

Minutes later, Charlotte finally spotted Carol standing near the front gates. But Hank was nowhere in sight.

The second Carol saw Charlotte, her face lit up, and she

rushed over to her. "Thank goodness!" she exclaimed. "I was beginning to think I never was going to find you."

Charlotte laughed. "I was looking for you, too."

"Well, now that we found each other, Hank asked me to give you a message. He said to tell you that he got a call from the hospital and had to leave."

"What a rotten shame," Charlotte said with feeling. "I know you two were having a good time. As for me, though, it's just as well. I was really looking for that son of mine to tell him that I have to be going."

Carol frowned. "Oh, darn! I was hoping you'd stay and keep me company. The evening is still young," she added in a wistful, coaxing tone.

For a moment, Charlotte was tempted to stay a while longer. Because Hank had interrupted their earlier chat, she'd only had time to ferret out a couple of facts about Carol. For one, she'd learned that Carol was a nurse who worked for one of Hank's associates. She'd also learned that Carol had once been engaged but had ultimately decided against marrying the man.

With Hank gone, Charlotte figured she just might be able to find out more. She might even be able to work the conversation around to the subject of children.

Charlotte glanced at her watch, then groaned. "The evening might still be young," she said regretfully, "but I'm not—not young, that is, and I have to be on a job by seven tomorrow morning."

"Well, you're certainly not old, either, not by today's standards."

Charlotte grinned. "I wish you'd help me convince my son of that. He thinks I need to retire and let him take care of me."

"I know," Carol told her softly. "But Hank just loves you, Charlotte. He really hates seeing you work so hard."

So they had discussed her, thought Charlotte. Interesting. Interesting indeed.

"And what do you think?" Charlotte asked.

"I think you should do what you want to do, and I've told Hank as much."

On impulse, Charlotte gave the younger woman a quick hug. "Carol, I think you and I are going to get along just fine."

Carol returned the hug eagerly. "I hope so. I certainly hope so."

Charlotte stepped back. "But hey, listen. Just because Hank and I have to leave doesn't mean you shouldn't stay and enjoy yourself."

Carol shook her head. "Nope! If you're not staying, then I'm not, either. It just wouldn't be any fun without Hank or you."

Bitsy Duhe lived on the same street as the vampire novelist Anne Rice. Charlotte glanced at the author's house as she passed it the following morning. Though vampires weren't exactly her choice of reading material, she still hoped one day to meet the famous lady who wrote about them. A grin tugged at her lips. She'd even had a fantasy or two about working for her.

A few houses farther down, Charlotte parked in front of Bitsy's house. Surrounded by huge azalea bushes filled with dark pink blooms, the house was a very old raised-cottage-style Greek Revival.

Bitsy was already outside, standing on the front gallery. As usual, Bitsy had on yet another of her flowered dresses. With her were two men dressed in jeans and matching khaki shirts.

Also as usual, Bitsy was talking a mile a minute. Even as she waved a greeting to Charlotte, her mouth never stopped moving.

Charlotte immediately recognized one of the men as Joseph O'Connor, a well-known Garden District gardener.

Joseph occasionally worked for Bitsy, but he also worked for several of Charlotte's other clients.

Who was the younger man with Joseph? she wondered. And why did the tall sandy-haired man look vaguely familiar? As far as she knew, Joseph worked alone most of the time. Of course, it was always possible that the gardener had finally decided to hire a helper, especially since he was getting on in years.

"But aren't we all?" Charlotte grumbled as she stepped out of the van.

After gathering the supplies she would need, Charlotte took a deep breath of the cool morning air. Too bad it wouldn't stay cool, she thought as she locked the van, then approached the steps leading up to the front gallery. By afternoon, the heat of the sun, combined with the humidity, would rival a sauna. And before the month of May ended, even the early mornings would be hot and muggy, typical New Orleans weather.

Even as Charlotte nodded at the two men when she passed them, the feeling that she knew the younger man grew even stronger. He was older than she'd first thought. Up close the fine lines around his piercing green eyes were more visible and defined, and she detected just a bit of gray around his temples.

Where had she seen him before?

Charlotte prided herself on her keen awareness of details, especially the faces of people she met and the names that went along with those faces. Being unable to recall where she'd seen the younger man before was puzzling. She should have been able to shrug it off, but for reasons she couldn't fathom, it disturbed her that she couldn't identify him.

Chapter Four

Though Bitsy's house was large, it wasn't hard to maintain. A strong believer in the old cliché, a place for everything and everything in its place, she was basically a neat lady. In spite of her efforts, however, the house, like its owner, was old. Coping with the accumulation of dust and cobwebs was an ongoing battle.

In the kitchen, Charlotte filled the sink with warm water and added a healthy measure of degreaser. Bitsy's kitchen was a nightmare, containing every modern kitchen gadget imaginable. She'd even had additional shelves built so she could display the vast collection, all of which seemed to draw dust and grease like metal drew magnets.

"Charlotte! Oh, Charlotte, where are you?"

Charlotte flinched at the sound of Bitsy's squeaky voice. Giving the electric juicer one last swipe, she then started wiping down the bread machine. She had hoped the older lady would spend a bit more time with the gardener and leave her in peace.

"Charlotte!"

"In the kitchen," Charlotte called out.

Seconds later, Bitsy bustled through the doorway. "Did you see my new carousel rotisserie?" She patted a large dome-shaped machine near the end of the cabinet. "It just arrived day before yesterday and makes cooking chicken a breeze. If you'll remind me before you leave, I'll give you a sample to take home with you."

"That's very generous of you, but—"

"Not generous," Bitsy said matter-of-factly. "Just practical. I don't like to eat frozen stuff, and I can't possibly eat the three chickens I experimented on by myself."

Charlotte hid a smile as she moved over to the sink to rinse out the washcloth she'd been using. It would never occur to Bitsy to cook only what she could eat, especially when she was trying out one of her new gadgets.

The sudden intrusion of noise from the lawn mower in the backyard should have made further conversation impossible. Not so with Bitsy. Though the old lady did move out of Charlotte's way and hurried over to the window instead so she could keep an eagle eye on the gardener, she kept right on talking, only louder.

". . . so glad . . . Brian finally . . . home. Joseph's arthritis . . . needs his son . . ."

Trying to follow Bitsy's ongoing monologue on top of the noisy mower was almost impossible. From the little Charlotte could make out, she deduced that the man she'd seen with Joseph was the gardener's son, Brian O'Connor. But Brian didn't much resemble his father, and discovering his identity still didn't explain why he seemed so familiar.

". . . such a shame . . . prison . . . didn't do it . . ."

Abruptly, the outside noise stopped. But Bitsy didn't miss a beat.

". . . poor boy wasted five years of his life stuck in prison, and all because of that awful Andrew St. Martin."

Charlotte's hand stilled at the mention of Jeanne's father, and she turned to face Bitsy. "But Mr. St. Martin died fifteen years ago."

Bitsy nodded. "Of course he did," she continued, seeming to relish Charlotte's undivided attention. "Andrew was murdered fifteen years ago, which was after the five years that Brian served in prison. He was murdered just about the time Brian was finally released."

Charlotte indicated that she understood with a nod, but Bitsy didn't slow down or miss a beat.

"Lordy me, I still remember when Brian was convicted and sent away," she continued. "Poor Joseph moped around for weeks. I felt so sorry for that man—for both of them. To this day he still claims that Brian didn't do it, that he was set up. He said that Brian might be guilty of a lot of things, but he wasn't a thief no matter what Andrew told the police."

Bitsy made a sound of disgust. "That Andrew was a piece of work, though. If I'm lying, I'm dying, but he was nasty through and through. Not only was he mean as a snake to Clarice and Jeanne, but he didn't care who got hurt just as long as he got what he wanted. And one thing he didn't want was Brian sniffing around his daughter."

Charlotte frowned. Following Bitsy's ping-pong monologue was like being lost in a maze. "Are you talking about Jeanne . . . and the gardener's son, before Andrew was murdered?"

Bitsy nodded her head. "Of course that's who I'm talking about. My goodness, Charlotte, pay attention. According to Joseph, Brian and Jeanne were planning on running off together, but old Andrew put a stop to it and got rid of Brian, all in one fell swoop. Claimed that Brian stole some valuable tools. Humph!" Bitsy took on an affronted look. "As if Andrew St. Martin ever touched any kind of tool in his life. Well, the tools were found in Brian's truck, all right, but Brian swore that Andrew put them there. Poor Brian might as well've been whistling Dixie. That boy never had a chance, especially since Andrew and the judge presiding over Brian's trial were big golfing buddies.

"But you mark my words." Bitsy shook her finger. "What

goes around in this life comes around, and people get paid back for the things they do. Yes, siree, old Andrew St. Martin got his."

"Because he was murdered?"

Again, Bitsy nodded, a smug look on her face. "Whoever did it broke right in through the French doors, robbed the safe, then bashed Andrew in the head. They found him the next morning slumped over his desk. Some say he had to be drunk as a skunk, since it didn't look like he'd put up much of a fight."

In her mind's eye, Charlotte had no trouble picturing the horrible scenario, and a sick feeling curled in her stomach.

But Bitsy wasn't through. She leaned closer to Charlotte in a conspiratorial manner. "They tried to pin it on his wife, Clarice, you know. Said she had either done it herself or hired it to be done, all because Andrew was getting ready to hand over everything to his new son-in-law, Jackson."

The old lady grinned. "Clarice fooled them all, though. She had an alibi. And since the murder weapon was never found, there wasn't a dad-gum thing they could do."

"Alibi? What kind of alibi?" Charlotte found herself asking.

"Not what. Who? Jeanne. Jeanne was Clarice's alibi. Swore that she and her mother were together that whole evening. Said Clarice had been sick with a stomach flu and she'd nursed her mother that whole night long."

What Bitsy had divulged was shocking. Though Charlotte kept reminding herself that half of what Bitsy said was probably pure gossip, she couldn't help being fascinated by the old lady's story.

"So what about Brian?" she asked. "What happened to him—after prison, I mean?"

"Joseph wanted him to come work with him, but Brian seemed to think it would be best if he went somewhere else, somewhere he could make a clean start. So he took off for

California—built up his own gardening service out there. But now that Joseph's arthritis is so bad, Brian finally agreed to come back and help his father out until next month, when Joseph plans to retire."

Charlotte frowned. "Seems to me that the police would have suspected Brian of the murder, seeing that it was because of Andrew that he was sent to prison in the first place."

Bitsy made a sound of frustration. "No, no, no. Brian didn't get out until the day after Andrew was murdered. Didn't I already say that?"

Bitsy had once confided in Charlotte that she worried about Alzheimer's and senility because of her advanced age, and she prided herself on her memory. Since the older lady was looking more distressed with each passing moment, Charlotte decided against pointing out that she had been vague about the specific date of Brian's release from prison. To Charlotte, the omission wasn't a big deal, anyway, but she sensed that it would be to Bitsy, so she simply shrugged instead and decided to change the subject.

"Is there anything in particular you want me to give extra attention to this morning?"

For a moment, Bitsy looked confused; then she brightened. "I'm putting my granddaughter in the pink guest room—the one with my doll collection in it. That's where she used to stay when she was a little girl. Just make sure you change the sheets on the bed and make sure you use lemon oil on everything. I just love the smell of lemon oil. . . ."

Bitsy immediately launched into a monologue on the advantages of using lemon oil versus the modern spray waxes, but Charlotte let the rest of what she said wash right over her. Gathering her supplies, she moved into the living-room area.

As usual, Bitsy followed her every footstep. And as usual, the only breaks she got from the old lady's constant chatter during the next four hours were the times that the phone rang.

*   *   *

By twelve, Charlotte had finished cleaning, and none too soon as far as she was concerned. At some point around midmorning, she'd felt the beginnings of a dull headache, and not even the two aspirins she'd swallowed had helped.

As she stepped out into the bright noonday sun, she groaned and squinted against the glare. No more Saturday-morning jobs, she silently vowed as she loaded the last of the cleaning supplies into the back of her van. And no more late Friday-night parties after working all day.

"Charlotte! Wait! Come back!"

The sound of Bitsy's voice was like fingernails on a chalkboard. Charlotte tensed. "What now?" she grumbled, slamming the back door of the van. She could always simply ignore the old lady, she thought. She could pretend she didn't hear her, jump into her van, and take off.

Then shame washed through her as she remembered the look of pride on Bitsy's face as she'd surveyed the spotlessly clean house. All the old lady wanted was for everything to be nice for her granddaughter's visit, and true to her word, she had paid extra for Charlotte coming in on such short notice.

With a weary sigh, Charlotte forced a smile, turned, and trudged back toward the house.

Bitsy met her at the bottom of the steps. "I forgot to give you these." She thrust a bulky paper sack toward Charlotte. "On top is one of those chickens I told you about. Beneath are some books I just finished. Don't worry, though. I wrapped the chicken in foil so it wouldn't leak on the books."

Charlotte accepted the sack and felt even more guilty about her uncharitable attitude. "Thank you," she said humbly.

Bitsy was a voracious reader, for she had little to occupy her time but gossip and doctors' appointments, and she was always passing along books to Charlotte. Their love of reading, specifically mystery books, was one of the few things they had in common.

"I'll have the chicken for my lunch, and I know I'll enjoy the books."

"There's a new Iris Johansen book in there," Bitsy told her. "And there's one by Tami Hoag. But there's also the latest one by that literary agent you like so much who writes."

"Evan Marshall?"

Bitsy nodded. "It's his second one, and it's even better than the first one."

Charlotte reached out and gently squeezed the old lady's arm. "Thanks again," she said. "And have fun with that granddaughter of yours," she added with feeling.

As Charlotte drove away, the weight of guilt she felt eased only marginally as Bitsy's earlier words came back to haunt her. *What goes around in this life comes around, and people get paid back for the things they do.*

Truer words were never spoken, she decided, and though she knew that it was a self-serving attitude, she made a silent vow to do her best to be kinder from now on. Not only in deeds but in attitude. After all, one day, all too soon, she would be an old lady, too.

Little did Charlotte know that her new vow would be put to the test so soon. As she turned the corner onto Milan Street, up ahead she spotted a car parked in front of her house, a familiar car that she recognized immediately.

Charlotte groaned and wondered if she dared drive past without stopping.

Chapter
Five

Nadia Wilson was waiting for Charlotte on the front-porch swing. There was no way Charlotte could drive past without being obvious and downright rude. Asleep in Nadia's lap was three-year-old Davy.

Charlotte parked her van and sighed deeply as she fought against building resentment. Though her headache had eased somewhat, she had still looked forward to a nice quiet Saturday afternoon . . . a little lunch, a bit of reading, and a long, relaxing nap.

A few minutes later, when Charlotte got a closer look at Nadia's red-rimmed, swollen eyes and blotchy face, all of her resentment instantly disappeared.

"Nadia, dear, what's wrong?" she asked softly, not wanting to wake the little boy.

Nadia looked up at Charlotte, and her eyes filled with tears. But when she tried to answer, Davy stirred, then shifted in her arms, and she made soothing noises to the little boy instead.

Davy's shirt was soaked with sweat. Recalling that the little boy had been ill the day before, Charlotte immediately motioned for Nadia to follow her. "Let's get Davy out of this heat first," she whispered.

The moment Charlotte opened the front door, cool air from inside rushed out to greet her, and Sweety Boy immediately launched into his regular routine of chirping and fluttering his wings as he pranced back and forth along his perch.

Charlotte shushed the little bird. "Not now, Sweety. Be quiet before you wake Davy." She pointed toward the bedroom. "Just put Davy in there," she told Nadia softly. "That way, we can hear him if he wakes up."

While Nadia settled Davy in the bedroom, Charlotte went to the kitchen and prepared two glasses of iced tea.

"Now what's this all about?" Charlotte asked the younger woman once they had seated themselves in the living room.

Again Nadia's eyes filled with tears. "Oh, Charlotte, I'm so sorry to bother you, but I didn't know who else to turn to." She took a deep, sobbing breath. "Ricco's been—he—he's been arrested."

For a moment, Charlotte was speechless. Though it was true that she didn't have a high opinion of Ricco Martinez, she'd never thought of him as the criminal type. Lazy, yes. But a criminal? "What on earth for?" she finally asked when she found her voice.

"Theft," Nadia told her. "Stealing graveyard artifacts."

For months the *Times-Picayune* had been filled with articles about a ring of drug-addicted thieves who were in cahoots with antique dealers. The thieves had systematically been robbing the city's old cemeteries, and thousands upon thousands of dollars had been made off the marble statues, urns, and benches that had been stolen.

Charlotte frowned. "But I thought that was old news and that all of the thieves had been caught."

Nadia nodded. "So did everyone else."

Charlotte shook her head, confused. "I don't understand. If all the thieves were caught, how could they accuse Ricco now?"

"I don't understand it, either. And since I'm not exactly a relative, no one will tell me anything, and they won't let me talk to Ricco, either. What we need is a lawyer, but Charlotte—" Again the younger woman's eyes filled, then overflowed, with tears. "I—I can't afford a lawyer, and D-Davy keeps asking about his daddy. What am I supposed to tell my son?"

At the mention of little Davy, Charlotte felt a tight fist squeeze her heart. She could well sympathize with Nadia's anguish over what to tell her son. She, too, had wrestled with the same question for years. But in the end, she'd simply opted for the truth and told Hank that his father had been a soldier, killed in the Vietnam war before he was born. Only many years later, when he'd become a man, had she finally told him that she and his father had never been married.

Charlotte reached out and squeezed Nadia's shoulder. "Hey, one thing at a time, now," she said softly. "If Ricco can't afford a lawyer, the court is supposed to appoint one for him—"

"When?" Nadia cried. "And how will I know if they won't tell me anything or let me talk to him?"

Charlotte gave it some thought for a moment. Then, making up her mind, she said, "Do you remember me talking about my nephew, Daniel?"

"The one I met at your Christmas party last year?"

Charlotte nodded. "That's right, y'all did meet. I'd forgotten about that. Anyway, Daniel is an attorney. Why don't I give him a call and see what he can find out for you?"

Nadia shook her head. "I—I don't know how I would pay him."

Again, Charlotte squeezed the younger woman's shoulder. "I know for a fact that sometimes Daniel takes on pro bono cases, so for now, don't worry about the money. But Nadia . . . I want you to promise me something in return."

"Anything, Charlotte. Anything."

"Not just anything," Charlotte told her. "And be careful what you agree to. What I want is for you to promise me that you will think seriously about your relationship with Ricco. Do you really want to spend the rest of your life with a man who does nothing but cause you heartache and worry?"

A stubborn, determined look crossed the younger woman's face, and Charlotte quickly shook her head. "No! Don't answer that question—not yet. All I want is for you to promise you'll think about it."

After a moment, Nadia finally nodded. "I'll think about it," she whispered. "I promise."

The forecast for Monday was afternoon thunderstorms. Determined to get in the daily walk that she usually reserved for the evenings, Charlotte had set her alarm clock for thirty minutes earlier than usual.

Dressed in shorts and tennis shoes, she hurried out the door. For once, she was glad it was Monday, glad to return to her regular routine.

After working Saturday morning for Bitsy and spending most of Saturday afternoon comforting Nadia, she never did get a nap. Not that she'd minded that much, especially once Davy had awakened from his nap. Having the little boy around was fun, but it was a mixed blessing. His presence made her yearning for a grandchild even worse.

Then, on Sunday, it had been her turn to host her family's weekly lunch after church, a tradition she and her sister had started when their children were young. It still amazed her that with their busy lives, her niece, her nephew, and Hank still adhered to the tradition.

She had planned to keep her promise to Nadia and talk to

Daniel about Ricco's situation after lunch. But Daniel had called early that morning to let her know he wouldn't be able to join them due to a nasty stomach virus.

The poor thing had sounded so awful over the phone that Charlotte didn't have the heart to bring up business, but she made a mental note to remember to call him in a day or two, when he was feeling better.

When Charlotte returned after her walk, she rushed through her shower and breakfast. Once she made sure Sweety Boy had plenty of water and birdseed to last the day, she was finally able to leave.

Traffic for a Monday morning on Magazine was surprisingly light. Charlotte figured that, unlike on Friday, today she'd arrive at the Dubuissons' right on time.

But Jackson Avenue was a different story. "What on earth?" she muttered, craning her head first one way, then another, to see around the line of vehicles that had slowed to a crawl ahead of her. Probably an accident, she figured when she finally spotted the swirling lights of police cars up ahead.

Charlotte began to have her doubts the closer she came to the swirling lights. She could see an ambulance and several police cars parked in the street. But other than the emergency vehicles, there were no signs of wrecked vehicles. So what was the problem?

She was still two cars away when she suddenly realized that an area had been cordoned off directly in front of the Dubuisson house. A policeman was directing traffic to a side street.

Warning spasms of alarm erupted within her, and her first thoughts were of Clarice. Was it possible that the old woman had suffered another stroke?

When the car in front of Charlotte turned off to the side street that the officer was pointing toward, Charlotte was finally able to drive her van closer. She rolled down her window, stopped, then signaled that she wanted to talk to the officer. At first, he resisted and continued motioning for her to move along. But Charlotte could be stubborn, too, and she refused to move, finally forcing the man to walk over to her van.

"Ma'am, you have to keep moving."

"I want to know what's happened."

He firmly shook his head. "This is police business. You have to keep moving," he repeated.

"But Officer, I work for the Dubuissons." She pointed to the house. "Please, can't you tell me what's going on?"

The obstinate man shook his head again. "All I can tell you is there's been a break-in and a murder."

Charlotte gasped as the meaning of the officer's words sank in. A break-in and a murder? At the Dubuissons'?

Icy fear twisted around her heart as the faces of Jeanne, Clarice, Anna-Maria, and Jackson flashed through her mind.

Oh, dear Lord, which one? she wondered. Which one of them had been murdered?

Chapter
Six

"Who-who wa-was murdered?" Charlotte choked out the words as her stomach knotted and dread welled in her throat. Surely not Anna-Maria . . . so young . . . so lovely . . . so full of life. But not Jeanne, either, she prayed. Or Clarice. And though she had never especially liked Jackson, she certainly didn't wish him dead, not *murdered*.

Such an ugly word, murder. Charlotte swallowed hard and tried to ignore the horrible mental images of violence swirling in her head.

"Who?" Charlotte repeated.

The officer shook his head. "Like I said before, ma'am, all I can tell you is there's been a break-in and a murder." His words were curt as he gestured toward the side street. "Move along now. You're holding up traffic."

One look at the unrelenting expression on the policeman's face told Charlotte that even though he knew who the victim was, he wasn't about to tell her. Further inquiries, she decided, would be a waste of time and energy.

Left with little choice but to do as he directed, she gripped the steering wheel to keep her hands from shaking and guided her van down the side street, away from the cordoned-off area.

Still in a daze, she'd driven almost half a block when, just ahead, she spotted a parking space. It would be a tight fit, but . . .

Making a split moment's decision, she flicked on the right-turn signal. No way was she leaving, she decided with a stubborn set of her jaw. Not until she found out which one of the Dubuissons had been murdered.

Slowing the van as she neared the parking spot and ignoring the blare of horns from the line of vehicles behind her, she maneuvered the van into the opening.

During the short walk back to Jackson Avenue, Charlotte spotted three different vans caught in the long line of traffic, each representing a major New Orleans television station. By the time she reached the cordoned off area, a crowd had already gathered.

Gawkers, the whole lot of them, she thought in disgust. Strangers, with nothing better to do than feed off someone else's misery. To them, the whole tragedy was simply entertainment, a brief diversion in their otherwise dull, boring existence. At least *she* had a real reason for being there, a personal stake in waiting around.

Charlotte didn't have to wait long. A blue Ford Taurus pulled up beside the young police officer who was directing traffic. Inside the car, seated on the passenger side, was a woman. Though Charlotte was standing at the back of the crowd of gawkers and only caught a glimpse of the woman's face, she would have recognized her anywhere.

A badge was flashed. Instead of the officer signaling for the blue Taurus to follow the diverted traffic, he allowed the driver to park beside a nearby police cruiser in the middle of the street.

Judith.

Charlotte's hopes rose as her niece and a man climbed out of the blue car. Now she would finally get some answers.

Ignoring the grumbling and rude glares of the people she

nudged out of her way, she shouldered her way through the crowd.

Judith Monroe was thirty years old, one of the youngest women ever to reach detective status in the New Orleans Police Department. In looks, Judith resembled her Aunt Charlotte more than she resembled her mother, and over the years, she'd often been mistaken for Charlotte's daughter rather than her niece. Though she was taller than Charlotte, both had the same honey-brown-colored hair and the same cornflower-blue eyes.

"Judith!" Charlotte cried out. "Hey, Judith, wait up! Over here!"

When Judith hesitated, turned, and searched the crowd, Charlotte slipped between the two metal police barricades and waved her arms. Ignoring the shouts of the uniformed officer, she made a beeline for her niece.

But the policeman was younger and faster than Charlotte. He caught her before she reached her niece.

"Oh, no, you don't," he said as he grabbed her by the upper arm and jerked her to a standstill.

"But that's my niece," she argued, trying to pull free of the officer's bruising grip while gesturing wildly at Judith with her free hand. "I have to talk to her."

"Hey, Billy," Judith called out as she hurried toward them. "Take it easy. That's my aunt you're manhandling."

Charlotte glared up at the young officer. "See, I told you she was my niece." When she tried once again to wrench free from his grip, he released her.

As Charlotte rubbed the red spot on her arm, stains of scarlet appeared on the officer's cheeks. Holding up both his hands in a defensive gesture, he shrugged and backed away. "Hey, Judith, how was I to know she was your aunt?" he said. "I was only doing my job."

Judith waved him away with a dismissive hand, then turned her attention to her aunt. "Aunt Charley, what on earth are you doing here?"

"Do you know that young man?"

Judith nodded. "That's Billy Wilson. We've had a couple of dates."

"Well, someone needs to teach him some manners."

"Aunt Charley." In an ominous tone, Judith drew out the pet name she'd always called her aunt, spacing the syllables evenly. "You didn't answer my question. What are you doing here?"

"The Dubuissons." Charlotte gestured toward the old mansion. "I work for them on Mondays, Wednesdays, and Fridays. I was on my way to work when, when—" Charlotte squeezed her eyes shut, drew in a deep breath, then swallowed hard. A moment later she opened her eyes, blinking several times against the brightness. "Which one, Judith?" she whispered. "Which one of them was murdered?"

"Oh, Aunt Charley . . ." Judith slipped her arm around her aunt's shoulder and squeezed gently in sympathy. Then, with a nudge, she guided her away from the crowd, toward the shade of a nearby oak that draped over the sidewalk. "I'm so sorry. I had no idea you worked for the Dubuissons. But it was Jackson, Aunt Charley. Jackson Dubuisson was the one murdered."

Though some of the tightness in Charlotte's chest eased a bit, she still felt sick at heart for the Dubuisson women . . . Jeanne . . . Anna-Maria . . . And yes, even Clarice, despite the old woman's rudeness and obstinacy. Losing a loved one or someone close was never easy under any circumstances, a fact she'd had to deal with personally more times than she cared to think about. But murder . . .

"According to the preliminary reports," Judith continued, "he was murdered sometime near midnight or early morning. His wife, Jeanne, was the one who found him in the library."

Charlotte shook her head. "Oh, poor, poor Jeanne. How awful for her."

"Yes, I'm sure it must be a terrible thing—"

"Hey, Monroe, you coming or what?"

Both women turned to face the man Charlotte had seen with her niece in the car.

"That's Lou—Louis Thibodeaux," Judith told her aunt. "Lou is my new partner till he retires at the end of the year."

Though Judith's new partner was a stocky man with gray hair and a receding hairline, Charlotte noted that for an older man, he was somewhat attractive in a rugged sort of way. At least his belly didn't hang over his belt like so many men her age, she thought.

"Go ahead, Lou," Judith called out. "I'll be along shortly."

Louis nodded, and Judith turned her attention back to her aunt. "I need to get to work now. You gonna be okay?"

Charlotte shrugged. "It's just such a shock."

"Do you need me to walk you to your van?"

"No." Charlotte firmly shook her head. "What I need is to see Jeanne Dubuisson, to talk to her."

Judith frowned, her expression filled with regret. "Oh, Aunt Charley, I can't let you do that, not yet. Go on home for now."

"But you don't understand. Jeanne has no one to—" Charlotte bit off the words spilling out of her mouth.

"What? No one to what? Aunt Charley."

"Nothing." Charlotte lowered her gaze. "Never mind," she said, realizing that there was no way she could explain about Jeanne, no way to explain that she had no one to confide in or turn to in a crisis, no one except possibly her maid. No, she couldn't explain, Charlotte decided, not without betraying the confidences that Jeanne had placed in her.

Charlotte tried another tack. "Surely you could bend the rules just this one time. I just need to talk to her for a moment, and I promise I won't get in the way."

"You know I can't, Aunt Charley. Not even for you."

One look at the strained expression on Judith's face and remorse shot through Charlotte. "Oh, hon, I'm sorry. I shouldn't have put you on the spot like that. It's just that—

that—" Charlotte shrugged, at a loss for words. How could she explain when she didn't quite understand it herself?

"It's just that you care about them," Judith offered softly, gently.

Charlotte nodded. "Yes—yes I do." She paused. "Maybe you could at least pass along a message for me. Would that be okay?"

Judith nodded. "I think that would be just fine."

"Just tell Jeanne to call me if there's anything I can do to help . . . anything at all."

Charlotte was used to staying busy. Since she had worked Saturday for Bitsy, she had expected to be off on Tuesday, her regular day to clean for the old lady. But she hadn't expected to be off two days in a row, and she found herself at a loss as to what to do.

For one thing, the house was quiet . . . too quiet. And lonely. Not even Sweety Boy's antics and chirps seemed to help.

There was plenty that needed doing, though, projects she'd been putting off due to lack of time . . . recording and totaling the month's receipts for tax purposes . . . taking inventory of her supplies . . . working on a bid for the Devillier job Cheré had told her about. And laundry, a large pile of dirty laundry that she'd had to ignore due to her unusually busy weekend, was still waiting for her beside her washing machine.

Charlotte tried to occupy both her time and her mind both days. Her daily thirty-minute walk helped somewhat, but concentration on anything for very long proved to be impossible. Her thoughts kept returning to the Dubuisson women. All she could think about was what Jeanne, Anna-Maria, and Clarice must be going through, how they were coping, and what, if anything, she could do to help ease their suffering.

But guilt plagued her, too, guilt for being so relieved that

Jackson had been the victim instead of one of the women. And she kept remembering the last time she had seen Jackson alive. In her mind's eye, she could still picture him dancing with Sydney Marriott on Friday night at the Zoo To Do, then, later, arguing with Sydney's husband, Tony.

And during those two days, as she waited, she kept hoping that Jeanne would call, yet dreading it at the same time.

By Tuesday afternoon, her nerves were stretched to the limit. Each time the phone rang, she felt a fresh wave of apprehension sweep through her.

Deciding that she'd just about had all she could stand and that taking yet a second walk might relieve some of the tension, Charlotte was lacing up her tennis shoes when the phone rang.

Once again, hoping the caller was Jeanne, she rushed to the phone and snatched up the receiver.

"Maid-for-a-Day, Charlotte speaking."

"Oh, Charlotte, I'm so glad you're home."

Bitsy. It was only Bitsy Duhe, and Charlotte almost groaned out loud with frustration.

"Don't you work for the Dubuissons?" the old lady asked.

Bitsy knew good and well that she worked for the Dubuissons, but Charlotte's vast experience in dealing with the old lady had taught her a few tricks about handling her. "Now, Miss Bitsy, you know I don't talk about my clients."

"Oh, Charlotte, don't be silly. Of course you talk about your clients. Why just Saturday you and I were discussing the Dubuissons."

Bitsy paused dramatically, and Charlotte rolled her eyes toward the ceiling. The temptation to point out that Bitsy had done all the discussing about the Dubuissons was strong. She was also tempted to point out that except for a couple of questions about Brian O'Connor, who wasn't a client, she'd simply listened. But Bitsy didn't give her the opportunity.

"And speaking of the Dubuissons," she continued, "that's

the reason I'm calling. Did you hear about Jackson? It's all over the news and made the front page of the *Picayune*."

Charlotte closed her eyes and sighed. "Yes, ma'am, I read the paper this morning."

"Well, my goodness, Charlotte, give me the scoop. I figured if anybody knew anything, it would be you."

Charlotte kept quiet on purpose and didn't answer. If she knew Bitsy, whether she answered or not, the old lady would keep right on talking, anyway. And she wasn't disappointed.

"The paper said a burglar broke in and killed him," Bitsy continued. "But I'd be willing to bet, when all's said and done, Tony Marriott was the one who did it, especially after that little show he put on Friday night. I've been thinking about calling the police myself—and you should think about it, too. After all, we were both eyewitnesses to that fight."

Charlotte shook her head and had to bite her tongue to keep from pointing out that about a hundred other people witnessed the altercation, too.

"So how was your granddaughter's visit," Charlotte asked in hopes of changing the subject.

"Oh, it was fine, but listen, Charlotte, I can't talk anymore right now. I think I'd better go ahead and make that call to the police. 'Bye now."

Before Charlotte had time to say anything, she heard the click on the other end of the phone line that indicated that Bitsy had hung up the receiver.

Charlotte took her walk, but it was just after the mechanical bird in the clock had finished singing the last of six cuckoos on Tuesday evening when the call from Jeanne finally came.

Chapter Seven

"**O**h, Jeanne, I'm so glad you called, and I'm so very sorry about Jackson."

"Thank you. I appreciate your sympathy."

Though Charlotte wasn't exactly sure what she'd expected Jeanne to sound like, a puzzled frown crossed her face when she heard the calm, matter-of-fact tone of the younger woman's voice.

"Are you okay?" Charlotte asked her.

"I think the standard answer is that I'm doing as well as can be expected under the circumstances."

Charlotte's frown deepened. Something wasn't right here, she thought. Was it possible that Jeanne might still be in shock? After all, what woman wouldn't be after finding her husband murdered? And different people reacted to traumatic events in different ways.

Then another thought occurred to her. Maybe Jeanne had been given something, some type of medication, to keep her calm.

"The reason I'm calling," Jeanne continued, "is to ask a favor. The police have finally finished gathering their evidence—thank God, they're finally gone. But they've left a mess, and I don't think I can—I just can't—"

The break in her voice, followed by the ensuing silence, was telling, and Charlotte found that she was relieved to know that Jeanne wasn't quite as cool or calm as she had first seemed. Surely, a certain amount of grief and emotion had to be healthier than keeping everything bottled up inside.

"I can come right over and clean it up for you if you need me to?" Charlotte offered.

A sigh of relief whispered through the telephone line, followed by a simple "Thank you."

"I'll be there in about twenty minutes."

"Twenty minutes will be fine, but I have to warn you, there are reporters all over the place. Maybe it would be best if you came in the back way."

Charlotte spotted the reporters camped in front of the house the minute she turned onto Jackson Avenue. The way they were standing around, clustered in small groups, reminded her of paradegoers during Mardi Gras, the kind who always arrived early so they could stake claims on the most advantageous spots to watch the parades.

Deciding the best bet was to park on the next block, she kept driving. "Bunch of vultures," she muttered as she drove past them. It was bad enough that the Dubuisson women had to cope with such a tragic loss, but to have to endure being held prisoners in their own home by the news media was the pits. Just the sight of the reporters made her angry enough to chew nails.

Still seething, Charlotte found a parking spot on Philip Street and grabbed her supplies. Ever wary of the reporters, she hurried down the street to the back entrance gate of the Dubuisson mansion.

The moment she pressed the buzzer on the gate, it clicked

open, so she figured that Jeanne must have been watching for her from the kitchen window.

Looking dry-eyed and stoic, Jeanne was standing at the back door when Charlotte crossed the deck. In contrast to her expression, for the first time that Charlotte could remember in the five years she'd worked for the Dubuissons, Jeanne looked almost rumpled. Her makeup was sparse and blotchy, and though the casual olive slacks and ivory blouse she wore weren't exactly wrinkled, the elegant, polished look that Charlotte had grown used to seeing was missing, all a sure sign of the turmoil that the poor woman had been through.

Charlotte almost reached out to Jeanne to give her a sympathetic hug, but she hesitated. One look at the rigid set of Jeanne's shoulders along with the strained expression on her face made Charlotte change her mind. "How are Anna-Maria and Miss Clarice?" she asked gently instead.

The line of Jeanne's mouth tightened. "Not well, I'm afraid." She signaled for Charlotte to come inside the house. "Anna-Maria went into hysterics yesterday when she found out." Jeanne firmly closed the door behind Charlotte and locked it. "The paramedics had to give her a shot to calm her down." Her gaze shifted toward the ceiling, and for a moment, a tinge of sadness flickered in her eyes. "She's upstairs in her room right now. Thank goodness she slept most of yesterday. But today was grueling, what with the police everywhere, asking all kinds of questions."

"And Miss Clarice? Where is she right now?"

Jeanne drew in a deep breath and sighed wearily. Once again the lines of her mouth tightened. "In her bed," she answered bluntly. "As usual, she's being her uncooperative self—refused to get up and has hardly touched a bite yesterday or today."

As understanding slowly dawned on Charlotte, her heart went out to the younger woman. No wonder Jeanne seemed so cold and aloof. She was hanging on to her own emotions by a thread. With the other women in the family so distraught, someone had to hold things together, and unfortunately for Jeanne, she was the one elected.

Though Charlotte had never experienced having a loved one murdered, she had experienced a situation very similar to Jeanne's when both her parents had died in a fatal airplane crash. Their deaths had left her with the total responsibility of caring for her sister, Madeline, then only fifteen, as well as Hank, who had been a toddler at the time. She could well remember that horrible, crushing feeling of being the person everyone else depended on.

"I'm afraid the police have left quite a mess."

Jeanne's words brought Charlotte back from thoughts of the past with a jolt, and she pushed away the painful memories, sealing them back into the compartment of her mind where they'd resided for more years than she cared to count. Past was past, and Charlotte had long ago discovered that in order to survive, she had to learn to live in the present.

"Where would you like me to start?" she asked.

"In the library." Jeanne turned and led the way through the dining room and into the foyer. "The rest can wait until tomorrow," she said as they walked down the hall toward the library. Halfway down the hallway, she suddenly stopped and turned to face Charlotte. "You will be coming tomorrow, won't you?"

When Charlotte nodded a confirmation, Jeanne seemed to breathe a sigh of relief.

At the doorway of the library though, Jeanne hesitated, just short of entering the room. "I—I'm not sure I can go in there," she said, staring at the opening. "Th-that's where it happened, where I found him. I didn't even realize he hadn't left for the office until I saw his briefcase still sitting on the floor in the foyer."

Charlotte felt her throat tighten, and she reached out and squeezed Jeanne's arm. "You don't have to go in."

Jeanne pulled her gaze away from the doorway, and her eyes filled with tears. She shook her head as if the action would hold the tears at bay. "Please," she whispered, her hands balling into fists. "Just clean it all up."

With one last entreating glance at Charlotte, she backed away, turned, then stumbled down the hallway.

Charlotte's first instinct was to go after her just to make sure that she would be okay. But after she thought about it for a moment, she decided that the best course of action was simply to do as the poor woman had asked, to clean up the mess.

The moment Charlotte entered the room, she wrinkled her nose against the sour odor that hung in the air like an invisible layer of fog. Death . . . and violence, she suddenly realized with a shiver. What she was smelling was death and the violence that had precipitated it.

No wonder Jeanne couldn't step foot in here, Charlotte thought as she gazed around the room. It was bad enough that the poor woman had been the one to find her husband murdered in the room. To make matters worse, the police had left the place in a mess.

Almost every surface in the small library was coated with a fine ashy film. Recalling the descriptions of the stuff from some of the police procedurals she'd read, she figured that the residue was the result of the police dusting for fingerprints.

Other than the fingerprint dust, one of the first things she noticed was the painting of the St. Louis Cathedral that hung between the built-in bookcases along the wall to her left. Instead of lying flat against the wall, the painting was sticking straight out, perpendicular to the wall.

Charlotte stepped over to the painting. Upon closer examination, she saw that it was hinged and hid a small wall safe; the door to the safe was open, and the safe itself was empty.

Funny, she thought. She'd known there was a safe somewhere in the house, and she'd dusted that particular painting many times. Even so, the hinges had been so well concealed that she never once suspected that it hid a wall safe. Whoever had installed it had done their job well.

She was still staring at the empty wall safe when a mosquito suddenly buzzed her head. When she swatted at the pesky insect, she noticed there were more flying around.

"What on earth—" She immediately searched for the source of their entry, and that was when she spotted the gaping black hole in the French door where one of the panes was missing. Small shards of glass littered the carpet in front of the doors, and as she stared at the hole, a terrifying realization washed over her. What she was looking at was the means of entry that had been used by the murderer.

Charlotte shivered and turned away to survey the room once again. She'd start with the desk first, she decided. Then she'd deal with the powder, glass, and the carpet.

The top of the desk was in shambles, with scattered papers, books, pens, several small framed photos, a collection of paperweights, and other odds and ends. In the midst of the clutter was a dark, uneven stain where it appeared that something had been spilled, then left to dry.

Charlotte began with gathering the papers. Only then did she notice that several of them were dotted with flecks of the same dark substance that was on the desk. As her gaze shifted between the papers in her hands and the stain on the desk, she suddenly realized what she was looking at.

Just clean it all up.

Charlotte shuddered with revulsion. No wonder Jeanne had fixated on the desk, she thought.

The dark stains had to be blood. Dried, congealed blood. Specifically Jackson Dubuisson's blood, which could only mean one thing. Jackson must have been murdered at his desk. Even as her stomach turned queasy, an eerie prickle of awareness marched down her spine.

Just being near the desk was dreadful enough. Charlotte

had to force herself to continue sorting through the blood-stained papers. Then she stacked the papers, along with the other items, in neat piles on the floor.

Armed with a small pail of warm, sudsy water, and rubber gloves, she scrubbed the desktop thoroughly. As she scrubbed, she tried to ignore the images flashing through her mind of Jackson slumped over the desk, his life's blood oozing from what could only have been a fatal head wound of some kind. And she tried to ignore the persistent whispers in the back of her mind, whispers that felt important, seemed even urgent, yet remained elusive.

But ignoring the images and the whispers proved almost impossible. By the time she'd rinsed and dried the desktop, then applied a coat of lemon oil and polished the wood, her hands were trembling.

After restoring the desk back to order, she found that the rest of her task was almost a relief. Once she'd completely dusted and wiped away all signs of the fingerprint powder, she gingerly picked up the larger pieces of broken glass and deposited them into a wastebasket.

Finally, all that remained to be done was to vacuum the carpet and she'd be finished. Then maybe, just maybe, the horrible, violent images that kept swimming in her mind and the urgent whispers would disappear.

But vacuuming would be noisy. And though the noise wouldn't disturb anyone upstairs, she wasn't exactly sure where Jeanne was at the moment.

Charlotte quickly walked through the downstairs rooms, searching for Jeanne's whereabouts. The last room she looked in was the back parlor. It was there that she finally located Jeanne, slumped over in a chair near the fireplace, her eyes closed and her breathing deep and even.

Poor thing must be exhausted, she thought as she tiptoed into the room and gently covered Jeanne with the crocheted afghan that was kept in a wicker basket near the sofa.

When Charlotte quietly left the room, she decided that

closing the doors to the parlor as well as closing off the library doors should muffle the sound of the noisy vacuum. After all, there was no sense in waking Jeanne until she was finished.

Though it wasn't the dirtiest or the messiest job Charlotte had ever tackled, cleaning up the library where Jackson had been murdered was by far the most horrible job she had ever been asked to do. Even so, once she'd vacuumed, all in all, it had only taken her a little over an hour to return the room back to order.

The only remaining problem was the gaping hole in the door. Charlotte decided that a piece of thick cardboard taped over the hole would have to suffice until Jeanne could call in someone to repair the broken glass pane. At least tape and cardboard might be enough to keep out the mosquitoes and bugs.

Charlotte had to rummage through almost every drawer in the kitchen before she finally located a roll of masking tape in the last drawer beneath the built-in oven. But where on earth was she going to find a piece of cardboard?

Then she remembered. In her van was a cardboard box that might be large enough to use. She should be able to cut off a piece that would be just about the right size.

The sudden peal of the doorbell in the quiet house gave Charlotte a start. With a frown of irritation and hoping the noise wouldn't wake Jeanne just yet, she dropped the tape into the deep pocket of her apron and hurried from the kitchen.

The ornate oak entry door, with its insets of narrow, leaded glass panels, was framed on either side by cut-glass window lights. Through the window light on her right, Charlotte recognized her niece's partner, Louis Thibodeaux. "Now what?" she muttered as she unlocked and opened the door.

Standing beside the detective was her niece. Behind the two detectives was a uniformed policeman. Judith frowned the moment she saw Charlotte; then she entered the foyer. Thibodeaux and the other man trailed after her.

"Aunt Charley, what are you doing here?"

Charlotte closed the door behind them, then faced her niece.

"Jeanne called me to clean up the mess your people left in the library."

Louis Thibodeaux's dark eyebrows shot up. "She did what?" His voice was a growl of disbelief as he glared at Charlotte as if she were a bug in need of squashing. Beside him, Judith groaned.

Charlotte glared right back at her niece's partner, not liking his tone or attitude one bit. "I don't think I stuttered, Detective Thibodeaux."

"Great! That's just wonderful," he said, each word dripping with sarcasm.

An uneasy feeling washed through Charlotte as she stared first at Louis Thibodeaux, then at her niece.

Judith narrowed her eyes and tilted her head. "Did you, Aunt Charley? Did you clean it up yet?"

When Charlotte slowly nodded, the affirming answer brought on another round of groans from both detectives as well as the uniformed policemen.

"Didn't you see the yellow crime-scene tape across the door?" But before Charlotte could answer, Judith answered her own question. "Of course you didn't, because Jeanne had probably already removed it."

The dire implication wasn't lost on Charlotte. If Jeanne had removed the crime-scene tape and directed Charlotte to clean up the library, then she must have something to hide. And if she had something to hide, did she also have something to do with Jackson's murder?

Charlotte shook her head in denial, but before she could protest aloud, Jeanne suddenly emerged from the back parlor.

"What's going on out here, Charlotte?" she asked. "Who's—" Jeanne froze, and her face clouded over with a look of pure distaste. "Why are these people back again?"

All eyes had turned toward Jeanne, but Louis Thibodeaux was the one who spoke first. "Mrs. Dubuisson, I'm afraid you're in a lot of trouble."

Chapter
Eight

For long seconds, Jeanne simply stared at the detective and made no response.

No matter what the implications, Charlotte refused to believe that Jeanne could have had anything to do with Jackson's murder. She was sure that there had to be a rational explanation for the misunderstanding about the crime-scene tape.

Louis Thibodeaux advanced menacingly toward Jeanne. "Why?" he asked, his eyes narrowing to dark slits. "Why would you purposely have that room cleaned when you knew we were coming back for one last look? Why—unless you have something to hide? What are you trying to cover up, Mrs. Dubuisson?"

Charlotte had every intention of staying put to hear Jeanne's explanation, but at that moment, Judith caught her eye. There was a look of warning on her niece's face, and with a sharp jerk of her head toward the dining room, she indicated that Charlotte should make herself scarce.

Feeling somewhat like a rat deserting the ship, Charlotte

grudgingly left the foyer. She was almost to the kitchen before she heard Jeanne finally answer the detective.

"No one said anything about coming back," Jeanne told him, her voice cold and blunt. "Besides, I was told they were finished."

"Who told you that?"

"I don't remember—one of the officers."

"Which one?"

In the kitchen, Charlotte hovered just inside the kitchen doorway. She hardly dared to breathe for fear of missing the ensuing argument between Jeanne and Judith's partner.

"There was no crime-scene tape." Jeanne insisted. "And how many times do I have to tell you that no one told me I shouldn't go in there."

Louis Thibodeaux's voice was a low rumble, and Charlotte couldn't make out exactly what he'd said in response, but she had no trouble hearing Jeanne's shrill retort.

"Stop it!" she cried. "No more questions, no more of your accusations, not without my lawyer."

From that point on, nothing but the sound of low murmurs came from the foyer. Unable to determine what was being said, Charlotte was almost ready to give up trying when she saw her niece appear around the corner, where the dining room opened onto the foyer, and stride purposefully toward her.

When Judith reached the kitchen doorway, she took Charlotte firmly by the arm and led her farther into the kitchen. "You should go on home now, Aunt Charley," she said, her voice low and urgent.

"But what about Jeanne? I think I should stay here until her lawyer comes."

Judith shook her head. "There's no need. Her lawyer isn't coming tonight. He's instructed her not to answer any more questions until tomorrow morning, when he can meet her at the station." She narrowed her eyes. "And get that stubborn look off your face, Auntie. Given the mood Thibodeaux's in, I—well I don't want to have to lock horns with him tonight over my aunt's part in this fiasco. Someone screwed up royally, and heads are gonna roll over this one. I just don't want it to be your head. And you know the old saying. Out of sight, out of mind."

Charlotte wanted to argue but knew that Judith was only trying to protect her, and she certainly didn't want to cause her niece any problems or have to deal with her rude partner. "I'll leave," she finally relented, "but only if you promise to call me later."

Judith shrugged. "I'll try, Aunt Charley, but I really can't promise. Oh, yeah, and another thing. If you haven't already done so, for now—for the duration of this investigation—I'd just as soon you didn't tell Mrs. Dubuisson that we're related. Believe me, it's better for everyone concerned if she doesn't know."

Judith never did call that night. Charlotte finally crawled into bed and turned off the bedside lamp at around eleven. After an hour of tossing and turning, her four-poster bed began to feel like a torture chamber; she felt every lump in the old mattress. With a groan and a vow that just as soon as she got a few extra dollars, a new mattress was going to the top of her list of things to replace, she switched the lamp back on.

She tried to read for a while, hoping that doing so would help relax her enough to sleep. But each time she grew drowsy and turned off the lamp, visions of the bloodstained desk, along with the argument between Jeanne and the detective, swam through her head.

Reading about such things in mystery novels was one

thing, but now, having actually experienced it, gave Charlotte a whole new appreciation for what her niece had to contend with on a day-by-day basis.

And so it went throughout the long, restless night. Consequently, when her alarm finally jangled the following morning, her head ached, and she could barely open her eyes.

Logic said that a good brisk walk would help clear her head. But Charlotte was in no mood for logic, and after hitting the snooze alarm twice, with a groan she finally forced herself to climb out of bed. By then there was barely enough time to dress, and she had to settle for a quick cup of instant coffee instead of waiting for a whole pot to brew.

Because of the reporters still camped out in front of the house, Jeanne met Charlotte at the back door again. Charlotte noticed that in contrast to the night before, there was no rumpled look about Jeanne this morning; yet even though she was dressed impeccably, complete with flawless makeup, a navy silk suit, and every hair in place, there was a weariness about her eyes that not even makeup could conceal.

"I have to leave for a while," she told Charlotte once they were inside. "I have some business that needs tending, and I—I also have to make funeral arrangements. For when they release Jackson's body," she added.

Charlotte set her supply carrier on the floor. Though she was well aware that Jeanne's so-called business included a trip to the police station, she recalled Judith's warning about revealing their relationship, so she simply nodded in response.

Jeanne shifted from one foot to the other, started to say something else, but hesitated. Then, as if gathering her courage, she straightened her shoulders. "I truly appreciate you coming last night," she said. "And I want to apologize for the misunderstanding with the police." She sighed deeply. "But I also need to ask another favor of you."

A sudden rush of sympathy for the younger woman gushed through Charlotte. With virtually no friends and little family left, Jeanne had no one she could turn to, no one but the maid. How sad that had to be for someone of her social status, someone who appeared to have everything that money could buy but no one to depend on in a crunch. Was it any wonder that she found it hard to ask for help?

Charlotte reached out, caught Jeanne's hand, and gave it a gentle squeeze. "You're welcome," she said softly. "No apologies necessary, and I'll be happy to do whatever I can to help out."

Jeanne attempted a smile, but the telltale quiver of her bottom lip betrayed her. "Thank you," she whispered. She cleared her throat as if the action would banish the strong emotion evident in her eyes. "James called late last night," she said. "He insisted that Anna-Maria should spend the day with him. At first, she didn't want to go anywhere, but he talked her into it. And frankly, I'm relieved. She needs his support now more than ever."

"Her fiancé sounds like a really nice young man." Charlotte offered.

"Yes," Jeanne nodded. "Yes, he is. He also offered to come with us to the funeral home later this morning. But with Anna-Maria gone and now I have to leave, well . . . I— I need someone to look in on Mother. There's a service I could call," she hastened to add, "one that specializes in sitting with elderly people, but when I mentioned it, Mother pitched a fit."

Charlotte held up her hand. "Don't say another word. I'll be happy to check on Miss Clarice for you while you run your errands."

* * *

Before Jeanne left, she brought down the wicker tray she used when she served Clarice her meals. From the looks of the food left in the dishes, the old lady had barely touched her breakfast.

"I'm worried about her," Jeanne confided. "If she keeps this up, I'll have to call her doctor."

"I'll watch her," Charlotte reassured the younger woman. "She's going to be just fine. Now run along and take care of your business."

Jeanne nodded, collected her purse and keys, and left through the back door.

Charlotte stood in the doorway and watched her cross the deck. After she'd closed and locked the door, it suddenly occurred to her that Jeanne's car was parked in the front driveway. She couldn't quite picture Jeanne catching the city bus or walking all the way to St. Charles to catch the trolley just to avoid the reporters.

Maybe she called a taxi, Charlotte thought as she peered out the window overlooking the backyard. But when a Ford Explorer instead of a taxi pulled up beside the back gate and Jeanne got inside, Charlotte grew even more curious.

She caught a quick glimpse of the driver when Jeanne opened the passenger door, but she didn't recognize the sandy-haired man due to the distance and the tinting of the vehicle's windows. So who was the driver? Charlotte wondered as she turned away from the window.

The answer came in a flash, and Charlotte rolled her eyes toward the ceiling. Her lawyer. "Of course, you silly woman," she murmured. The man had to be Jeanne's lawyer.

Charlotte decided that the best place to start cleaning was in the kitchen.

Though the Dubuissons' house was never really dirty, Charlotte had worked out a schedule of sorts to keep it that way. Mondays were for general cleaning, which included dusting, mopping, vacuuming, and laundry. Wednesdays were reserved for the deeper cleaning: baseboards, inside windows, and the refrigerator. Fridays were much like Mondays, except on Fridays, Charlotte always put fresh sheets on all of the beds.

Charlotte removed several small dishes of leftover food from the refrigerator. Then she wiped down the inside and rearranged the contents. As lagniappe, a little extra service she liked to provide, she made a list of condiments that needed replenishing. To the list she added eggs, bacon, and milk.

Once she'd wiped down the outside of the refrigerator with a degreaser, she decided it was time to check on Clarice.

She climbed the stairs and approached the old lady's room. She'd expected to hear the television, but for once there was no canned laughter or clapping from a TV audience, the usual sounds of the game programs that Clarice always watched.

From the doorway, she saw that the television set was silent and dark. And so was the rest of the room. All of the blinds were closed, and the curtains were drawn. Only tiny slivers of morning light peeped between the closed slats of the blinds, just enough for Charlotte to make out Clarice's huddled form beneath the covers on her bed.

It took a moment for her eyes to adjust to the dim room. As she continued staring at the huddled form, she was finally able to detect movement indicating that the old lady was still breathing. Clarice was probably just fine, Charlotte figured. But with an older person, one could never be sure. Maybe she should take a closer look just to be sure. After all, she had promised Jeanne she would check on her mother for her.

Charlotte was halfway to the bed when she heard the sounds . . . sobs . . . low, muffled sobs.

Under other circumstances, she might have assumed that

the old lady was simply grieving over the death of her son-in-law, but after hearing Clarice and Jeanne's argument and her talk with Jeanne on Friday, Charlotte found it hard to believe Jackson's death could be the reason for Clarice's tears.

"Miss Clarice?" Charlotte stepped closer to the bed. "What's wrong?" She reached out and touched what she thought was the old lady's shoulder. "Are you ill? Are you in pain?"

"Go-go a-away," the old lady whimpered, cringing beneath Charlotte's touch. "Just leave me alone."

Charlotte withdrew her hand and shifted uneasily from one foot to the other. Should she leave? Or should she stay? What if the old lady was ill and didn't know what she was saying? What if she left her and Clarice had another stroke?

"I don't think I can," she finally said. "I don't think I can leave you like this, Miss Clarice. Won't you please tell me what's wrong?"

Then a thought occurred to her. Maybe Clarice had had a change of heart. Maybe now that Jackson was dead, she was having trouble coping with her feelings about him. "Sometimes sharing things makes a burden lighter," Charlotte said gently.

From beneath the covers came a loud snort followed by Clarice's muffled voice. "And sometimes sharing makes great fuel for gossip, eh, Charlotte? Be sure and tell all your friends about poor old crippled Clarice, locked away in her room, grieving for her dead son-in-law."

"I don't gossip," she told the old lady bluntly. Clarice's accusation stung and insulted the very principle that Charlotte had upheld for years, but rather than being affronted, she found herself amused. At times, Clarice reminded her of a child, one minute crying, the next, pitching a temper tantrum.

Charlotte reached down and switched on the bedside lamp.

Suddenly, Clarice threw back the covers and struggled to

sit up. "I don't want that light on," she cried, promptly switching it off.

But in that brief moment, Charlotte got a good look at the old lady, and what she saw was a shock. Clarice appeared haggard and unkempt. The old lady's thin hair was a tangle of dirty gray wisps, there were dark circles around her rheumy eyes, and the front of her wrinkled nightgown was spotted with what appeared to be food stains.

"And I ain't grieving," Clarice shouted. "Not for that worthless piece of—"

"Miss Clarice! Shame on you. You shouldn't speak ill of the dead," she told her.

"I'll speak any way I want to speak. Besides, none of it matters anymore." She squeezed her eyes shut, and a sob caught in her throat. "It-it's all going to hell in a hand basket, anyway. Everything that Andrew tried to do." She bowed her head and began to shake it from side to side as she clutched the sheet in her hands. "It-it's all th-that O'Connor boy's fault. If he'd just stayed where he belonged, none of this would be happening."

Charlotte frowned. "O'Connor? Brian O'Connor?"

"He did it," Clarice moaned. "Just as sure as I'm sit'n here, he did it. Sneaking around down on the porch . . . think'n nobody knows he's down there snoop'n around, spying. Well, I know—know all about what he's been up to."

Charlotte could hardly believe her ears. What's more, she wasn't sure just how much of the old lady's ramblings she should believe. Clarice never went downstairs, so how could she know that anyone was on the porch? "Miss Clarice, are you saying that Brian O'Connor killed Jackson?"

"Who else?" she cried. "Ever since that summer he was here helping his daddy with the gardens, he wanted my Jeanne. Hated Jackson 'cause she married him instead."

Suddenly, a moan erupted from the old lady's lips, a moan of pure anguish that sent chills chasing up Charlotte's arms.

"Oh, my poor, poor Anna-Maria," she sobbed. "What's she gonna do when she finds out she's got a murderer for a daddy."

Charlotte frowned, finding it harder and harder to follow Clarice's irrational ravings. "But Jackson's the one who was murdered, so how could he be the murderer?"

"No, no, no!" Clarice jerked her head from side to side, emphasizing each word. "Not Jackson, you ninny. Brian O'Connor. He's Anna-Maria's real daddy."

Shock waves washed over Charlotte, and she was stunned speechless. Brian O'Connor was Anna-Maria's father?

But Clarice hadn't finished, it seemed, and Charlotte could do nothing but stand there and listen. While she was truly mesmerized by what the old lady was revealing, Clarice's logic was baffling. She'd accused Charlotte of being a gossip, yet here she was now, telling her all the family secrets. Maybe Jeanne was right, after all. Maybe the old lady was going senile.

"He thought he was so smart," Clarice continued. "But my Andrew was smarter. That stupid boy actually thought he could get that airhead daughter of mine to run off with him—and she probably would have, too, if Andrew hadn't of stopped him. Stopped him good, too. No one ever defied Andrew and got away with it. He had that boy's butt thrown in jail.

"But chickens come home to roost," Clarice added. "They always do." She sniggered. "Or maybe I should say roosters. That O'Connor boy just couldn't stay away. And Jackson got his. Serves him right, too." She suddenly laughed. "The Good Book says that the love of money is the root of all evil. Well, my Andrew loved money, and so did Jackson. Andrew used it to threaten Jeanne and used it to bribe Jackson. Told Jackson if he'd marry Jeanne and pretend that Anna-Maria was his baby, he'd make him a partner." Clarice laughed again, a maniacal sound that gave

Charlotte the creeps. "And now look at the both of them. Both dead. And what good's all that money now?"

Both dead . . . both dead . . . Charlotte shivered. The persistent whispers she'd heard in her mind from the night before were back, and so was the eerie prickle of awareness. But like the night before, when she'd first realized that Jackson had died at his desk, the whispers were just as elusive now as they had been then. And now, as she had last night, Charlotte tried once again to ignore them.

"You're right," she told Clarice, hoping she could calm her. "The money's not much good to either of them now."

Charlotte should have let it drop right then and there. For the sake of keeping the old lady calm, she should have completely changed the subject. Yet in spite of her good intentions, her curiosity was aroused, and she found she couldn't simply drop it. Too many unanswered questions crowded her mind, demanding answers.

"Just one thing, though, Miss Clarice. I'm curious. Later on, after Brian got out of prison, why didn't Jeanne simply divorce Jackson and go off with him, especially after Mr. Andrew's death?"

Clarice covered a yawn even as she shook her head. "Too late by then," she mumbled, leaning her head back against the pillows. "By then, Anna-Maria thought Jackson was her daddy, and Jackson threatened Jeanne. Told her if she ever left him, he'd make sure that little girl found out who her real daddy was, said he'd tell her all about how her real daddy was nothing but a no-account jailbird, then he'd tell everyone else."

Charlotte shuddered inwardly. Only a truly cruel man would even threaten something so mean and contemptible.

The old lady yawned again, and her eyes drifted shut. "Truth ever came out, my Anna-Maria would never be able to take her rightful place in New Orleans society." Clarice sighed, then murmured. "Be too big a scandal. Nobody suitable would have married her."

As Charlotte stood there, trying to absorb all that Clarice had revealed, the old lady's breathing slowed until it became deep and even. But her last words kept swirling through Charlotte's head. *Nobody suitable would have married her....* *Nobody suitable would have married her....* The more she thought about the implications of such a statement, the angrier she grew.

Just like Jeanne, Charlotte had never married the father of her child, so did that make him unsuitable? According to Clarice's screwed-up standards, it did. Never mind that he was a devoted, loving son. Never mind that his morals were above reproach. And never mind that he had become a well-respected, much sought-after surgeon, a doctor who people entrusted their very lives to.

Charlotte glared at the old lady, now fast asleep and completely oblivious to the turmoil her careless words had caused. Why was she letting such hogwash get to her? she wondered even as she reminded herself that Clarice's priorities were not only way off but out-and-out wrong.

Having come from working-class people, Charlotte had never been a part of, nor had she been able to understand, all of the rites of passage connected with so-called New Orleans wealthy society. Coming-out parties, the debutante thing, all designed to showcase young women of wealth, to parade them in front of young men who were their so-called contemporaries. To Charlotte, it was a lot of rigmarole that amounted to nothing truly important.

Love, responsibility, family, and friends were what was truly important. Putting food on the table and paying the bills were important. And above all, one's faith in God was the most important.

Clarice emitted a raunchy snore, and a slow smile pulled at Charlotte's lips. People like Clarice, people of wealth and social standing, were no better than anyone else. They just had more money. So why were they held in such esteem by those who had less money? *The love of money is the root of all evil*.

Charlotte grimaced. No truer words were ever written. Of course, to be fair, she thought, she supposed that if she'd grown up on the other side of the fence, she might feel very differently about the importance of such things.

Charlotte tiptoed out of the room and pulled the door closed behind her. She might feel differently, but she couldn't imagine that she actually would. She was simply too practical-minded. Always had been.

From behind the closed door, the old lady snored peacefully. Outside in the hallway, Charlotte fretted over what Clarice had revealed.

Was any of it true? Or was it all simply the fabrications of a confused old lady? Was Brian O'Connor truly Anna-Maria's father instead of Jackson? Could he have murdered Jackson in cold blood as some sort of retribution for the past? Men had killed for a lot less.

But why now? Why, so many years later?

Charlotte thought about calling her niece and telling her what Clarice had said about Brian O'Connor. Then she thought about all of the questions Judith would be obligated to ask, questions that could prove both embarrassing as well as stressful to Jeanne, especially if none of it was true.

And proof. Judith would want some kind of proof. But short of asking Jeanne to confirm or deny what Clarice had revealed, there was no way of proving that the old lady was telling the truth. Judith would more than likely write it off as simply the ramblings of an embittered, senile old woman.

No, Charlotte finally decided. She just couldn't do that to Jeanne. Not only would doing such a thing be a betrayal of confidence, but telling tales on clients was highly unprofessional, in Charlotte's opinion. Besides, even if she asked Jeanne, more than likely she would deny everything, especially if what Clarice had said were true and she had sacrificed herself by settling for a loveless marriage so that she could protect her daughter's paternity. Jeanne already had enough to contend with, anyway, she decided.

With a heavy sigh, Charlotte trudged down the hallway. As long as she was already upstairs, she could make a start at cleaning the other bedrooms.

When Charlotte entered Anna-Maria's room, she was shocked at what she saw. Normally, the girl was tidy and took pride in both her surroundings and her appearance, but the pink-and-white princess room, as Charlotte thought of it, looked as if a hurricane had blown through it.

Several pairs of jeans, a pile of T-shirts, along with an array of lacy bras and panties, were strewn across the floor near the closet. The embroidered silk duvet was in a jumble on the bed, spilling onto the floor. On the dresser was a collection of dirty glasses and mugs. The mugs were empty, but a couple of the glasses still contained a dark liquid that she suspected was Coke, since that was Anna-Maria's drink of choice. Charlotte counted four plates stacked together on the floor in front of the dresser. The top plate had a half-eaten slice of pizza on it, and from the uneven way the plates beneath were stacked, she suspected they still contained food, too.

By the time that Charlotte finished cleaning Anna-Maria's room, it was almost noon, time for lunch, and she almost panicked. With Jeanne gone, it would be up to her to fix Clarice's noonday meal.

After a quick peek at the old lady, Charlotte hurried down the stairs, her hands filled with the dirty glasses and dishes from the girl's room.

Thank goodness Clarice was still sleeping, she thought. Maybe she would have time to come up with something really appetizing for her, something that would entice her to eat. And wouldn't that be a nice surprise for Jeanne, for her to know that her mother was finally eating again.

But what to fix? she wondered. What would Clarice be more likely to eat? Charlotte was almost to the kitchen door when she heard a noise and suddenly froze.

Someone was in the kitchen.

Visions of the broken pane of glass in the library and the bloodstains on the desk danced in her head. She gripped the dishes tighter to keep them from rattling.

Chapter Nine

Charlotte fought down the panic that was making her legs weak. Should she stay, or should she run? And if she ran, then what about Clarice?

She wanted to run. Oh, how she wanted to run, screaming into the streets. But there was no way in good conscience that she could leave the poor defenseless old lady at the mercy of the intruder.

The police. What she needed to do was call for help . . . call 911. A phone. Where was the closest telephone, the one that was farthest away from the kitchen?

Her eyes glued to the kitchen doorway, Charlotte slowly took a step backward. If she could just get to the back parlor without alerting the intruder, then—

Charlotte froze when she heard footsteps from the kitchen . . . decisive footsteps headed her way.

"Who's out there?" a voice called out.

Jeanne's voice. No intruder. Just Jeanne.

Relief washed over Charlotte like a warm spring shower. "It's Charlotte. Jeanne, it's just me."

Jeanne stepped into the doorway. "My goodness,

Charlotte! What are you doing sneaking around out here? I thought you were upstairs. You gave me a terrible fright."

"That makes two of us," Charlotte quipped. "I heard a noise in the kitchen and thought— Well, I thought—"

"You thought, and I thought—"

Charlotte nodded. "I'm sorry I frightened you. I was just on my way to fix lunch for Miss Clarice." She nodded at the wicker tray Jeanne was holding. "But I see that you beat me to it."

"Yes—yes I did, and I'm the one who should apologize. I should have let you know I was home again. How is Mother, by the way?"

Charlotte hesitated, shifting from one foot to the other one. Now would be the time to tell Jeanne about the things that her mother had said. Jeanne really needed to know. But one look at the shadows of fatigue beneath the younger woman's eyes and she knew she couldn't do it; she just couldn't add to her worries, not right now.

"She was still sleeping a few minutes ago when I looked in on her," Charlotte told her instead. "And speaking of sleep. When was the last time you slept? You look really tired."

Jeanne shrugged, then shifted her gaze to stare at the floor. "I'm beginning to wonder if I'll ever sleep again," she said. "And I am tired."

"Of course you are, you poor thing." It was bad enough that Jeanne had to cope with her husband being murdered and deal with making arrangements for his funeral, but she'd also had to contend with being questioned by the police like some ordinary criminal as well, thanks to Judith and Louis Thibodeaux. "Anyone would be tired after going through what you've had to go through," Charlotte told her gently. "Tell you what." She set the glasses and dishes she was holding down on the dining-room table. "Why don't you let me carry that tray up for you and you go take a nice long nap."

She reached to take the tray from the younger woman, but Jeanne shook her head no.

"That's very kind of you," Jeanne said, "but there's something I have to discuss with Mother . . . something that I really need to take care of first."

Charlotte let her hands fall to her sides, and she stepped back. "Well, if you're sure . . ."

Jeanne gave her a weary smile. "At this point, I'm not really sure about anything."

"All the more reason you need to rest," Charlotte insisted.

Jeanne sighed. "I know you mean well, and there's nothing I would like more right now. But you know what they say—no rest for the weary. Maybe later, though—after I make sure that Mother eats. Then maybe I'll lie down for a while. But I do appreciate your concern," she added.

Charlotte knew when she was beaten, knew when to give in. "In that case"—she turned and picked up the dishes she'd set on the table—"I'll just put these in the dishwasher; then I'll go ahead and clean your bedroom. That way I won't have to disturb you when you do decide to rest."

A few minutes later, when Charlotte entered the master suite, one quick glance around the room told her that cleaning it wouldn't take long. In comparison to Anna-Maria's room, the suite was inordinately neat. In fact, except for one of Jackson's shirts tossed carelessly across the foot of the bed and a pair of his shoes on the floor near the dresser, the room looked almost exactly the same as she'd left it after cleaning on Friday, as if no one had occupied the room since then.

"Now that's strange," she murmured, gazing at the king-sized bed.

Only one side of the bed had been slept in. The left side. Jackson's side. Charlotte knew it was Jackson's side because it was next to the alarm clock, and she'd once overheard Jeanne talking and laughing with Anna-Maria about how

Jackson insisted on sleeping next to the alarm clock, since she had a bad habit of turning it off instead of hitting the snooze button.

The other side of the bed, Jeanne's side, was unused. The comforter was still smooth and in place, as were the pillow shams and throw pillows.

So where had Jeanne slept?

She could understand that after Jackson's murder it might have been too painful for Jeanne to sleep in the same bed that she'd shared with her husband. Even now, some forty-odd years later, Charlotte still couldn't pass the Pontchartrain Hotel without having qualms.

The one and only time she'd ever slept with Hank's father had been in that hotel. Unlike Jeanne, she didn't know what it was like to sleep with a man for almost a lifetime or even have a husband. And though she'd never regretted that one night of indiscretion for a moment, nor had she regretted the results of that night, just looking at the place conjured up painful memories of what could have been . . . what should have been, if not for a foolish war.

For years after his death, she'd fantasized about how her life might have been if he'd lived. In her dreams, she'd pictured a perfect marriage, one patterned after that of her own parents, one of a loving, caring couple with the same aims and goals. Only as she'd grown older had she come to realize that reality and fantasies rarely meshed. Her parents' marriage had been the rare exception to the rule, from what she'd seen.

Just because one person loved another didn't mean they were necessarily suited to marriage. Her son had loved his ex-wife; her sister had claimed to love both of her ex-husbands. And just because a couple were wealthy and socially compatible didn't guarantee everlasting happiness or harmony, not if Clarice and Jeanne's marriages were gauges to measure by.

Charlotte sighed deeply and shook her head in an attempt

to shake loose the grip of her painful past. Wondering or even speculating whether she and Hank senior would have had a successful marriage was a waste of time and energy. She'd do better to concentrate on the present instead of the past.

Charlotte stared at the bed. So where had Jeanne slept Friday and Saturday? Why hadn't she slept with her husband?

"And why are you standing around daydreaming when there's work to be done," she muttered. When and where Jeanne slept, or even with whom she slept, was none of her business.

Even though nothing was really dusty, Charlotte dusted and polished all of the furniture surfaces, anyway, then moved on into the bathroom. There she emptied the wastebasket into a plastic garbage bag first, then cleaned the vanity mirror. Next, she wiped down the marble sink and countertop. After she'd scrubbed and disinfected the toilet, she did the same to the bathtub.

Her last chore was to clean the tiled shower. But when she pulled the bottle of tile cleaner from her supply carrier, she groaned, realizing it was almost empty.

Thanks to her restless night and having overslept, she hadn't bothered to check on the cleaners in the supplier carrier, as she normally would have.

"Wonderful," she muttered. "Just wonderful." Now she'd have to waste time on a trip out to the van to refill the bottle. Ordinarily, a trip to the van wouldn't have bothered her, but because of all of the reporters, now she had to walk clear over to the next block. With a firm grip on the empty container and dark thoughts about the news media in general, she stomped out of the bathroom.

As Charlotte approached the door leading into Clarice's rooms, she suddenly stiffened when she heard the raised voices coming from inside. Since the door was half-open, she slowed her steps to a halt just past the opening.

Jeanne and Clarice were at it again.

"You have to, Mother!" Jeanne insisted, an edge of desperation in her tone. "You have to go."

"I don't want to, and besides, you know I can't get up and down the stairs," Clarice whined.

Charlotte frowned as she recalled scrubbing up the scuff marks on the tile in Clarice's bathroom, then scrubbing up the ones that looked exactly the same on the stairs.

"That's bull, and you know it," Jeanne retorted. "I'll get Max to help you down the stairs, just like he does each and every month for your doctor's visit. Besides, what will everyone think if you don't show up for your own son-in-law's funeral?"

"What will everyone think?" Clarice's indignant voice was a high-pitched squeal. "Since when do you care what everyone thinks?"

"Mother, please, don't start that again. Not now. You have to go, and that's all there is to it."

"For your information, missy, I don't have to do anything I don't want to do. I didn't like that two-timing gigolo while he was alive, and unlike some people," she said, sarcasm dripping with each word, "I refuse to be a hypocrite and pretend I'm grieving now that he's dead."

"So what about Anna-Maria? Don't you even care what she thinks?"

Charlotte didn't wait around for Clarice's answer. She figured she'd already heard more than she should have heard. Even so, the harsh, angry words of the two women rang in her ears all the way down the stairs, through the house, and out the back door.

Clarice might insist she wasn't grieving, might claim to have disliked Jackson, but if she wasn't grieving, then what on earth was going on with her? Why had she declined to get out of bed, and why had she declined to eat the food brought to her?

Charlotte noticed a group of people huddled together just across the street from the back gate as she walked the half a block to her van. Were they reporters, or were they simply gawkers wanting to get a look at the murdered man's house? From her vantage point, she couldn't tell.

Probably gawkers, she thought with disgust as she unlocked the van and climbed inside. Of course, they could simply be one of the many guided walking tours that roamed the city. Tourists were always wandering around through the Garden District.

Charlotte set about refilling the bottle of tile cleaner, then climbed out of the van. She was locking the door when she saw a man break free from the group and stride purposefully toward her.

"Hey!" he called out. "Hey, lady, can I talk to you a minute?"

Something about the slim but powerfully built man set off warning bells, and Charlotte always heeded warning bells. She firmly shook her head and walked briskly toward the back gate.

"Wait up, lady. I'm a reporter for the *Times-Picayune*. I just want to ask a couple of questions."

Again Charlotte shook her head. "Go away. No one here is interested in answering any of your questions." She picked up her pace, but she could still hear him behind her.

She was almost to the gate when he suddenly darted past her, stepped in front of her, and pivoted, blocking her path. "How long have you worked for the Dubuissons?"

Charlotte shook her head. "Go away." She tried sidestepping to get around him, but he grabbed her supply carrier.

"Come on, lady. Just a couple of questions."

Sudden anger shot through her. "Let go!" she demanded.

"Don't you want your name in the paper?"

Charlotte glared at the man. Gripping the supply carrier with both hands, she shouted, "No! Now let go!" She yanked hard, and he lost his hold. She feigned to the right. Before he could regain his balance, she jerked back to the left and bolted through the gate opening.

Charlotte knew that the gate would automatically lock once it was pulled into place, and she quickly slammed it shut.

With the locked gate between her and the man, she still didn't breathe easy until she reached the steps leading to the deck.

"Aw, come on, lady," he called out.

His hands clutched the cast-iron bars on the other side, giving him the appearance of being behind the bars of a jail. "Give me a break here. All I wanted was to ask a couple of questions."

"Go away," she yelled, "or I'm calling the police." With one last, wary look at the reporter, she hurried across the deck. Once inside the house, she shoved the door shut and locked it, but her heart was still racing.

"Charlotte?"

The abrupt sound of Jeanne's voice gave her a start. Charlotte whirled around to see the younger woman standing in the doorway of the kitchen.

"What's going on? Did I hear voices outside?"

Still so angry that she could hardly talk, Charlotte nodded as she shoved away from the door. "Just an obnoxious reporter," she told her, "looking for a story."

A haunted expression came over Jeanne's face. "Aren't they all?" Her voice quivered, and if possible, she suddenly looked even more exhausted than she had earlier.

"Now, don't you worry one minute about that man out there," Charlotte told her, her protective instincts flaring. "I'll fix his wagon good. I'll call my niece—"

I'd just as soon you didn't tell Mrs. Dubuisson that we're related. . . .

"The police," Charlotte quickly interjected to cover the slip. "If he doesn't go away soon, I'll call the police—or just as good, I'll call a friend of mine who's a managing editor with the *Picayune*." Making a mental note to phone Mary Johnson to complain about the reporter, she motioned toward the general direction of the foyer. "You go on back upstairs now. Go to your room and take a nap. Turn the ringer off the phone," she added, "and I'll answer it if anyone calls and take messages for you down here."

"Sounds wonderful," Jeanne said. "But I don't think I'll be able to sleep. It's like I'm too tired now, if that makes any sense."

Charlotte nodded. "That happens sometimes. What about something to help you sleep? Doesn't Miss Clarice have a prescription for something like that?"

Jean wrinkled her forehead in thought. "Yes, I'm sure she does, but—"

"Normally, I wouldn't suggest that anyone take someone else's prescription drugs," Charlotte hastened to add, "but I'm sure that whatever Miss Clarice is taking would be mild enough and safe enough for you to take, too."

The younger woman nodded. "I've taken sleeping pills before, so that's not really a concern."

"Tell you what, then." Charlotte moved closer to Jeanne. "Let's get you tucked into bed and I'll go ask Miss Clarice for one of those pills for you." She placed her hand at the small of Jeanne's back and urged her back through the dining room and into the foyer. That Jeanne willingly went along with her and didn't argue or resist was telling. The woman was past exhaustion, inside and out.

It was only when they reached the door to the master suite and Jeanne hesitated that Charlotte had misgivings. Maybe she should have suggested that Jeanne sleep in the guest room or even on the sofa in the back parlor.

The guest room.

Of course. All the while, she'd been speculating as to where Jeanne had slept over the weekend, but since she hadn't cleaned the guest room yet, she'd never once even considered the logical answer, that Jeanne had more than likely been staying in there.

"Ah, Jeanne, maybe you'd prefer to nap in the guest room instead?"

Jeanne slowly turned to face Charlotte, her eyes bright with unshed tears. "How did you know?" she whispered.

Not exactly sure what the younger woman was asking, Charlotte simply shrugged. "I didn't," she hedged. "I just figured you might find it more—er, ah, comfortable, given the circumstances."

Jeanne nodded. "You're a very kind person, Charlotte LaRue. And yes, I think I would rest better in there."

From that minute on, Charlotte was like an old mother hen hovering over a baby chick as she urged Jeanne toward the room across the hall. "You go in and get undressed, and I'll bring you in a gown."

When Charlotte returned with one of the long-sleeved silky gowns and matching robe that Jeanne preferred, she glanced around the spacious room while the younger woman changed. The bed was rumpled, as if it had been hastily made up, a couple of slacks and blouses were draped across one of the overstuffed lounge chairs, and cosmetics littered the dresser top, all evidence that Jeanne had indeed taken up residence in the room.

Once again, as it had earlier, a curious thought niggled at the back of her brain. Why all weekend, though? Why would Jeanne have chosen to sleep in the guest room instead of with her husband, especially since Jackson wasn't murdered until either late Sunday night or early Monday morning?

After she made sure that Jeanne was tucked into bed, she told her, "I'll get one of those sleeping pills for you and be right back."

When Charlotte approached the door to Clarice's rooms, it was still partially open, and there were no sounds coming from within. Thinking that the old lady could be in the bathroom, Charlotte peeked around the edge of the door.

Jeanne had opened the blinds, and the afternoon light poured into the room. But Clarice wasn't in the bathroom. The old lady was still in her bed, her head thrown back against a pillow, her eyes closed, and her mouth wide open.

All that arguing must have worn her out, Charlotte thought as she eased inside the doorway, her gaze still focused on Clarice.

But something wasn't quite right. Charlotte narrowed her eyes and stared harder at the old woman, specifically at her chest region. Shouldn't her chest be moving up and down, even a little bit? she wondered, staring harder.

An eternity of time seemed to pass, and Charlotte held her own breath even as her whole being slowly filled with dread.

Why wasn't Clarice breathing?

Chapter Ten

Charlotte was close to the panic stage. Then, suddenly, Clarice's whole body seemed to shudder. She drew in a noisy, gasping breath, and within moments, she resumed the deep, even rhythm of sleep, accompanied by loud, raunchy snores.

It was only then that Charlotte drew in a deep breath of her own and released it with a sigh of heartfelt relief. Sleep apnea, she belatedly realized as she tiptoed across the room. Another client she'd once worked for had suffered from the sometimes deadly condition, and Charlotte recalled that temporary suspension of respiration was one of the main symptoms.

Quite simply, the brain sometimes malfunctions while the person sleeps and doesn't send the right signal to the body to breathe. Since Clarice, more than likely, had a milder form of the condition, Charlotte made a mental note to bring the matter to Jeanne's attention just in case she hadn't already noticed.

Inside the bathroom, Charlotte flipped on the light switch. To make sure she wouldn't disturb Clarice, she eased the door closed behind her.

"What a mess," she murmured as she glanced around. Dirty towels and washcloths, along with dirty clothes, were piled on the tile floor in the corner. But it was the marble countertop around the sink that was the worst. There were more soiled washcloths, wadded up and thrown carelessly in the sink, a couple of dirty glasses, and a tube of toothpaste without the cap, the toothpaste oozing out of the tube onto the countertop.

In addition to everything else, as always, a fine film of talcum powder dusted the countertop and the floor. From her years of working for the Dubuissons, Charlotte had come to know certain idiosyncrasies about each of the family members. One of the things that she'd learned about Clarice was that the old lady literally bathed in the lilac-scented talcum powder after her shower each day.

Inside the closed-up room, the flowery scent was overwhelming. Charlotte felt a sneeze coming on, sniffed to stave it off, then twitched her nose as she stared at the countertop. Then she frowned. Something was different about the powder. Mixed with the talcum was a more coarse type of powder that Charlotte didn't readily recognize.

So what could it be? she wondered as she reached out and traced an invisible pattern through the residue. Had Clarice changed brands? It certainly smelled like the old lady's usual brand.

She rubbed her forefinger and thumb together. No, she thought, noting the gritty texture of the substance. It definitely wasn't all just talcum.

Charlotte never had been able to walk away from a mess. With one last puzzled look at the powder and a shrug, she quickly set about gathering the towels, washcloths, and clothes that were on the floor and on the countertop. After stuffing them into the hamper, she replaced the cap on the toothpaste, then thoroughly rinsed out the dirty glasses.

From underneath the cabinet, she selected a clean washcloth. After wetting it beneath the faucet, she wrung it out, then wiped down the countertop. Wadding it up into a ball, she dropped the soiled washcloth into the hamper, then turned her attention to the array of prescription-medicine bottles lined up at the back of the counter.

Charlotte picked up three different vials and read each of the labels before she finally found the one she was looking for. Though it took a moment to wrest off the childproof cap, she finally got it open and shook out one of the phenobarbital tablets. Peering down into the vial, she noted that there were only two tablets left.

She filled one of the glasses with water, and with one last glance around and a silent promise to do a more thorough job of cleaning once Clarice woke up, she left the bathroom. As she tiptoed back across the bedroom, she noted that Clarice's breathing still appeared to be normal.

In the guest room, Jeanne was in the bed, her eyes staring up at the ceiling, when Charlotte reentered.

"I took one of your mother's phenobarbital tablets," she said as she walked over to the bed and held out the pill.

Jeanne shifted her gaze to Charlotte, accepted the tablet, then raised herself up off the bed, using her elbow for a prop.

"There are only a couple of tablets left, though," Charlotte told her, "so you might want to call in a refill."

Jeanne's eyebrows shot up in surprise, but she popped the tablet into her mouth and washed it down with the water Charlotte gave her. "I can't believe I forgot to get that refilled," she said a moment later as she lay back against the pillow. "I guess with everything that's happened, it just completely slipped my mind."

"That's certainly understandable," Charlotte agreed. "Would you like for me to call it in for you? While I'm at it, I could check out Miss Clarice's other prescriptions, too, in case any of the rest also need refilling."

Jeanne closed her eyes and slowly shook her head from side to side. "That's really sweet of you to offer, Charlotte," she murmured. "But no, I'll take care of it . . . later . . ." She turned over on her side and snuggled farther down into the bed. "After I've rested for a while," she added, her voice barely above a whisper.

Charlotte checked to make sure that the ringer of the telephone on the bedside table was turned off, then quietly left the room. With both Jeanne and Clarice asleep, there wasn't much more she could do upstairs, not without making noise that might disturb them. She knew that the laundry was piling up, but she decided that Friday would be soon enough to catch up on the washing.

Out of the master suite, she retrieved her supply carrier, but as she eyed the small tables in the upstairs hallway, she remembered that she had wanted to make a phone call to Mary Johnson. Figuring that now was as good a time as any, she left her supplies by one of the tables and hurried down the stairs to the kitchen.

Mary Johnson was the oldest daughter of Claude and Lydia Johnson, a couple who had been Charlotte's clients for years, up until they had both retired. After retirement, Lydia had decided that since they needed the additional exercise, anyway, it would do them both a lot of good to clean the house themselves instead of hiring someone.

After a series of transfers, Charlotte finally got Mary on the line. "Mary, this is Charlotte LaRue."

"Oh, Charlotte, it's so good to hear from you. How have you been?"

"I'm doing fine," Charlotte answered. "And you? And your mom and dad?"

Mary assured her that everyone was doing just great, and Charlotte propped her hip against the cabinet while she listened to her friend bring her up-to-date about her parents' latest hobby.

"I tell you, Charlotte, I never thought I'd see the day when my mother and father would be hitting every garage sale and flea market around. You should see all the junk they've collected."

"Sounds like they're having fun," Charlotte told her. And as she listened to Mary describe some of the items her parents had discovered at a particular junk sale, she felt a small pang of envy. One of these days Hank would finally win, she thought. She would have to retire. But unlike the Johnsons, there would be no one for her to share new hobbies with, no one to share anything with. . . .

Charlotte gave herself a mental shake. Retirement day was still a long way off as far as she was concerned, and feeling sorry for herself was a totally useless waste of energy and time.

"Listen, hon," she interrupted when Mary paused, "I know you must be busy, and I won't keep you but a moment more. But I was wondering if you might be able to help me out with a little problem I'm having."

Once Charlotte had explained about the rude reporter, Mary was outraged. "I'm so sorry that happened, Charlotte, and I'm pretty sure I know who the man is. We've had other complaints about him, if he's the one I'm thinking of. And for the record, he's not a regular employee. He's just a free-lance writer we've occasionally bought stories from. I'm afraid there's not much I can do about it, but I'll try. If he makes a pest of himself again, please feel free to call the police on him, with my blessing."

Charlotte thanked her friend, and quickly reminding Mary to say hello to her folks for her, she ended the conversation. But as she trudged back up the stairs, she couldn't help thinking about the conversation and how different her life might have been if not for Vietnam.

"Woulda, shoulda, coulda," she grumbled, removing her duster from the supply carrier. And while she dusted and polished the small tables in the upstairs hallway, she began mentally listing all of her blessings and the positive forces in her life in a concerted effort to stave off the shadows of the past.

By the time she moved on to the staircase, she was feeling somewhat better. The scuff marks were there again, she noted, staring at the stairs. Funny, she thought. They looked just the same as the last time she'd dusted and polished the staircase.

Charlotte's brow furrowed in puzzlement. Maybe she'd been mistaken; maybe the marks hadn't been made by Clarice's walker, after all. She supposed that they could have been made by someone's shoes. Perhaps she should check out the ones that Jeanne wore around the house. In the long run, though, what difference did it make? she finally decided. Either way, the marks still had to be scrubbed up.

It seemed to take an eternity to finish the stairs. By the time she was finally done, she'd lost count of how often she'd been interrupted by the phone ringing. Her legs ached from running up and down the stairs. Her apron pocket was filled with messages she'd taken, mostly from well-meaning acquaintances calling to express their condolences or others wanting to know if funeral arrangements for Jackson had been made yet.

It was getting close to the end of her workday when she finally finished cleaning the downstairs rooms. Jeanne and Clarice were still sleeping.

Though cleaning could be physically demanding and tiring, for the most part it was mindless work, the kind that allowed a person to daydream or occasionally indulge in fantasies.

Charlotte found that cleaning was an excellent time to review all the tiny details as well as the problems that running her own business required. There were always things like quarterly taxes, health insurance, and employee time schedules to contend with. Many times after a day's work, she found that she was not only physically exhausted but mentally tired as well.

The only chore left to do was to sweep off the gallery; in Charlotte's opinion, sweeping was the most mindless work of all. At times, she even found the rhythm of the swish-

swish of the broom restful, and she welcomed the mental break as she moved onto the porch to begin the task.

Outside there was a cloud cover that painted the sky gray. Though it was still hot and muggy, at least it wasn't as unbearable as the last time she'd swept the porch.

She had finished almost half the front lower gallery when it suddenly struck her that the pattern of the debris strewn across the porch was almost identical to the one that she'd swept away on Friday.

Charlotte stopped sweeping and stood motionless. Frowning, she stared at the leaves and dried grass. On Friday, she'd decided the debris was the result of the gardener's tracking the stuff across the porch in search of a cool, shady place to rest.

Her frown deepened. The gardener came on Tuesdays, and the police didn't finish their investigation until late Tuesday, too late for the gardener to come.

So who had tracked up the porch this time?

Then it dawned on her, and she chuckled. The police. Yes, of course, she thought as she resumed sweeping. The police were probably all over the place, looking for clues, so of course they were the ones who had tracked it up this time.

But as she turned the corner of the porch and the cast-iron bistro set came into view, she slowed to a standstill again. One of the chairs had been moved closer to the double French doors, in almost the same exact position that she'd found it in on Friday. Once again Charlotte envisioned someone sitting in the chair, someone watching, or listening to, the goings-on inside the library.

Someone listening . . . watching . . . waiting . . .

Charlotte shivered. Could she have been mistaken about the gardener, after all? Could that someone have been Jackson's murderer instead, casing the place?

Chapter Eleven

The slamming of a car door drew Charlotte's attention away from the chair, distracting her for the moment. Surely that wasn't the police coming back again, she thought as she hurried back around to the front gallery to investigate. But if it was, then maybe she should tell them about the chair and her suspicions.

Then a vision of the pushy reporter she'd encountered earlier popped into her head. She wouldn't put it past him to have come back with a whole camera crew in tow.

Charlotte turned the corner of the gallery just in time to see Anna-Maria walk around the front end of a black sporty Jaguar. Charlotte backed up a step and watched as a dark-haired man climbed out from the driver's side and slammed the door. He was dressed in a royal blue polo shirt, tucked neatly into light tan chinos, and all Charlotte could do was stare. She'd never seen a man with such perfect features, features that bordered on being almost too beautiful to belong to a man.

Though Charlotte had never met Anna-Maria's fiancé, she assumed that the strikingly handsome young man had to be James Doucet. Her assumption was confirmed when he caught Anna-Maria by the hand and pulled her into his arms for a long, slow kiss. Charlotte's throat tightened. The kiss was obviously so full of tenderness and love that it almost brought tears to her eyes.

But that was good, she thought, good that Anna-Maria's fiancé wasn't afraid to show how much he cared for her. Would it be enough, though? If what Clarice had said was true, if Brian O'Connor was Anna-Maria's birth father instead of Jackson and the truth ever came out, Anna-Maria was going to need all the loving support she could get to make it through such a traumatizing revelation.

For Anna-Maria's sake, Charlotte could only hope that James Doucet truly loved her with the kind of love that would be strong enough to weather the turbulent storm that was brewing on the horizon.

The young couple were obviously so caught up in the moment that neither seemed to notice they were being observed. But what if they did catch her watching them?

She knew she shouldn't be embarrassed. After all, they were out on the street in plain sight for anyone to see, for Pete's sake . . . anyone, including that awful reporter.

Charlotte shuddered. A newspaper reporter was one thing, but what if the couple got the idea that *she* was spying on them? Just the thought made her cheeks burn with embarrassment, and she quickly eased back around the corner to the side porch.

She took her time sweeping away the remaining debris as she listened for some indication that the couple had finished with their good-byes. Then, suddenly, the roar of a lawn mower coming from the property next door intruded, drowning out all other noises.

With a frown of irritation, Charlotte automatically turned toward the source of the noise. At that moment, she caught a glimpse of a man pushing a lawn mower on the other side of the tall hedge of ligustrum that bordered the cast-iron fence separating the properties.

Charlotte recognized the man right away as Joseph O'Connor, the gardener that Bitsy Duhe used. Was Brian O'Connor helping his father today? she wondered. She shaded her eyes with her hand against the afternoon glare and tried to see in between the breaks in the hedge.

As if the very thought of the man had conjured him up, he suddenly appeared just above the hedge. At first glance, he looked as if he were suspended in midair, floating along the top of the tall hedge. Then Charlotte saw that he was standing on a ladder and in his hands was a piece of equipment she recognized as a gas hedge trimmer.

But Brian O'Connor's attention wasn't on trimming the hedge. Instead, his gaze seemed riveted on the street in front of the Dubuissons' house.

Anna-Maria and James, Charlotte suddenly realized. Brian O'Connor was watching Anna-Maria and James say their good-byes.

Seeing Brian once again reminded her of what Clarice had said earlier. Was it true? Was Brian O'Connor Anna-Maria's birth father? Why would the old woman say such a thing if it wasn't true? And if Brian O'Connor was the young woman's birth father, did he know that he was? she wondered.

Abruptly, the noisy lawn mower sputtered, then died. At that moment, a movement on the street caught her eye, and Charlotte recognized the black Jag driving slowly away.

But Brian O'Connor's gaze was still zeroed in on the front of the Dubuissons' house, his head slowly turning, as if watching the progress of someone. He was watching Anna-Maria.

The sound of the Dubuissons' front door opening and closing reached Charlotte's ears. Only then did Brian O'Connor look away to focus on the piece of machinery in his hands. For long seconds he simply stared at it. Even with the distance between them, Charlotte could see that his expression was tight with strain, as if he were fighting some demon from within.

Then, in an abrupt, almost angry motion, he yanked on the starter cord of the hedge trimmer. One pull was enough, and the piece of machinery came to life with a high-pitched whine.

He knew, thought Charlotte as she watched him crop off the uneven growth of the hedge with swift, precise strokes. Why else would he have been watching Anna Maria so intently?

Sneaking around down on the porch . . . think'n nobody knows he's down there snoop'n around, spying.

Charlotte let out a disgusted sigh. "Why indeed?" she muttered as she shook her head. "There you go again, imagining things that just aren't so." And all because of an old lady's ranting and ravings, an old lady who was probably going senile to boot.

The truth of the matter, plain and simple, was that Anna-Maria was a beautiful young woman, the kind who would attract any man's attention, even a man old enough to be her father.

But even as Charlotte tried to dismiss the whole incident, she couldn't completely forget it, not entirely. Nor could she forget the things that Clarice had told her earlier.

Inside the house, Charlotte found Anna-Maria in the kitchen. She was pouring herself a glass of wine.

Charlotte smiled at the young woman. "You doing okay, hon?"

Anna-Maria held out the glass of wine as if making a toast. "Sure, I'm okay. I'm just fine and dandy, like everyone else in this household. Another couple of glasses of this and

I'll feel even better, though." As if to emphasize the point, she took a healthy swallow.

The girl was hurting, hurting badly. Charlotte recognized the signs immediately, for she, too, had once been in the young woman's shoes. She had also wished for something, anything, to take away the pain. Her smile faded.

"Alcohol is a depressant, you know," she told her softly, gently. "It won't help, not in the long run."

For several moments, Anna-Maria simply stared at Charlotte, her expression unreadable. Then, to Charlotte's surprise, she turned to the sink and poured the drink down the drain. "You're right, of course," she said, carefully placing the glass on the countertop. She faced Charlotte again. "But I—I—" Her lower lip quivered, and tears welled up in her eyes. "I don't know what else to do," she whispered in a choked voice. "I can't stop thinking about it. I—I—" She covered her face with trembling hands, and a deep sob shook her body.

Charlotte quickly closed the gap between them and pulled the young woman into her arms. "There, there," she murmured, gently patting her back. "I know it hurts, but it's going to be okay," she soothed.

Anna-Maria buried her face against Charlotte's shoulder and continued to sob.

"I'm just so sorry you have to go through this," Charlotte told her. "I lost my father, too, when I was about your age, and I know how you feel."

The young woman lifted her head, and with tears still streaming down her face, she stared at Charlotte. "You—you did? Your d—dad was murdered, too?"

"No," Charlotte said. "He wasn't murdered. But he and my mom were both killed in an airplane crash. For years they had saved to take their dream vacation, a trip to Hawaii. Then, when they were finally able to . . ." Charlotte swallowed hard to ease the sudden tightness in her throat. She could still see the face of the television reporter, still hear his voice as he told about the fatal flight going down in the Pacific.

"They died? Both of them?"

Again, Charlotte nodded. "Strange as it may sound, though, I've always drawn comfort from the fact that they were together when it happened. I like to think that's the way they would have wanted it."

"Oh, Charlotte, that must have been terrible for you. It's bad enough I've lost my dad, but I can't even imagine losing my mom, too, and at the same time."

"You're going to get through this," Charlotte assured her. She squeezed the young woman's shoulders and stepped back. "It's going to hurt, and it won't be easy, but you will survive. Just take one day at a time and keep looking forward, not backward. None of us can change the past, and we can't predict the future. All we truly have is today."

Anna-Maria sniffed and scrubbed at her eyes, then crossed her arms, hugging them close as she nodded. "I'm trying. Really I am. But—"

"No buts, now," Charlotte said firmly, wagging her finger at the younger woman. "One thing in particular that helped me was keeping busy. If you can stay busy, then you don't have a whole lot of time to dwell on things." She offered the girl a smile. "And speaking of staying busy, there's something you can do right now." She glanced at her watch. "I'll be leaving in a few minutes. Your mother and grandmother are both upstairs. Your mom hasn't been resting well, so she really needs to sleep. I'd feel a whole lot better about leaving if I knew you were keeping an eye on them for me."

"Do you have to go right now?"

There was a desperate edge in the young woman's voice, and Charlotte hesitated, torn between leaving and staying. She was tired and ready for her workday to be over, ready to kick back and relax. But she also cared about these people, truly cared about them.

Unbidden, a conversation she'd once had with Hank suddenly came to mind. *Be careful dealing with these people, Mother. Business is business, and these people you work for are part of your business. They're clients. They're not your friends.*

In spite of her son's warnings, to her the Dubuissons weren't just clients. She'd watched Anna-Maria grow up. For years she'd observed and admired Jeanne's devotion to her mother. Charlotte loved her son with all her heart and was proud of him, but she'd often wished that she'd had a daughter, too, one just like Jeanne.

Maybe she could stay just a little longer, after all. "Tell you what," Charlotte told Anna-Maria, smoothing down her apron. "Why don't I fix us a nice cup of coffee, some of that New Orleans blend with chicory that you like so well."

Charlotte's hands stilled over the pocket of the apron, the slight bulge and rustling sound reminding her of the phone calls and messages she'd taken. She withdrew the messages. "I took some calls while your mother was sleeping." She handed the slips of paper to Anna-Maria. "We can go over them while we drink our coffee. Just in case you can't read my handwriting," she added with a grin. "And after I'm gone, then you can take over that chore as well."

Anna-Maria nodded, and a tentative smile pulled at her lips. "Thanks, Charlotte."

She had just finished brewing the coffee when the phone rang. "Why don't you answer it this time while I pour the coffee," Charlotte told Anna-Maria. "There's a notepad on the counter there if you need to take a message."

The younger woman only hesitated a moment, then answered the call. "Hello . . . yes, she's still here . . . just a moment." She turned to Charlotte and held out the phone. "It's for you."

"For me?" Charlotte rolled her eyes upward and gave an exaggerated oh, well shrug, a gesture that made Anna-Maria really smile.

Wondering who on earth would be calling her at the Dubuissons', she set down the coffeepot, then took the receiver. "Charlotte speaking."

"Ms. LaRue, this is Detective Thibodeaux with the NOPD."

At the sound of the detective's deep, raspy voice, Charlotte stiffened.

"I'd like to ask you a few questions," he continued. "Either you can come down to the station or I can come by your house."

She wasn't sure why, but just the thought of being alone inside her house with the menacing detective made Charlotte's insides knot up. "I'll come to the station," she blurted out. "I can be there in about a half an hour or so."

Chapter
Twelve

An hour later, when Charlotte turned onto Milan Street, she immediately spotted her niece's tan Toyota parked in front of her house.

She'd gone to the Sixth District police station, but when she'd arrived, she'd been told that Detective Thibodeaux had been called out on another homicide. He'd left word for her that he would be in touch. And though it was like waiting for the other shoe to drop and Charlotte wondered what kind of questions he was going to ask, she was vastly relieved that she didn't have to deal with the man right away.

Charlotte slowed down the van at her driveway. At any other time, she would have been delighted by a midweek visit from Judith, but given the circumstances surrounding their encounter the night before at the Dubuissons' house, not to mention the call from Judith's partner, she felt only dread.

The words *official police business* kept running through her head.

But Charlotte had always tried to look for something positive in every situation; she supposed that she should be grateful that the car sitting in front of her home belonged to Judith and not Louis Thibodeaux.

Charlotte pulled into her driveway and parked beneath the shed. Everyone in her family knew that Charlotte kept a spare key hidden beneath the fat ceramic frog in the flower bed near the front corner of the house. Since Judith was already inside instead of waiting on the porch, Charlotte figured she'd been there a while.

The moment Charlotte stepped through the front door, Sweety Boy let out a series of chirps and whistles and fluttered around inside his cage, all orchestrated, she knew, to get her attention.

"That bird is something else, Aunt Charley."

Judith was seated on the sofa. An open briefcase, along with several stacks of papers, were spread out around her. "I've been here about a half an hour, and there hasn't been a peep out of him. He's barely even moved off his perch, and now look at him."

"What can I say?" Charlotte grinned. "He knows who hands out the birdseed."

Ignoring the bird's antics for the moment, Charlotte deposited her purse on the small table near the door. "I would say that this is a nice surprise," she said as she slipped off her working loafers and stepped into a pair of soft suede moccasins she wore around the house. "But I have a feeling that this isn't strictly a social visit. And by the way, I waited for you to call last night."

Judith had the grace to look sheepish for a moment. "I'm sorry I didn't call, Aunt Charley, but I did say I probably wouldn't have time, and I didn't get home until late. I figured you were probably already asleep. You're right, though," she continued. "I'm afraid this isn't a social visit. But Auntie, you know I wouldn't bother you if it wasn't necessary. We have to question everyone who is even remotely connected to the family."

Charlotte nodded. "I understand. What I don't understand is why I have to be questioned by your partner, too."

"You've seen Thibodeaux?"

Charlotte shook her head. "Not yet, but he tracked me down at the Dubuissons'." She went on to explain about his phone call and what had happened once she'd arrived at the precinct.

Judith looked puzzled. "I'm pretty sure he knew that I was going to talk to you," she said.

"Maybe because I'm your aunt he doesn't think you can be objective enough."

"No, he knows better than that." Judith paused. Then, after a moment, she shrugged. "He probably just misunderstood."

Though she didn't think Judith looked quite convinced, Charlotte let it slide. "If you don't mind, I'd like to shower first and change clothes," she told her. Charlotte headed toward the bedroom. "Just give me ten minutes," she called over her shoulder. "And there's a fresh pitcher of tea in the refrigerator. Fix us both a glass."

Though Charlotte had chosen the navy uniforms and white aprons that she and her employees wore with careful consideration, there was a downside to her choice. While the cotton-knit material always looked neat and was comfortable and practical, it also absorbed odors, more specifically the odors of the cleaning chemicals they sometimes used. She'd learned early on that showering and changing the minute she got home was much more practical than risking a possible allergic reaction to the chemicals.

While Charlotte showered, she thought about the reason for Judith's visit, and she suspected she already knew what type of questions her niece was going to ask. Since she worked for the Dubuissons, it was only logical that her niece was going to ask her about the family and their relationships with each other.

Charlotte stepped out of the shower, dried off, then went in search of something to wear. With dread building inside her, she selected a well-worn sweatshirt and matching sweat-pants from the closet and dressed.

As she'd told Clarice earlier that day though, she never gossiped about her clients. It was a matter of principle and pride that clients trust her and her employees. Whatever went on in a client's home stayed there. But gossiping about clients and a murder investigation involving the police were two vastly different things. Unlike lawyers and doctors, she didn't have the legal luxury of pleading privileged information.

Back in the living room, Charlotte seated herself on the opposite end of the sofa from Judith. "I'm pretty sure I know what you want, hon," she said, accepting the glass of iced tea that Judith handed her, "but I won't pretend I like it."

"I'm sorry, Aunt Charley. I know all about your privileged-information policy. But I'm getting nowhere fast with this case, and I have to explore every angle." Judith pulled out a small notebook from her briefcase and flipped through it to a page filled with notes; then she shifted on the sofa to face Charlotte. "At approximately one A.M. Monday morning, someone either broke in or made it appear that they broke into the Dubuissons' home through the French doors leading out onto the porch. We've already established that the front gate was unlocked. Would you happen to know why the gate was left unlocked?"

"Did you ask Jeanne?"

"Yes, Auntie, I did. But I'd like to hear your answer."

"Well, there's no big mystery, hon. Jackson often worked on the weekends, and if he was going to be late, she'd leave the gate unlocked so as not to be disturbed when he came home."

Judith nodded. "That's what she said."

Charlotte tilted her head, a puzzled look on her face. "Why did you say 'made it appear' earlier?"

Judith waved away the question without looking up. "I'll get to that in a minute," she said, her gaze still on her notes. "There were a couple of papers—deeds and stuff—left on the desk, the kind that would be kept in a safe, so I figure that the safe was probably already open. Of course, any good thief worth his salt could crack that particular kind of safe," she added. "But I don't think that was necessary in this case.

"We also found a half-empty bottle of Scotch on the desk and not much sign of a struggle. We already know that the Scotch was a new bottle, a gift from Jackson's partner, Tony Marriott. Supposedly it was a peace offering of sorts for an argument they'd had."

Judith shifted again on the sofa, a sure sign she was under stress, and Charlotte almost felt sorry for her. Anytime her niece was worried or in an uncomfortable or tense situation, she resorted to what Charlotte thought of as the nervous fidgets. The girl simply couldn't keep still.

She looked up at Charlotte. "The way I figure it," she continued, "Jackson was either passed out and came to while the killer was robbing him or he was well on his way to a drunken stupor, too drunk to put up a fight but sober enough to identify the intruder. Why else would the intruder have bashed him in the head?"

. . . bashed him in the head . . . A sudden prickly feeling of déjà vu came over Charlotte as she listened to her niece's description of the murder scene. Each detail was almost identical to what Bitsy had told her about Andrew St. Martin's murder, a murder that had occurred over fifteen years earlier.

It was Charlotte's turn to fidget while her niece paused to take several swallows of her tea. Was it possible that Judith didn't know about Andrew's murder? Fifteen years ago, Judith would have still been a teenager, but surely someone with the police department had already recalled the incident. Surely someone older who had been around for a while had already pointed out the similarities of the two murders. Someone like Louis Thibodeaux.

Judith had to know, she decided, and Charlotte couldn't think of any good reason to bring up the matter. But there were several reasons not to. For one, with her being the Dubuissons' maid, if she did bring it up, Judith might become even more suspicious of the family than she already was.

While Charlotte continued her mental debate, Judith set her glass down and picked up her story where she'd left off. "But all of that is how it *could* have happened," she said. "Personally, I think it was an inside job. And so does Thibodeaux. We both think it's possible the whole thing was staged . . . the broken glass, the fact that Jackson Dubuisson was bashed in the head and not shot . . ." She waved her hand. "Et cetera, et cetera.

"Assuming that the murder wasn't simply a random burglary gone sour, so far we have two definite suspects. Right now, Tony Marriott and Jeanne Dubuisson are our best bets."

"No!" Charlotte shook her head adamantly. "Not Jeanne," she protested. "Jeanne wouldn't hurt a flea."

"Now don't get all upset, Aunt Charley." Judith reached over and patted her shoulder. "We always look at the spouse as a suspect in a murder case. And you'd be surprised at what people are capable of doing, even the seemingly nice ones. But if it will make you feel any better, so far we haven't uncovered a motive for Jeanne Dubuisson to have killed her husband. Not yet."

Charlotte nodded slowly, not because she agreed with Judith, at least not about Jeanne's having killed Jackson. But she did understand what Judith was telling her. It was exactly the same thing Bitsy had said about Clarice's being the main suspect in Andrew's murder.

"We'll know more once the autopsy is done," Judith said, then glanced up at the cuckoo clock on the wall. "The coroner should be finished by now, and if I'm lucky, I'll have that report tomorrow morning."

"So what about Tony Marriott?" Charlotte asked. "Why is he a suspect?" Though she could pretty much guess why, she was curious to hear the official reason the police suspected him.

"He and Jackson had an altercation Friday night at the Zoo To Do. Witnesses say that Tony accused Jackson of having an affair with his wife. He also made some other accusations as well."

"Like what?" Charlotte asked.

"Primarily, he made noises about Jackson systematically transferring funds out of the firm into his own personal account."

"I was there Friday night," Charlotte confessed, "and I saw them having words. But I wasn't close enough to hear what they were saying," she hastened to add.

Judith suddenly grinned. "Hank won out and made you go, after all, huh?"

Charlotte rolled her eyes upward toward the ceiling. "You, of all people, should know how persuasive that son of mine can be."

"You're right about that." Judith laughed. "I can't tell you how many times I got into trouble growing up all because my dear cousin talked me into doing something I shouldn't have done." She paused for a moment, a faraway look in her eyes, and her expression softened. "We had some good times, though, despite the circumstances, didn't we, Aunt Charley?"

"Yes," Charlotte assured her, knowing exactly the circumstances that Judith was referring to. "Yes, we did," she confirmed. Then, gently, knowing how painful the subject could be, she asked, "Have you seen your father lately?"

"No, not in a while, not since he married again." Judith suddenly grimaced and made a sound of disgust. "Can you believe? This is his fourth marriage, and each time, his wives just keep getting younger and younger. This time he married one younger than I am."

Charlotte winced at the bitterness in her niece's voice, bitterness resulting from years of hurt and neglect by a father who didn't know the meaning of the words love and responsibility.

"Have you mentioned this to your mother yet?"

Judith shook her head that she hadn't. "You know how she gets," she said. "I just couldn't bring myself to tell her, not this time."

Charlotte nodded in agreement. She loved her sister dearly, but she would never understand the love-hate relationship that Madeline had with her ex-husband. Though it had been years since he had run off with another woman and left Madeline with two small children to raise by herself, each of the two other times he'd remarried had thrown her into a tailspin of depression. The kids had still been young then, and Charlotte was the one who had taken care of Judith and Daniel until Madeline was able to snap out of it.

Abruptly, Judith shook her head as if the action would wipe away the disturbing thoughts of her father and mother. Then, with a sigh, she squared her shoulders. "In the meantime, though," she said, "I've still got a case to solve." She flipped through the notebook to a clean page and reached for a pen in her briefcase. "So," she said, pen poised in her hand, "what kind of relationship did Jeanne and Jackson Dubuisson have? Did they get along? Did they argue?"

"Like I said earlier, he worked a lot," Charlotte answered diplomatically. "I rarely ever saw them together," she explained. "Mr. Dubuisson was always gone by the time I got there, and I always left before he got home."

"Come on, Aunt Charley, you know what I mean."

Torn between keeping her client's confidence and divulging what she knew, Charlotte hesitated.

He's stealing you blind.

Clarice's accusation rang in Charlotte's ears, and she winced. "Well, I never heard them argue," she said truthfully.

"Aunt Charley. Surely Jeanne Dubuisson mentioned her husband to you once in a while."

"She never actually complained, mind you. All she ever said was that he worked a lot even when he was home."

Judith made a sound of frustration. "This is getting us nowhere fast. Okay, forget her for now. What about the old lady?"

"What about her?" Charlotte hedged.

"Did she get along with her son-in-law? Did she like him, hate him? What?"

"She's an old lady," Charlotte answered. "She has her good days and bad days."

"That's not what I'm asking, and you know it. Please, Aunt Charley, don't make this any harder than it has to be."

Charlotte stared at her niece. "You're right. It's just that—I—I—" She shrugged away the explanation. "Never mind." She lifted her chin. "Miss Clarice was very vocal in her opinions about Jackson. She didn't like him or respect him. But like I said, she's an old lady . . . maybe even a bit senile at times." And that was all Charlotte intended to say on the matter.

"The girl . . ." Judith checked her notes. "I believe Anna-Maria is her name. How did she get along with her father?"

When Charlotte glared at her niece, Judith held up her hands in defeat. "Okay, okay. Forget the daughter. But Aunt Charley, is there anything—anything at all—that you *can* tell me about the Dubuisson family or their friends that might help?"

Charlotte thought about Brian O'Connor and what Clarice had said about him. Still she hesitated. But which would be worse? To maintain her loyalty and keep what

Clarice had told her to herself or breach that loyalty in hopes of protecting the family from further allegations?

In an attempt to stretch the tense muscles in her neck, she tilted her head first to one side and then the other. Maybe, she thought, just maybe, there might be a way she could tell what she knew without compromising her principles.

"There might be another suspect," she finally said. "Mind you, I said might," she emphasized when she saw Judith's eyes brighten with interest. "But I won't tell you how I know, so don't ask."

"Okay, Aunt Charley. Fair enough . . . for now. So—who is this suspect?"

"There's a man named Brian O'Connor who my source claims is the murderer," Charlotte began, and as she repeated what she'd been told by Clarice, Judith jotted down notes, only interrupting Charlotte's story to clarify a couple of the facts.

"And you're sure you can't tell me who gave you this information?" she asked when Charlotte had finished.

"I'd rather not," she answered. "I can't see what purpose it would serve at this stage."

"Hmm . . ." Judith tapped the notebook with the pen. "I suppose you're right, but I might have to insist that you do so at some point if any of what you've told me about this Brian O'Connor turns out to be true. But even if it's true, even if he is Anna-Maria Dubuisson's real father, that's not much of a motive for murder." She paused. "And another thing. Why now? Why would he have waited so long to get his revenge?"

Judith's questions weren't really directed at Charlotte and didn't require a response, but sharp pangs of guilt nagged at her. "If it helps," she said, "I can't see how it's much of a motive, either. And to be honest, I don't consider the information that reliable, considering the person who told me. But be that as it may, I still felt obligated to pass it along."

Judith shoved her fingers through her hair and flounced around to a different position on the sofa. "Don't worry about it, Aunt Charley. You did the right thing by telling me, and I'll check it out. Discreetly, of course," she added. "But at this rate, this case is going nowhere fast. And frankly, right now, I'm at a dead end—Oops! Sorry, Aunt Charley, no pun intended. All I meant was that both the primary suspects have alibis."

Hoping that Judith would tell her more about the alibis, Charlotte raised one eyebrow and directed a pointed look at her.

"Okay, okay. I really shouldn't," she said, "but I don't guess it would hurt to tell you. None of it is a big, dark secret, anyway. Tony Marriott claims he and his wife were on their sailboat in the middle of Lake Pontchartrain at the time. And of course, his wife corroborates the story."

"Well, I can't imagine Tony would be stupid enough to murder Jackson, anyway," Charlotte exclaimed, "especially not after what happened on Friday night. As a lawyer, surely he would realize that there were too many witnesses to his altercation with Jackson."

Judith nodded. "Exactly my conclusions, too."

"And Jeanne?"

"Mrs. Dubuisson's mother swears that she and her daughter were watching a late-night television movie together. Says she wasn't feeling well and Jeanne didn't want to leave her alone."

"Sounds like something Jeanne would do," Charlotte said. "She's very devoted to her mother."

"Yes, well, at first I thought it was a little strange that neither of the women heard anything." She gave a one-shoulder shrug. "But the way that house is built, and if they were both upstairs with a television set going, it's possible, I suppose."

Judith paused and stared with unseeing eyes at a point just beyond Charlotte's head. "The case is young yet, but the whole thing has me stumped. Brick-wall time," she said, unable to mask her frustration. "I'll check around about this Brian O'Connor person. But unless we can come up with a murder weapon or discredit either Jeanne Dubuisson's or Tony Marriott's alibis, I'm afraid this is going to be just one more of those lovely unsolved cases that already clutter my files."

Chapter
Thirteen

Normally, Charlotte tried to keep Thursdays free from commitments so she could catch up on paperwork or do whatever was needed to keep her service running smoothly as well as take care of personal errands. But with the two un-expected days off on Monday and Tuesday, she'd already done everything. Thursday loomed before her like a vast wasteland of unending time.

"And Hank wants me to retire," she muttered as she pulled on her walking shoes. Without her work, what would she do all day long?

Go crazy, she thought as she tied the laces into double knots, then headed for the front door. "Absolutely crazy, crazy, crazy," she told Sweety Boy as she paused in front of his cage.

But Charlotte knew there was more to her restlessness than having nothing to do. She could always find *something* to do if she really wanted to. And if all else failed, she could always catch up on the latest movies she hadn't seen in the theater. It had been a long time since she'd indulged in one of her afternoon movie marathons.

The trouble was, she didn't want to do anything. After Judith had left, she'd tried watching television, but even with eighty-some-odd cable stations to choose from, nothing had held her interest for very long. She'd finally selected a book from the fresh batch Bitsy had given her and tried reading for a while.

But nothing had worked, and she'd spent a restless night tossing and turning and replaying in her mind the conversation she'd had with her niece about the relationships between the members of the Dubuisson family.

"One thing I can do, though," she told the little parakeet. She poked her finger into the cage and wiggled it. "I can clean out that nasty cage of yours." As if agreeing, the little bird nodded his head up and down and made chirping noises; then he hopped closer to her finger.

Charlotte rubbed the back of his head. "Now say, 'Bye-bye, Charlotte,' " she instructed. The parakeet pushed against her finger with his head and made a gurgling noise. "Come on, boy, you can do it. Say it. Say, 'Bye-bye, Charlotte.' "

"Crazy."

Charlotte froze when she heard the garbled sound. "Did you just say, 'Crazy'?" She stared at the little bird and narrowed her eyes. The parakeet cocked his head and stared back. "No way," she whispered, pulling her finger out of the cage. "Bad enough I talk to myself. Now I'm hearing things as well."

Outside, the sky was overcast, and the warm air was heavy and humid, a sure sign of rain. The narrow street was quiet, with little traffic, since most of Charlotte's neighbors had either already left for work or hadn't ventured out yet.

Across the street, her neighbor's black-and-tan Doberman suddenly spotted her. He bared his teeth and, with a low warning growl, strained against the leash that kept him tied to the front porch. Then he began to bark.

Charlotte glared at the Doberman. "Be quiet, Prince," she commanded in a firm, loud voice. "It's just me, you silly mutt."

Prince immediately stopped barking and began to whine instead. Ignoring the dog, Charlotte took a few minutes to do some warm-up stretches, then she struck out down the sidewalk and headed toward the intersection of Milan and Magazine.

But with every step, no matter how hard she tried to clear her mind and concentrate on coordinating the swinging of her arms and her breathing with her pace, nagging thoughts of Jackson Dubuisson's murder kept interfering.

Judith had said she would have the results of the autopsy today. Charlotte wondered what, if anything, the report would turn up. She also wondered if Judith would share what the report said if she called and asked.

Half a block from home, a sudden prickly uneasiness came over her. At first, she ignored the feeling, telling herself that she was being silly. Milan Street was a perfectly safe street, one that she knew like the back of her hand. But with each step she took, the uneasy feeling persisted and grew worse.

Someone was watching her.

Without breaking stride, and trying not to be too obvious, she casually glanced around, her gaze taking in both sides of the street within her view.

Nothing. There was nothing out of the ordinary, nothing more sinister or threatening than the roots of the oak trees protruding through the cracked sidewalk.

When she chanced a quick look over her shoulder, however, she immediately spotted the source of her discomfort.

A blue Ford Taurus was cruising slowly behind her. The car was just far enough back so that the noise of the vehicle had blended in with the sound of traffic passing on Magazine Street.

Because of the distance and the car's tinted windows, she

didn't recognize the driver right away. But something about the outline of the driver made her suspect that the person behind the wheel was male.

The minute the driver realized she'd spotted him, he gunned the engine and drove past her. Though the side windows of the car were even more darkly tinted than the windshield, Charlotte got a good glimpse of the driver.

Detective Louis Thibodeaux.

Maybe he wouldn't stop, she prayed, and held her breath.

When he pulled the vehicle over to the curb, just ahead of her, then stopped, her nerves tightened like the strings of a violin. Charlotte released her pent-up breath and slowed her pace. He was waiting for her, she suddenly realized, waiting for her to come to him. Why, the man didn't even have the decency to get out of his car. He was sitting there, waiting, as if she were some street hooker.

Charlotte felt her temper flare. It would serve him right if she ignored him and just kept on walking. Or even better, she could pull an about-face and head the other way. That would show him.

In the end, she did neither. Still fuming, and ignoring the tiny voice inside her head that said she was overreacting, out of sheer stubbornness she stopped several feet behind the detective's car. If he wanted to talk, he'd have to come to her, she decided.

With her hands on her hips, she glared at the parked vehicle and tapped her foot impatiently while she waited. Finally, after what seemed like forever, the car door swung open, and the detective climbed out.

Louis Thibodeaux was dressed in neatly pressed khaki pants and a solid brown shirt with a buttoned-down collar, the sleeves rolled halfway to his elbows. Though he wasn't a tall man, there was something about his stocky appearance that made him seem large and intimidating, and she couldn't stop thinking about the way he'd harangued and bullied Jeanne when he'd questioned her.

"I hope I didn't scare you," he said. "I spotted you walking down the street right after I pulled up to your house."

Charlotte chose to say nothing, for she wasn't about to admit that he had frightened her.

"I wanted to apologize about missing our meeting yesterday."

Charlotte wasn't sure exactly what she'd expected, but it certainly wasn't an apology.

"I'd still like to ask you a few questions," he continued.

"What kind of questions?" she blurted out. "I don't know what I can tell you that I haven't already told my niece. And now isn't really a good time for me," she quickly added. Of course, no time would be good for her as long as *he* was asking the questions, but she couldn't say that.

"There are just a couple of points I want to clarify."

Charlotte tilted her head and raised one eyebrow as if to say, So go ahead.

"Could I buy you a cup of coffee while we talk? There's a coffeehouse not far on Magazine."

To be fair, the man was trying to be civil, but just the thought of climbing into the car with the detective made her insides feel all jittery. *No way,* she decided. "What is it you want to know, Detective?" she demanded.

Dark eyebrows furrowed over his equally dark eyes as he stared at her for several seconds. She was sure that the gesture was intended to intimidate, so just to show him that it didn't work, she pasted on her friendliest smile while she waited for his answer.

"I want to know how the daughter and her father got along."

"You mean her stepfather, don't you?"

"That hasn't been established yet." The detective's voice became a growl of impatience. "I think you know exactly what I mean, but just for the sake of clarity, how did Anna-Maria Dubuisson get along with Jackson Dubuisson?"

"I'm afraid I can't help you there, Detective," she said

sweetly. "It was rare that I ever saw them together, since, as I told my niece, most of the time Mr. Dubuisson was already gone to work by the time I arrived and I had usually finished and left before he got home each evening."

Louis Thibodeaux studied Charlotte for several seconds before he asked his next question. Though there was nothing menacing in the way his dark eyes looked at her, she was certain it was a deliberate action on his part, designed to throw her off balance.

"What do you know about the daughter's boyfriend?" he finally asked.

"Nothing, I'm afraid. I've never met the young man." This time she paused. After all, she thought as she studied him, turnabout was fair play. "Any other questions, Detective?" she finally said.

He glared at her, but before he had a chance to respond, the radio in his car crackled to life. He stepped over to the window, and after listening a moment, he said, "The rest will have to wait. I have to answer this call. I'll be in touch, though," he told her as he opened the door and climbed inside.

As she watched his vehicle roar off down the street, she repeated the detective's parting words. "I'll be in touch." She mimicked his growling tone. "Yeah, and I can't wait," she muttered sarcastically when his car disappeared around the corner.

Thirty minutes later, sweaty, winded, and still annoyed by Louis Thibodeaux's surprise appearance, Charlotte turned back down the block leading back to her house. Abruptly, she stopped dead in her tracks and groaned.

"Just what I need this morning," she grumbled.

Parked in front of her home was a red Dodge Neon she recognized all too well. Her sister's Neon.

Why wasn't Madeline at work, where she was supposed to be? Charlotte wondered. As she forced herself to put one foot in front of the other, a feeling of dread weighed down each step. An early-morning visit from her sister didn't bode well and could only mean one thing: Madeline was in some kind of trouble . . . again.

Over the years, Madeline had moved back in with Charlotte at different times. The reasons varied and ranged from too much debt to failed relationships.

At least she had the good sense to lock the door behind her this time, thought Charlotte when she tried the front doorknob and found she had to use her key to get inside.

Charlotte unlocked the door, but even before she opened it, she heard the muted squawks and protests of Sweety Boy coming from the other side. She groaned again, knowing exactly what she would find when she got inside.

Just as she'd expected, the little parakeet was hopping from one side of the cage to the other, banging against the wire cage, his wings flapping in protest. Birdseed was scattered everywhere.

"Hey, boy, I'm home now," Charlotte told him softly, reaching through the cage with her finger to pet him. "Just calm down," she soothed as she stroked his breast. "There, there, that's a good Sweety Boy, my good little watch bird."

After a moment, the little parakeet hopped on Charlotte's finger and began preening his ruffled feathers. Satisfied that he had finally settled down, Charlotte nudged him off her finger onto his perch and went in search of her sister.

"Madeline?" she called out.

"In the kitchen," her sister answered in a lackluster voice that made Charlotte wince.

When she entered the room and saw Madeline seated at the breakfast table, her hands wrapped around a coffee mug, the feeling of dread she'd had earlier grew even stronger.

There were dark circles beneath her sister's eyes, her

toffee-colored hair looked as if it hadn't seen a brush in days, and she was dressed in a faded T-shirt and stained sweatpants.

"That bird hates me," Madeline told her.

Charlotte walked to the refrigerator.

"Every time I come over here, he goes into conniption fits," Madeline continued. "Why, this time he even called me crazy! Is that the kind of thing you've been teaching him— to call your sister crazy?"

Charlotte couldn't help herself as she burst out laughing. "That's silly," she said, almost choking on the words. "Sweety Boy doesn't talk."

"Humph! Sounded like he said crazy to me."

"Well, if the shoe fits . . ."

"Thanks a lot, Charlotte. I can always count on you to come up with pithy words of wisdom."

Madeline's smile belied her sarcastic words. Charlotte simply shook her head and grinned as she opened the refrigerator and removed a carton of orange juice. "It has to be the perfume you wear," she said, for lack of any other excuse, though from the looks of her, she doubted that her sister had bothered with perfume.

Charlotte took a glass out of the cabinet and poured the juice. "I think I read somewhere that birds are really sensitive to odors." She held out the glass. "Want some?"

"Humph! Can't be perfume. I'm not wearing any." Then Madeline shook her head. "No, thanks."

With a shrug, Charlotte returned the carton of juice to the refrigerator, then seated herself at the table across from her sister. "Maddy, why are you here?"

"Well, excuse me," Madeline replied in her most indignant tone. "Can't I visit my own sister?"

Charlotte ignored the question. "Why aren't you at work?"

Her sister dropped her gaze, focusing on the coffee she was holding, and took her time answering. "I got fired," she finally said, her voice just above a whisper. She glanced up. "But it wasn't my fault."

It never is, thought Charlotte. For years she'd blamed herself for her sister's irresponsible ways. She'd spoiled Madeline after their parents' deaths, then made excuses for her sister's reckless actions, setting a pattern that had unfortunately continued into adulthood.

Charlotte no longer blamed herself, though, and hadn't, not for a long time. She had finally made peace with her guilty conscience, had finally decided that she'd done the best she could with what she had at the time. It had taken awhile, but she'd ultimately reached the point where she could accept the fact that Madeline was a grown woman who knew right from wrong. How she lived her life had to be up to her.

She gave her sister a pointed look. "So whose fault was it?" she asked bluntly.

Maddeline colored slightly and glanced away. "I never could fool you, could I?"

Charlotte reached out and patted her sister's hand. "What happened, Maddy?"

"Johnny got married again."

Charlotte stiffened and jerked her hand away. For long seconds, all she could do was stare at her sister as she battled for patience as well as control over her rising temper. But neither was forthcoming, and she lost the battle.

"What on earth does your ex getting married again have to do with you getting fired?" she said through clenched teeth.

"I was absent too many times without an excuse."

"Aw, Maddy, give me a break. It's been over twenty years since he left you. Do you know how absurd all of that sounds?"

Suddenly, Madeline slapped her hands against the table and propelled herself out of the chair. "Yes, Charlotte!" she shouted as she leaned across the table and glared at her. "I'm well aware of how absurd that sounds, and I certainly don't need you to point it out. I came over here thinking—thinking—" Her voice died away, and she shook her head. "To tell the truth, I don't know what I was thinking," she mumbled as she collapsed back into her chair. Crossing her arms on top of the table, she laid her head down on top of them.

"Maddy, honey, you need some help—some professional help."

Madeline raised her head. "I never told you," she whispered, "but I tried that several years ago. It didn't work."

"Maybe you didn't go to the right doctor," Charlotte suggested.

"Well, I can't afford to go to any doctor now, so what's the point? Besides, I wouldn't know who to go to even if I could afford it."

Charlotte thought a minute and chose her words carefully. "I'll ask Hank to help you locate the right doctor. I can lend you the money if needed, but I'm sure you won't have any trouble getting another job. Good CPAs are hard to find, especially ones who are as qualified and experienced as you are."

Even as Charlotte hesitated, waiting for her sister's reaction, the gem of an idea began taking root. Excitement began to build the more she thought about it, and suddenly she knew that she had the perfect solution to her sister's job situation.

"Hey, Maddie, what about starting your own company? I'm sure that Hank could make recommendations to some of his colleagues, and so could Daniel." She rushed on. "For that matter, so could I."

Madeline slowly straightened back into a sitting position, a thoughtful expression on her face. "Do you really think I could?"

"Of course you could."

"But wouldn't something like that take a lot of money? I have bills to pay—rent, utilities, a car note . . ."

Remembering how often she had cautioned Madeline about saving for a rainy day, Charlotte fought down frustration and disappointment. How many times had she stressed that a single woman needed to have a financial cushion?

Charlotte thought about it for a minute, and though she knew she might regret it, she made the offer, anyway. "You could always move back here. The other half of the double isn't rented right now, anyway. And I could spring for the utilities for a couple of months until you got on your feet."

"I could get a small-business loan, too," Madeline said, excitement building in her voice. "I already have a computer and the programs I'd need." A smile broke out on her face. "Oh, Charlotte, why didn't I think of this years ago?"

Charlotte laughed, but refrained from pointing out that she was the one who had thought up the idea. "Tell you what," she said. "I just happen to have the afternoon free. If you want to get started on cleaning out the other half of the double after lunch, I'd be glad to help."

Madeline nodded enthusiastically. "If we can get it cleaned today, I could get Daniel and Hank to help me move in by the weekend. That would save me having to come up with next month's rent on my apartment. And tomorrow I could go to the bank and talk to them about a small loan— Oh, Charlotte, this is great! I haven't felt so good in a very long time."

While Madeline chattered away, making all kinds of enthusiastic plans, Charlotte fixed them breakfast and tried not to begrudge the extra money her sister's plans were going to cost her.

Over poached eggs, whole-wheat toast, and fresh Ponchatoula strawberries, she listened to her sister mapping out a list of things to be done while she tried to ignore the niggling doubts already forming in the back of her mind.

To make a business successful demanded a great deal of hard work and dedication and a lot of self-discipline. Would Madeline be able to handle the responsibilities that running a business required? Or would she revert back to her old, irresponsible ways? Charlotte had lost count of the times she'd had to bail her sister out of financial disasters, and with her own retirement looming so near, she really couldn't afford to take too many more risks.

Only time would tell, she finally decided as she stood on the front porch and watched her sister drive away.

If worse came to worse, Hank would take care of you.

Charlotte shuddered and walked back inside, locking the door behind her. She loved her son with all of her heart, and she knew he meant well, but having to rely on him—or anyone, for that matter—was simply out of the question. Charlotte LaRue could take care of herself.

Back in the kitchen, she cleared the table, stacked their dirty dishes into the dishwasher, then turned on the dishwasher. At least her sister's visit had taken her mind off the Dubuissons for a while . . . and off of dark thoughts of Louis Thibodeaux and his probing questions. Madeline's visit had also solved another dilemma as well. Now she knew how she was going to spend her afternoon, she thought as she walked into the living room and eyed Sweety Boy's dirty cage with distaste.

Though she tried to change the paper in the bottom of the cage daily, at least once a week she washed his food pot and the water trough and tubes in hot, sudsy water. She also removed and thoroughly cleaned the perches and swing by scraping them with sandpaper, just as the vet had suggested. In addition, she always made sure that she sprayed the little bird with a special parasitic spray. The whole process took about an hour and was her least favorite chore, one that she tended to put off as long as possible.

As she stared at the cage, an idea began to form. She was certain that Judith would want to know about her mother's new employment plans. Why not use the news to her advantage. Telling her niece the news would give her a legitimate excuse to call her, and of course, after telling Judith about her mother's new plans, she could work the conversation around to Jackson's autopsy report.

Charlotte went to her desk and looked up the phone number to the Sixth District police station in the phone directory. Cleaning the birdcage could wait until later, she decided as she punched out the number. And in the grand scheme of things, what was a clean birdcage compared to finding a murderer?

Chapter Fourteen

"**I** would like to speak with Detective Judith Monroe," Charlotte told the woman who answered the call.

"I'll see if she's available, ma'am. Please hold."

Charlotte drummed her fingers against the desktop while she waited. When the same voice came back on the line a minute later, she was told that Detective Monroe wasn't available at the moment. "Can someone else help you, ma'am?" the woman asked.

A mental image of Louis Thibodeaux popped into Charlotte's head, and a wave of apprehension swept through her. "No," she blurted out. "I'll call back again later." She quickly hung up the phone. The very last person she wanted to talk to or have to deal with was her niece's partner. There was just something about that man that rubbed her the wrong way.

By the time that Charlotte showered, washed and dried her hair, and dressed, it was late midmorning. Again she tried calling her niece, and again she was told that Judith wasn't available.

She had just made up her mind that, like it or not, she was going to have to clean the birdcage, after all, when the phone rang.

"Saved by the bell," she murmured, snatching up the receiver. "Maid-for-a-Day. Charlotte speaking."

"Hi, Charlotte, this is Nadia."

Nadia . . . Oh, no. Charlotte squeezed her eyes shut and wished the ground would suddenly open up and swallow her. She'd completely forgotten to call Daniel about Ricco.

She'd intended to talk to her nephew about the matter on Sunday, but after Daniel had called to say he had a stomach virus and wouldn't be able to come, she'd put it off.

"Charlotte? Are you still there?"

"Yes, hon," she answered, feeling worse with each passing moment. "I'm still here, and I'm afraid I owe you a big apology."

"Your nephew wouldn't take Ricco's case." It was a flat statement, filled with disappointment.

"Ah . . . well, you see, I haven't asked him," Charlotte told her. "Not yet, anyway. I'm hoping you'll forgive me, though, after you hear why."

Charlotte explained about Daniel's illness first. Ordinarily, she wouldn't have discussed the Dubuissons' problems with anyone, but Jackson's death had made the news, so as she told Nadia about Jackson's murder, she figured she wasn't truly breaking her confidentiality code.

"Since Monday I haven't been able to think straight with everything that's happened," she said when she'd finished her explanation.

The line was silent for several moments. "How awful," Nadia finally said. "And I think I have problems. Funny thing is, I remember reading about that in the paper, but I guess I didn't realize that the Dubuissons were your clients."

"Yes . . . well, but that's still no excuse for me forgetting—not really. I'm so sorry, dear. Just as soon as we hang up, I promise I'll give Daniel a call."

True to her word, Charlotte called her nephew the moment she finished the conversation with Nadia. She was relieved when his secretary put her right through.

"Aunt Charley, what's up?"

"First things first, hon," she said. "We missed you Sunday. How are you feeling?"

"I missed seeing all of you, too, and I'm feeling a heck of a lot better than I did Sunday morning. I'm still a bit queasy now and then, but at least I'm no longer paying homage to the porcelain god in the bathroom."

Charlotte burst out laughing. "Oh, Daniel, only you could make a joke about such a thing." Even as a small boy, Daniel had been the clown of the family. Charlotte had often wondered if her nephew's antics were his way of dealing with the hurt of his father's abandonment. At least Daniel's way was healthier than his sister's, she thought. Poor Judith had bottled up all of her resentment until it had turned bitter. Resentment without a release always turned bitter. Then there was Madeline . . .

No, she decided. She wouldn't go there. Not now, not so soon after their little confrontation. Just thinking about her sister's obsessive behavior only made her crazy.

Daniel cleared his throat. "So, Aunt Charley, you said, 'First things first,'" he said. "Other than worrying about your favorite nephew's health, was there another reason you called?"

"I need a favor, dear. You remember Nadia Wilson, don't you?"

"Sure I do. She's the tall, dark-haired woman who works for you. The one with the little boy named Davy. A really nice lady, if she's the one I'm thinking about."

"Yes, she is a nice lady," Charlotte agreed. Then she launched into an explanation about Ricco's situation and

Nadia's predicament. "Such a shame," she added when she was finished. "She really doesn't deserve the way she's been treated by Ricco or the police, and it's doubly hard on her with little Davy crying for his daddy."

"Yeah, that's a tough one," Daniel agreed. "You know I can't promise anything, but you can tell Nadia that I'll check into the matter for her. And for little Davy," he added. "But I have to tell you, this Ricco sounds like a real loser."

"He's not exactly one of my favorite people," Charlotte admitted, "but Nadia is, and I'd appreciate whatever you can do."

"Hey, Aunt Charley, anything for you. After all, what good is having a favorite nephew if he can't help out once in a while?"

"You won't get an argument out of me on that one," Charlotte quipped. "So, will I see you next Sunday?"

"You know it! I'll be there with bells on. Now, before you hang up, why don't you go ahead and give me Nadia's phone number?"

Charlotte gave him the number, then hung up the receiver. Daniel was a sweetheart, and he was right. He was her favorite nephew. Never mind that he was her only nephew, she thought with a smile.

Charlotte's smile quickly turned into a frown, and she groaned. Why hadn't she thought to tell Daniel about his mother's decision to start her own business? Later, she finally decided, her finger hovering above the REDIAL button on the phone. She'd call him back later, but first she needed to phone Nadia.

After a quick call to Nadia to let her know that Daniel had agreed to look into Ricco's case, Charlotte checked the cuckoo clock and saw that it was almost noon. Daniel would more than likely be on his way out to lunch by now, she figured, so she'd have to call him later.

Charlotte glared at the phone, then eyed the birdcage. "I'm not calling the police station again," she told Sweety Boy. "And I'm not cleaning that cage today, either. One more day won't hurt you. But what I am going to do is track down that niece of mine."

The Garden District was under the jurisdiction of the Sixth District New Orleans Police Department. The station, a modern, two-story maroon brick building trimmed in blue and tan, was located on the corner of Martin Luther King Boulevard and South Rampart. It was a new building and a vast improvement over the old headquarters that had been located on Felicity Street.

As Charlotte pulled into the parking lot behind the station, she glanced around at the cars parked there and right away spotted a vehicle that looked like Judith's.

Once she'd parked, she hesitated. Dropping by had seemed like a good idea at the time, but now that she was actually there, she wondered about the prudence of her decision.

That Judith was busy was obvious, since she hadn't been able to take phone calls. Maybe she shouldn't disturb her, after all, Charlotte thought.

Checking the clock on the dashboard, she noted that it was already half past twelve. Before she could change her mind, she quickly gathered her purse and climbed out of the van.

After all, the girl had to eat, she told herself as she locked the van and hurried down the sidewalk that ran alongside the building, a smile on her lips. Surely she could take a moment to talk to her favorite aunt.

Inside the building was a large glass-fronted foyer area that contained a wall of vending machines, two closed doors, and an elevator. Since there were no signs to give directions, by a process of elimination, Charlotte chose the elevator and rode it up to the second floor. Sure enough, when she stepped out of the elevator, directly to her right was what appeared to be an information desk.

"May I help you, ma'am?" a young uniformed female officer asked.

"I'm here to see my niece, Judith Monroe. She's a homicide detective."

"Do you have an appointment?"

Charlotte frowned. "Well, er . . . no—no I don't, but I'm sure she'll see me."

At that moment, a door opened near the beginning of a hallway several feet away, and Judith walked out. When she glanced Charlotte's way and saw her aunt, a puzzled look crossed her face.

"Aunt Charley?" She approached Charlotte. "What are you doing here?"

"I could say I just happened to be in the neighborhood and decided to drop in and say hello, but that would be a lie. I tried calling you"—she shrugged—"but never could get through, so since it was lunchtime, I—" Charlotte looked around and noted that several officers were watching the two of them and listening to their conversation. "Could we talk somewhere a little more private?" she suggested.

"Will this take long? I'm really, *really,* snowed under here."

"It's about your mother."

When Judith's eyes widened with alarm, Charlotte felt an immediate stab of guilt.

"Is she okay? Nothing's happened to her, has it?"

Charlotte quickly shook her head and patted her niece's shoulder. "No, no, dear, nothing like that. This is good news."

The look of relief on Judith's face only made Charlotte feel worse. "Like I was saying, I thought since it was lunchtime, maybe you could join me for a bite to eat—my treat—and then we could talk."

"I'm sorry, Auntie, but there's just too much work still to be done on the Dubuisson case. As much as I'd like to, I

can't. Until this thing is solved, I won't have time for anything."

Charlotte narrowed her eyes. "You need to eat, dear, and I
insist. If you can't go out to lunch, then I'll order us something to be brought here. You can still work while you eat, if
you have to." She paused. "And you can just get that look off
your face, young lady. I won't take no for an answer. Now,
where's a phone I can use?"

With a weary sigh, Judith motioned toward a long hallway. "Follow me."

Judith led the way to a large rectangular-shaped room divided by several shoulder-high, back-to-back partitions.
Each partition was further divided into work stations.

"This is as private as it gets around here," she told
Charlotte with a wave of her hand that took in several other
officers seated at work stations. "Over here," she said. "You
can use that phone." She pointed to an area in the second
row of partitions. "When the food comes, we'll talk."

She seated herself at the work station next to the one
she'd pointed out to Charlotte. Picking up a pen, she immediately began sorting through a stack of neatly organized
files and jotting down notes on a tablet of paper.

Charlotte eyed with distaste the area Judith had told her
to use. Besides a computer monitor and keyboard, there
were stacks of files and papers strewn all over the top. There
were also what appeared to be several wadded-up candy
wrappers, a coffee mug still half-filled with coffee, a half-
eaten sandwich, and French fries sitting on top of a paper
sack.

She set her purse down near the phone on top of a stack
of papers, then rummaged through the purse until she found
her address book.

"I believe Georgio's delivers, and it's just around the corner," she said absently as she thumbed through the book
until she located the name and number of the restaurant she

was looking for. "How about an oyster po-boy?" She punched out the phone number. "If I remember right, that used to be one of your favorites."

Her face a picture of concentration, Judith nodded without looking up and continued poring over the files and writing down notes.

Once Charlotte had placed the order, she seated herself at the desk. Despite Judith's telling her they would talk when the food arrived, now that she was actually there, it was all Charlotte could do to contain her curiosity about the autopsy report.

Patience, she cautioned herself. She'd wait until the food came, and while they were eating, she'd begin by telling Judith about Madeline's new career plans. Then she'd work the conversation around to Jackson's murder and the autopsy report.

When Judith continued working and didn't look up or say anything, Charlotte began to wonder if her niece had forgotten about her even being there.

Should she interrupt Judith, or should she simply wait? Charlotte wondered as all around her officers came and went, computer keyboards clicked away, and the phones rang. Probably best to wait, she decided.

With nothing better to do at the moment, Charlotte glanced around and took in the details of the room. One whole side of the long room was a bank of uncovered windows. The windows, along with the white walls and light gray tiled floor, conspired to give the room an open, airy atmosphere.

Except for the cluttered work stations, the place appeared, for the most part, to be clean. No dust that she could see, and the floor looked freshly mopped and waxed. Yep, clean, all except for . . .

Her gaze zeroed in on the desk area in front of her. Disgusting, she thought. Totally disgusting. Compared to

Judith's neatly organized area and the rest of the room, it was a pigsty, and whoever usually sat there had to be a slob, she decided.

Whoever sat there . . .

Louis Thibodeaux. Of course. Who else?

That's just great, she thought. Not only was the man rude and abrasive, but he was a slob to boot. She shuddered, then her gaze flew to the doorway. She didn't remember seeing him when she came in, but what if he showed up while she was there? She'd never get Judith to tell her anything if he was around.

"Earth to Aunt Charley."

With a start, Charlotte suddenly realized that Judith was talking to her.

"Oh, sorry, hon. Did you say something?"

"Are you okay? You looked a little sick for a moment there."

Charlotte waved away Judith's concern. "I'm fine. Just woolgathering, I guess," she added, then laughed. "Having one of those senior moments."

Judith smiled but still didn't look quite convinced. "What was it, now, that you wanted to tell me about Mother?"

"She's decided to go into business for herself. She's going to move into the other half of the double and work there."

"In other words, she got fired."

Charlotte frowned. "Well, yes, as a matter of fact she did, but how did you know?"

"I know my mother, and after all, I am a detective, Auntie. The way I figure it, she found out about my father's new wife, got all depressed, probably didn't show up for work, and ended up getting fired."

"You got all that just from her deciding to go into business for herself? I'm impressed."

Judith grimaced. "Don't be. Like I said, I know my mother."

"Oh, honey, how did you get to be so cynical at such a young age?"

Judith shrugged. "Comes with the territory." She looked as if she wanted to say more, but at that moment, the phone on her desk trilled.

Judith answered it, but her conversation was short, and as she hung up the receiver, she said, "The food's here. The delivery boy is waiting by the front desk."

"That was fast." Charlotte stood and grabbed her purse. "I'll go take care of it," she said, then motioned toward the stack of files in front of her niece. "You just go ahead with whatever you're doing."

Judith stood. "I'll have to come with you, Auntie. They don't like civilians roaming around on their own."

The huge po-boys were made with freshly baked French bread overstuffed with fried oysters and dressed with lettuce, onions, mayonnaise, and thick slices of tomatoes.

"Just one of these would have been more than enough for the both of us," Judith said as she bit into her sandwich. "Hmm," she groaned with pleasure, and Charlotte smiled.

"I'd be willing to bet that you didn't eat breakfast this morning, now, did you?"

Judith shook her head and managed to say, "No," and chew at the same time, all without opening her mouth.

By the time she had eaten her fill, Charlotte couldn't stand the suspense a moment longer, but even so, she didn't want to appear too eager. "So, did you get that autopsy report back on Jackson," she said, striving for an offhanded attitude as she carefully wrapped the remainder of her sandwich and stuffed it back into the small paper sack.

Judith was still chewing, but she nodded, then swallowed. "That's why I've been up to my eyeballs around here. From the size of the wound, it appears that the official cause of death was the result of a blow to the head from some type of heavy blunt instrument." Judith took a drink out of her canned Coke.

"We suspected as much, of course," she continued, dropping the empty can in a wastebasket beside her desk, "but there was so little blood splatter that we weren't sure. What we didn't know was that the weapon used measures about four inches wide. Even so, there were no fibers or anything embedded in the wound to give us a clue as to exactly what type of weapon was used."

Judith stared into space at a point just past Charlotte's shoulder, her face a picture of concentration, and Charlotte could well imagine gears and wheels turning in her niece's head. "It also seems that our Mr. Dubuisson was full of barbiturates," she said, almost as if she were thinking out loud. "Not enough to kill him but just enough to knock him out."

Judith's voice trailed away, and a sick feeling spread through Charlotte. "Why?" she asked.

Judith suddenly frowned as if she'd just remembered her aunt's presence. "Why did someone kill him if he was already unconscious?"

Charlotte nodded.

"That's the million-dollar question right now. But if what we suspect holds true, then we just might be on the right track to catching his killer."

Charlotte tilted her head. "You know who did it?"

"Let's just say that we think the barbiturates were in the bottle of scotch. It's being analyzed now. And I personally think that papers were missing out of the safe because there was something in there that had to do with the money Jackson had been taking from the firm, money that—"

"Tony Marriott?" Charlotte exclaimed. If Tony Marriott was on the hot seat now, that meant that suspicion had shifted from Jeanne. "But what about his alibi?"

"Yes, well, that is a sticky point, and unfortunately, no

fingerprints other than Jackson's were found on the bottle. Louis is down at the marina now trying to find someone who might be able to blow holes in Marriott's alibi."

"Well, if anyone can bully the truth out of someone, that partner of yours can."

Judith frowned thoughtfully. "You don't like him very much, do you?"

"Like who?"

"Come on, Aunt Charley. You know who I mean. Lou— Louis Thibodeaux, my partner."

Charlotte shrugged and felt her cheeks grow warm. "What's to like? Or dislike," she quickly added. "I don't even know the man."

Judith's eyes narrowed. "Or could it be that you like him a little too much?" she said shrewdly.

Charlotte felt a full-fledged flush inching up her neck and tasted a hot denial on her tongue. Then she recalled some old saying about a person protesting too much and decided against reacting to Judith's question at all. She made a show of checking her watch instead.

"Good grief," she said. "Look what time it is." She abruptly stood and gathered her purse and the sack with her leftover sandwich. "I'm supposed to help your mother clean up the other half of the double this afternoon. Hopefully, Hank and your brother can move her in this weekend. But she's already upset Sweety Boy once this morning, and I don't want him upset again."

Charlotte knew she was babbling, but she couldn't seem to stop. But even worse was seeing the knowing grin spreading on Judith's face.

"He's not married, you know," Judith told her. "And he'll have a pretty decent pension once he retires."

"That's enough, young lady. It's not nice to tease an old woman."

"You old? Ha! That's a funny one if I ever heard one."

"Getting older by the moment," Charlotte groused. "Only five more months and I'll turn the big six-o."

Judith shoved out of her chair and walked over to Charlotte. "You'll never be old, Aunt Charley." She hugged her. "And I'm sorry for teasing you." She pulled away and smiled. "Forgive me?"

"Of course," Charlotte replied, then grinned. "After all, you are my favorite niece."

Judith laughed. "Just like Daniel's your favorite nephew and Hank's your favorite son."

Judith walked Charlotte back down the hallway to the elevator by the front desk. To Charlotte's surprise, her niece stepped into the elevator with her, then punched the first-floor button.

"I'll ride down with you," she said as the doors closed. "Besides, I almost forgot to tell you that we haven't caught up with Brian O'Connor yet, but we did talk to his father. I'm afraid that's another brick wall, though. His father claims that Brian took him to visit some out-of-town relatives that night. Like everyone else involved in this case, he has an alibi, too."

Charlotte just shook her head. "You certainly have your work cut out for you, don't you, hon?"

Judith nodded. "Goes with the territory. It's in the job description."

The elevator arrived at the first floor, and the doors slid open. Charlotte stepped out, but Judith stayed inside, her finger on the OPEN button. "Speaking of jobs," Judith said. "Specifically my mother's new so-called career."

Charlotte raised her eyebrows. "What about it?"

"Well, I know it's none of my business, and I love her dearly, but we both know how my mother operates." Judith grimaced. "I guess what I'm trying to say is, just don't let her take advantage of you, not again." She paused, and suddenly looking uncomfortable, she added, "And one more thing, Auntie. I know I don't have to say it, but I really shouldn't have discussed the details of this case with you—policy and all that—so—"

Charlotte nodded, then made a zipping motion with her finger across her lips. "My lips are sealed."

Chapter Fifteen

Charlotte was climbing into her van when a familiar-looking blue Ford Taurus pulled into an empty parking space beside her. When the driver's door opened and Louis Thibodeaux got out, she cringed, recalling Judith's teasing. For a split second, the urge to duck down out of sight came over her.

But Charlotte never had been the type to hide or run from a confrontation of any kind, whether real or imagined. Still thinking about Judith's teasing remarks, she ignored the butterflies jumping in her stomach and forced herself to sit there and wait, just to see if he would notice her.

He didn't notice her . . . or anything else for that matter. He didn't even glance her way. His craggy face was a picture of intense concentration as he hitched up his pants, then strode purposefully toward the station house.

She waited until he disappeared around the corner of the building before she started the van. Feeling relieved yet oddly disappointed, she drove out of the parking lot and into the street.

Or could it be that you like him a little too much?

Charlotte thought about Judith's words all the way down Martin Luther King Boulevard to St. Charles Avenue. While she waited at the stop sign for a break in the traffic, she wondered if it were possible to be both repelled and attracted to someone at the same time.

"I'm too old for this stuff," she muttered, tapping her fingers impatiently against the steering wheel. Besides, if she'd guessed right and the messy desk next to Judith did belong to Louis Thibodeaux, the man was a total slob. What's more, she'd had her love of a lifetime with Hank's father. Though she'd had several relationships since, when all was said and done, no one had ever measured up to the memories of her son's father. No one had ever even come close to tempting her into the more permanent institution of marriage.

The blast of a car horn shook her out of her reverie. Ignoring the little voice that said she could be wrong, that the desk might not have been his and Louis Thibodeaux might measure up if given a chance, Charlotte pulled onto St. Charles Avenue.

For the rest of her drive home, Charlotte shied away from thinking about her niece's partner and tried concentrating on what she'd learned from Judith instead. As she dissected each piece of information about the ongoing investigation into Jackson's murder, especially the part about the barbiturates in the Scotch, something niggled at the back of her mind. But the more she tried to pinpoint what bothered her about it, the more elusive it became.

Then there was Brian O'Connor, she thought, slowing to a stop for a red light. She could still see the intent look on his face as he'd watched Anna-Maria and James. Had she imagined it, or had that look been more than simple curiosity or admiration for a pretty girl?

Sneaking around down on the porch . . . spying.

Spying on whom? Charlotte wondered as Clarice's accusations came to mind. Spying on Anna-Maria because he'd somehow found out that she was his daughter? Or spying on

Jackson to learn his habits because Brian had more sinister things on his mind? More sinister things, like murder?

Of course, both possibilities hinged on whether she could believe Clarice. Had she been mistaken in dismissing the old lady's accusations?

Working for the Dubuissons' neighbors would have certainly presented Brian many opportunities to spy on both Anna-Maria and Jackson. It would have also afforded him knowledge about the layout of the house.

But what about motive? she wondered. Did he have a motive, enough to commit murder? After all, according to Bitsy, it was Andrew St. John who had framed Brian and had him sent to prison, not Jackson.

Still . . . if what Bitsy Duhe had told her was true, how would Brian have felt, knowing he'd been cheated out of the woman he loved and a daughter as well, a daughter who didn't even know he existed and had grown up thinking another man was her father?

But why now? she wondered as she watched the cars cross the intersection in front of her. Why would Brian have waited so long to do something about it? And what about his alibi? According to Judith, Brian's father had given him an alibi. But wouldn't any parent do the same if they suspected their child was in trouble?

The traffic light finally turned green, and Charlotte accelerated. The whole thing was a puzzle, she decided, a giant puzzle with too many missing pieces.

When Charlotte turned down her street, she expected to see Madeline's car parked in front of her house. But there was no sign of her sister's jaunty red Neon. Though she wasn't exactly surprised—Madeline had never been that dependable—Charlotte felt a twinge of disappointment in spite of herself.

Now what? she wondered as she unlocked the door and let herself inside. Should she call Madeline or simply wait until she heard from her? She could always go ahead and start on the rooms, anyway. The last time she'd cleaned them had been over six months ago, right after the last renters had sneaked out while she was at work without paying her the two months back rent they owed. If nothing else, she could at least air out the place.

"What would you suggest I do?" she asked Sweety Boy.

The little bird's only answer was to ruffle his feathers and prance back and forth on his perch.

"Well, you're no help," Charlotte told him as she slipped off her shoes and stepped into her moccasins.

Out of habit and because she thought Madeline might have called, she checked her answering machine. The blinking light indicated she had three messages, and Charlotte hit the PLAY button.

"Hi, Charlotte, this is Nadia. I just thought I'd let you know what a wonderful man your nephew is. He's already arranged for Davy and me to see Ricco, and what's more, he's agreed to take Ricco's case. Thanks again for your help, and I'll talk to you later."

As the machine beeped and the next message began, a smile pulled at Charlotte's lips. Nadia and Daniel. Now those two would make a perfect couple, she thought.

"Hi, Mom." The sound of her son's voice on the answering machine instantly wiped away her matchmaking thoughts. "Just checking in, since I haven't heard anything out of you in a few days," he said. "Guess you're busy, though, like everyone else, huh? You don't have to be, you know. If you weren't so stubborn, I— Never mind. Just give me a call when you get a chance. I love you."

"I love you, too," she murmured as the machine beeped, signaling the end of Hank's call and the beginning of the final message.

"Charlotte, there's been a change of plans."

At the sound of her sister's voice, Charlotte rolled her eyes toward the ceiling.

"Would you believe," Madeline continued, her recorded voice breathless with excitement, "my old boss just called and wants me to come back to work? He says the office manager should never have fired me without consulting him. Between you and me, though, I suspect his offer has more to do with the fact that I work on certain special accounts for him that are— Well, let's just say the IRS would have a field day if they knew the truth about them. Anyway, isn't that great! But hey, Charlotte, thanks, anyway, for the offer to help and for—for just being there. You're the greatest. Talk to you later."

The machine beeped, signaling the end of the message, but all Charlotte could do was stare into space with unseeing eyes as her sister's message spun through her head.

"Yeah, I'm the greatest, all right. The greatest chump." Just like that, she thought. One minute her sister was starting her own business, and the next, she's not.

"And speaking of business, what's that business about special accounts?" she muttered. "And the IRS?" Charlotte frowned. What on earth was Madeline thinking? And what in the world had her sister gotten involved in this time?

Charlotte's frown deepened. "And why am I standing around talking to myself, for Pete's sake?" It was a bad habit she'd gotten into of late, one she really needed to work on breaking.

Charlotte returned Hank's call but was told he was in with a patient. She left her name with his receptionist and made a mental note to try again later if she didn't hear from him.

For the remainder of the afternoon, she tried to stay busy and not worry about her sister's troublesome message.

She went next door and opened all the windows to let the rooms air out. Then she let Sweety Boy out of his cage and began the distasteful task of cleaning it. Meanwhile, she kept telling herself that Madeline was no longer a helpless little girl. Her sister was a grown woman, responsible for herself. If she got herself into trouble with the IRS over some questionable bookkeeping, then it was no one's fault but her own.

But no matter how hard Charlotte tried not to worry and how much she scrubbed and cleaned Sweety Boy's cage, she couldn't get her sister's message out of her mind.

It was almost six by the time that Charlotte took a break. She had just sat down in front of the television to watch *JAG* while she polished off the last of the leftover chicken gumbo from Sunday's lunch when the phone rang.

In spite of the fact that *JAG* was a rerun, it was one of the few programs she truly enjoyed, and she was hungry, so she decided to let the machine take a message.

"Charlotte, this is Jeanne Dubuisson. I really need to talk to you—"

The moment she heard Jeanne's voice, Charlotte set down the bowl of gumbo, then rushed over to the desk and grabbed the receiver. "Hang on, Jeanne," she said as she switched off the answering machine. "Sorry about that," she told her. "Now what can I do for you?"

"Oh, Charlotte, I'm so glad you're home. Jackson's body has finally been released. We're having the funeral tomorrow at eleven. But Anna-Maria and I have to be at the funeral home by eight, so there won't be anyone who can let you inside the house when you get here in the morning."

"What about leaving me a key somewhere?" Charlotte suggested.

"Why, yes, I suppose I could. Tell you what. I'll leave it under that big potted plant that sits on the right side of the front door."

"And don't forget to leave the front gate unlocked, too."

"Good point. Lately I've been so forgetful that I'd better write myself a note." Jeanne hesitated. "I'd like to ask another favor, too," she said after a moment had passed. "I'm really going to need some help after the service, when everyone congregates at the house—you know, with the refreshments and drinks. I'm having the food catered, but the catering service I'm using doesn't supply anyone to serve the stuff. I'd be willing to pay you extra."

"There's no need for that," Charlotte said. "I've already told you I'll help in any way I can. I'm just so sorry all of you have to go through this."

"You're a good person, Charlotte LaRue, and I don't know what I'd do without you. Just so you'll be watching for him, the caterer promised he would deliver everything around ten."

"I'll be ready for him," Charlotte assured her.

The line hummed with silence for a moment, then Jeanne cleared her throat. "I really hate imposing on you like this," she said, "but there's just one more little thing I need help with, too. Mother still refuses to attend the services, and she won't hear of me getting a sitter. The way she's been acting lately, I—Could you—I mean, would it be too much of an imposition for you to come a little earlier than usual, and would you mind checking on her while we're gone?"

"Of course I don't mind, and it's not an imposition. I'll be there, so just stop worrying—and try to get a good night's sleep. Tomorrow will be a hard day for you."

"Lately, they're all hard, but I'll try. And thanks, Charlotte. See you tomorrow."

Charlotte hung up the receiver. Outside, thunder rumbled in the distance, signaling the rain that the dreary day had promised. Charlotte quickly sent up a prayer that the storm would pass over quickly. Funerals were hard enough on the family involved on a good day. A cloudy, rainy day always made things seem worse.

Chapter
Sixteen

The day of Jackson Dubuisson's funeral dawned bright with sunshine, but the air was heavy with steamy humidity left over from the stormy night.

Charlotte had set her alarm clock fifteen minutes earlier than usual so that she would still have time to take her daily walk before going to work. By the time she'd finished the walk and stepped into the shower, she was dripping with sweat.

Sweat was good for you, though, she grudgingly reassured herself as she stood under the tepid spray of water, rinsing off a rich lather of soap. She'd once read an article somewhere that sweating opened up the pores and helped the body rid itself of impurities.

Charlotte switched off the faucets and reached for a towel. So if it was so good for you, why did she still feel so icky even after taking a shower? Whoever had written that silly article had never lived in New Orleans, she figured.

* * *

Charlotte kept her promise to Jeanne and arrived early. When she approached the front of the house, she was vastly relieved to see that there was no sign of the reporters who had kept vigil for the past four days.

They were probably all at the funeral, hovering around the church like a flock of vultures, just waiting to pick up some juicy tidbit to exploit.

Thankful that she could finally park in her usual spot, Charlotte pulled the van over to the curb near the corner. When she climbed out of the vehicle, an old battered truck pulled alongside the curb of the house next door and parked.

Charlotte immediately recognized the truck as belonging to the gardener, Joseph O'Connor, but the lone man who climbed out of the truck was Brian, not Joseph.

He acknowledged her presence with a brief nod; then, after he'd unloaded a wheelbarrow, he immediately began stacking it with bags of what looked like fertilizer out of the back of the pickup.

Where was his father? she wondered as she watched Brian heave the large bags out of the truck bed.

Though he was some distance away, with each movement he made she could still see the muscles in his arms and back straining beneath the black T-shirt he wore.

What was it that Bitsy had told her about his father? Something about his being ill? No, not exactly ill, she thought as she walked to the back of the van.

Charlotte climbed inside and began gathering the supplies she would need. Bitsy had said Joseph sometimes had problems with his arthritis and that it was the reason Brian had moved back to New Orleans.

But was that the real reason? Was Brian simply being a good, dutiful son, or did he have another, more sinister agenda for returning to his hometown, one that included revenge and murder?

Supply carrier in hand and her mind whirling with the implications of her thoughts, Charlotte climbed slowly out of the van. As she slammed the door and locked it, she toyed with the idea of using the old gardener's condition as an excuse to start up a conversation with his son.

But to what purpose? The moment the question popped into her mind, she immediately realized how far-fetched and silly the whole idea was. If Brian did realize that Anna-Maria was his daughter, he wasn't about to discuss it with someone he'd only met a few days earlier. And if he'd cold-bloodedly murdered Jackson Dubuisson, he would be a fool to confess his crime to anyone, let alone the maid from next door.

Chiding herself for being such a nosy-rosie, Charlotte pocketed the keys, then walked briskly to the front gate. At the gate, she reached out and tugged on the latch. The latch held fast and didn't budge, and Charlotte sighed. Had Jeanne forgotten to leave the gate unlocked, after all? Charlotte pulled down hard on the handle one more time, just to make sure, but it still didn't open.

She glanced up toward the upper gallery, her hand still gripping the handle. What now? she wondered, searching for a solution to the dilemma. She could always use her cell phone to call Clarice and ask her to throw the inside switch that unlocked the gate. But in order to do so, the old lady would have to go down the stairs to where the switch was located, near the front door.

No, Charlotte decided. Even if Clarice agreed to go down the stairs, which she was sure she wouldn't, she couldn't take the chance that the old lady might slip and fall. She'd have to think of something else.

But what? she wondered as a frisson of real concern coursed through her. Clarice was in the house, all alone. What if she had another stroke? What if she slipped going to the bathroom, or what if . . .

Charlotte shook her head and tried to block out all of the negative thoughts churning through her mind. *Think positive,* she commanded herself. *There has to be a way to get in.*

"Is there something wrong, ma'am?"

Charlotte almost jumped out of her skin at the sound of the unexpected male voice directly behind her. When she spun around, the sight of Brian O'Connor standing within touching distance unnerved her even more.

"Hey, take it easy," he told her. "I didn't mean to startle you."

Feeling more than a little flustered, Charlotte stared up at the tall, sandy-haired son of the gardener. As she tried to regain control over her momentary panic, once again she was taken aback by a vague feeling of familiarity, the same kind of feeling she'd had when she'd first met him at Bitsy Duhe's house.

It was his eyes, she decided. Those startling green eyes . . . just like . . . like . . . Of course! she thought. No wonder he seemed familiar. Anna-Maria's eyes had that same piercing green quality to them, with just a hint of a bruised look about them. Like father, like daughter?

When Charlotte suddenly realized that too much time had passed and that he was looking at her strangely, she blurted out, "The gate is locked. Jeanne—Mrs. Dubuisson, that is— was supposed to leave it open for me, but I guess she forgot." To emphasize the point, Charlotte rattled the latch. When several strained moments passed again and Brian simply continued to stare at her, Charlotte became uncomfortable under his scrutiny.

She'd wanted to talk to him, question him, but now that she had the opportunity to do so, she didn't have the foggiest idea as to how to proceed.

"I really need to get in," she finally said, for no other reason than to fill in the silence. "Everyone's at the funeral home, all except Miss Clarice. And she's by herself "—she waved her hand toward the house—"inside, and I promised Mrs. Dubuisson that I'd keep an eye on her."

Why on earth was she babbling on so? she wondered. Because he made her nervous, came the answer. Because deep down, in the dark recesses of her mind, she suspected that he could very well be the person who had murdered Jackson Dubuisson.

"I think there's another way in," he finally said. Seeing her speculative look, he quickly clarified his statement. "While I was trimming the hedges the other day, I noticed that there's a gap in the fence on that side. Two of the metal bars must have rusted through. I've been meaning to mention it to Jean—Mrs. Dubuisson—but with everything that's happened, I didn't want to bother her right now. I think the gap is probably large enough to squeeze through, though, if you're willing to try it out."

Had he tried it out? Had he squeezed through the gap, sneaked onto the porch, smashed in the pane of glass . . .

"Show me" was the only thing that Charlotte could think to say. Anything to end the awkward conversation, anything to stop the wild speculations roaring through her mind.

Just as Brian had predicted, the gap in the fence was big enough for Charlotte to squeeze through . . . and big enough for someone larger to squeeze through, too, she thought. . . . *Sneaking around . . . spying . . .* Someone like Brian O'Connor?

"Thank you," she told him once she was safely standing on the other side of the fence.

"No problem," he said. "And if you don't mind, be sure and tell Mrs. Dubuisson about the fence."

"I'll tell her," Charlotte assured him, eager to end the encounter. "Thanks again," she added, then turned and hurried toward the front steps.

At the mention of Jeanne's married name, there had been no hesitation this time, she noted. Too late, though, she thought. He'd already slipped up the first time and almost called her Jeanne. Of course that in itself was no big deal, she silently argued, playing devil's advocate. After all, according to Bitsy, the two were once in love with each other.

When Charlotte reached the porch, she glanced nervously over her shoulder to see what Brian was doing. She wasn't sure what she'd expected him to be doing, but to her relief, he had returned to the truck to finish unloading the bags of fertilizer.

Charlotte released a heavy sigh. Had she done it again? she wondered. Had she once again allowed her overactive imagination to get the best of her? After a moment, she decided that maybe she had. Maybe she was making a mountain out of a molehill and had let Bitsy Duhe's gossip get the best of her.

With a shake of her head, Charlotte turned her attention back to the problem at hand. Since Jeanne had forgotten to unlock the front gate, she worried that she might have forgotten to leave the key to the door, too. When she lifted up the edge of the potted plant next to the door and felt beneath it, Charlotte sighed with relief when her fingers connected with the small piece of metal.

The moment she stepped inside the foyer, she wrinkled her nose at the distinct odor hanging in the air. Bacon, she decided as she set down her supply carrier. Someone had fried bacon earlier, and the scent of bacon, like the smell of fried fish, always seemed to hang around forever.

Air freshener would take care of the smell, but the first order of the day was to check on Clarice—just a quick peek to make sure the old lady was okay and to ease her mind. Then she needed to get a move on before the caterers delivered the food or before someone decided to show up at the house early.

Halfway up the staircase, the muted sound of voices, followed by canned laughter, drifted down. Clarice's television. Not wanting to startle the old lady, Charlotte called out to her before she reached her door.

"Miss Clarice! It's Charlotte." She waited a moment, then peeked around the door. "Good morning," she told the older woman.

As usual, Clarice was still in bed, and though she looked a bit more tidy than the last time Charlotte had seen her, she also appeared to be a bit flushed.

"Are you feeling okay this morning?" Charlotte asked her.

The old lady totally ignored her question. "You're late," she said, her gaze never wavering from the TV set. "You were supposed to be here fifteen minutes ago."

Good old Clarice, Charlotte thought. Rude as ever. "Yes, well, I had a little problem getting in," she explained, thinking that the old lady sounded a bit breathless as well as looking flushed. Maybe she should take Clarice's temperature just to make sure she wasn't running a fever. "Jeanne must have forgotten to leave the front gate unlocked."

"Sounds like that airhead daughter of mine."

It was hard to bite back the stinging retort that popped into her head, hard to keep from telling the old lady that she was an ungrateful old grouch who should be thankful she had such a kind, loving daughter like Jeanne. But Charlotte reminded herself that Clarice was just that, an old woman.

"Yes . . . well, I just wanted to let you know I'm here," Charlotte told her, noting with relief that the flush seemed to be fading. Just excitement, she figured, or agitation because she'd been late showing up. Besides, she thought, Jeanne would never have left her mother unattended if she'd suspected she was ill.

"I'll be cleaning the bottom floor first," Charlotte said, "but if you need anything, just call out."

Charlotte waited a moment longer for some kind of response, but when Clarice kept watching the TV and said nothing, Charlotte finally left the room.

Downstairs, as Charlotte entered the kitchen, she quickly glanced around, mentally listing the chores that needed taking care of by priority.

There were unwashed dishes in the sink. A dirty plate and

fork, along with the morning newspaper, cluttered up the breakfast table, and on the counter next to the stove top sat a carton of eggs and a package of bacon.

She walked over to the stove, a frown on her face. A dirty skillet was on one of the burners, and a film of grease was splattered all over the stove top. Someone had definitely fried bacon.

Strange, she thought as she reached out to remove the frying pan. When Jeanne cooked, she always cleaned up after herself. Charlotte couldn't recall her ever having left such a greasy mess.

The moment Charlotte touched the handle of the skillet, her frown grew deeper. She released the handle and gingerly tapped the pan itself. Sure enough, the pan was still warm.

"Now that's really strange," she muttered as she took hold of the handle and poured the grease into a nearby garbage pail, then placed the skillet in the sink. By her calculations, Jeanne and Anna-Maria had to have left well over thirty minutes earlier, plenty of time for the pan to have cooled off.

Charlotte squirted a dab of liquid detergent in the pan, then filled it with water to soak. After she turned off the faucet, she walked over to the table to retrieve the plate and fork. Back at the sink, she rinsed the plate before placing it in the dishwasher. It wasn't until she had actually stacked the plate in the dishwasher that it suddenly dawned on her that the leftover egg yolk on the plate had rinsed off beneath the spray of water without her having to scrub it, which meant it hadn't congealed yet, which, in turn, meant that it hadn't been that long since someone had eaten the plate of food.

For several moments, Charlotte stood staring out the window above the sink as she tried to put her finger on just exactly what was bothering her about the messy kitchen. Then she recalled a conversation between Jeanne and Clarice . . . Clarice saying something about wanting bacon . . . *lots of bacon, fried nice and crisp.*

"Of course," she murmured. The obvious answer was that

Clarice had decided to fix her own breakfast after her daughter and granddaughter had left. But Clarice didn't cook as far as Charlotte knew, and she didn't go up and down the stairs by herself, either.

Or did she? Charlotte wondered, remembering the scuff marks she'd had to scrub off the steps. And if Clarice could negotiate the stairs without assistance, why pretend otherwise all this time?

The grandfather clock in the foyer chimed the half-hour, the sound penetrating Charlotte's reverie, and she felt a momentary panic. At the most, she only had a little over an hour and a half before the caterers showed up.

Other than the dirty dishes and the grease-splattered stove top, the kitchen was basically clean, and it didn't take her long to load the dishwasher, then wipe down the stove top, the countertops, and the appliances.

Charlotte chose to use the broom instead of the noisy vacuum cleaner just in case Clarice might call out or need something. Then she mopped the room.

The dining room only took minutes to clean. Charlotte dusted the huge antique table and matching China cabinet, but she decided against taking the time to wax or polish the furniture. Instead, she concentrated on the sideboard, since it would be used to hold the food brought in by the caterers.

Once she was finished with the dining room, she moved to the parlor. After eyeing the large room, she decided that all it needed was straightening and a bit of dusting. Though she would have normally vacuumed, too, she decided to make a quick check on Clarice first before running the noisy machine.

From the sound of Clarice's television filtering down the stairs, Charlotte recognized a popular game show. Knowing that the old lady sometimes napped about midmorning, she decided against calling out to her this time as she quietly approached the bedroom door.

When Charlotte peeked around the corner of the open

doorway, it took a moment for the sight before her to register in her mind.

She'd expected to see Clarice dozing peacefully. But Clarice wasn't asleep. The shock of what she did see hit her full force, and her mouth dropped open.

Chapter
Seventeen

Clarice was standing beside the bed, her back to the door-way, and in each of her hands was a small barbell.

Charlotte clamped her hand over her mouth to stifle the giggle bubbling up in her throat. Dressed in her flannel nightgown, her thin gray hair sticking out like porcupine quills, the old lady looked ridiculous, all hunched over, straining to lift the weights.

But Charlotte's amusement swiftly grew into amazement as she watched Clarice slowly lift first one arm, then the other. But from the way her arms quivered, Charlotte could tell that the exertion was a strain.

Weight training? Clarice worked out with weights? What a hoot! she thought. As long as she'd been employed by the Dubuissons, Charlotte couldn't ever recall seeing Clarice do any kind of physical exercise despite Jeanne's efforts to persuade her otherwise. In fact, the old lady balked at even the suggestion of doing anything physical.

But as Charlotte continued watching the older woman, she recognized immediately that Clarice was no stranger to using the weights. She knew exactly what she was doing.

As she continued to observe the old lady and felt her own arms strain with each curl the old lady achieved, a peculiar feeling deep inside took root and grew. She wasn't sure how she knew, but instinct told her that the old lady probably wouldn't appreciate having an audience.

Charlotte quickly backed away from the door, then retraced her steps to the top of the stairwell. The thing to do would be to ignore what she saw, to simply take care of what she was hired to do and mind her own business.

Still . . . there was something about the whole thing that bothered her, and like a pesky fly that wouldn't go away, her curiosity finally got the best of her. What would happen if . . .

Before she could change her mind, Charlotte called out, "Miss Clarice, you doing okay in there?" Charlotte took her time walking back to the bedroom door.

When she looked inside the room, Clarice was back in bed, the covers pulled up to her chin. Her wrinkled face was flushed, reminding Charlotte of how it had looked when she'd first arrived and checked on her, and the barbells were nowhere in sight.

Either Clarice had hidden the weights under the bedcovers or she had shoved them beneath the bed. But the truly bizarre thing about the whole incident was that the old lady was lying there with her eyes closed; of all things, she was pretending to be asleep.

But why? Charlotte wondered as she stared at the old woman. Why would she hide the fact that she was weight lifting or that she was stronger than she pretended to be? To what purpose?

When the answer first popped into her mind, Charlotte almost laughed out loud at the absurdity of the notion. At first, she dismissed the idea totally as but one more example of her own overactive imagination.

But as she backed out of the doorway, a prickly feeling danced along the nape of her neck, and her mind was bombarded with what could only be described as instant replays of different scenes that had occurred over the past week.

. . . the arguments between Clarice and Jeanne over Jackson . . . the coarse, powdery substance in Clarice's bathroom . . . the almost-empty sleeping-pill bottle . . . the description of the murder weapon in the autopsy report . . . the scuff marks on the stairs . . . the smell of bacon and the messy kitchen . . .

In a daze, Charlotte slowly walked back to the stairwell. By the time she reached the first step, her knees were weak from the enormity of the implications.

At the stairs, she gripped the rail, then sank down to sit on the top step. Was the notion absurd? Had Clarice killed her son-in-law?

In and of itself, yes, the notion was absurd. Clarice was a crippled old woman who wasn't strong enough to overpower a man Jackson's size.

But given all of the facts, no, the notion wasn't that far-fetched. It would have been difficult but not impossible for Clarice to have spiked the scotch with the sleeping pills. Once the bottle had been opened, all she had to do was add the powder.

She also had access to the perfect murder weapon. According to what the autopsy report had revealed, the bar-bells were just about the right size.

Charlotte shivered and glanced back toward the old lady's door. Fifteen years earlier, Andrew St. Martin had been murdered in what was eerily similar, by all accounts, to the way Jackson was killed. Was it simply a weird, unfortunate coincidence, or was there a more logical reason? she wondered. Could it be that the same person who had murdered Andrew had also killed Jackson?

Could the murderer have been Clarice? Was it possible that she had killed both her husband and her son-in-law?

According to what Bitsy had said, the police had thought

it was possible when Andrew was murdered. Clarice had been the number-one suspect in her husband's death. But Jeanne had provided her mother with an alibi, so there was no way of proving it. Jeanne was very devoted to her mother, but did her devotion include covering up the murder of her own father and now her husband as well?

As for motive . . . Though Charlotte certainly didn't condone murder in any shape or form, she could understand the motive Clarice might have had for killing Andrew, especially if he'd been abusive to her and Jeanne. But what about her motive for killing Jackson?

He's stealing you blind . . . and Jackson got his . . . serves him right too . . .

The only logical answer that Charlotte could think of was the oldest reason in the world: a mother protecting her child.

Clarice might be old and appear to be senile at times, but she was well aware of the loveless relationship between Jackson and her daughter. She'd accused Jeanne of being weak . . . spineless, and on more than one occasion, she'd made it crystal clear that she didn't trust her daughter's husband. If Clarice had somehow found out that Jackson was also cheating on Jeanne, then . . .

Charlotte suddenly remembered Clarice's accusations against Brian O'Connor. The old lady had accused him of killing Jackson, had said he was sneaking around, spying. Charlotte had a growing suspicion that Clarice, in fact, had been the one sneaking around and spying.

Had the old lady's accusation simply been a ploy calculated to throw suspicion on Brian and divert suspicion away from Jeanne and herself? And if it had, why had Clarice revealed all of that stuff to her instead of telling the police?

When the answer came to her, Charlotte almost groaned out loud. Clarice knew. Somehow she'd found out that Judith, a police detective, was Charlotte's niece. And if she knew, then it was possible she'd counted on Charlotte to reveal the information about Brian. If Clarice had revealed it directly, the police might not have taken it seriously, but if the information was revealed indirectly . . .

Charlotte suddenly got the feeling that she'd been had. Big time. But was Clarice that clever, that devious? Had she used her?

With a weary sigh, Charlotte pulled herself up and stood. Suddenly, she felt old, very old and tired, as she trudged down the stairs.

Speculating about Clarice's guilt was one thing. She could speculate till doomsday, but to what end? Just thinking about blowing the whistle on the old lady made her queasy. For one thing, Clarice wasn't just any old lady; she was Jeanne's mother and Anna-Maria's grandmother. She was also an affluent woman who was well known and respected throughout the city.

So she should get away with murder?

The nagging voice of her conscience made Charlotte cringe. No one should get away with murder.

But what if she was wrong? What if she went to Judith, told her what she knew, told her what she suspected, and then found out she'd been mistaken about everything?

Charlotte shuddered. The repercussions of such a mistake would be catastrophic. Not only would she lose a long-term client, but the Garden District, in spite of its size, was truly a small community. Word would travel like wildfire. Even now, she could hear the whispers and gossip. She could kiss her little cleaning service good-bye. Why, she'd be lucky to ever work again.

No, she decided. All she had right now was what the movies and mystery books termed as circumstantial evidence. All she had were unproven speculations. Before she could go around accusing someone of murder, she'd need proof, real proof, the kind that would stand up in a court of law.

Proof, like the residue from the crushed phenobarbital tablets.

At the foot of the stairs, Charlotte groaned and almost tripped over the last step. In her mind's eye she saw herself cleaning Clarice's bathroom, wiping off the cabinet top, possibly destroying the only evidence that could substantiate her suspicions.

Then, like a lightbulb going off in her head, she suddenly remembered that she had never gotten around to doing the laundry. The washcloth she'd used to wipe up the powder was still in Clarice's dirty clothes hamper. Surely the residue on the washcloth was still detectable.

There was also the prescription bottle itself. If the pills were used, the pill count and the date the prescription was filled wouldn't jibe, would they? Unless . . . Charlotte almost groaned again. Unless Jeanne had remembered to get the prescription refilled.

The grandfather clock in the foyer chimed its quarter-hour signal, and Charlotte's pulse jumped. Time was flying, and she still needed to vacuum the main parlor before the caterers arrived. And soon after the caterers, people would start trickling in from the funeral service.

If she wanted to get the evidence, she needed to do it now, while she had the opportunity. But was that what she wanted?

Her head swirled with doubts, and a war of emotions raged within her. She tapped her fingers impatiently along the top of the stair rail. "What to do . . . what to do," she murmured.

Chapter
Eighteen

No one should get away with murder.

Charlotte calculated that if she hurried, she could get the evidence and still have time to vacuum the parlor.

In the movies she'd seen and in the mystery novels she'd read, the police always wore plastic gloves when gathering evidence at the scene of a crime. She also recalled that as they gathered it, they used either paper or plastic bags to store it. Charlotte always kept a small box of disposable plastic gloves in her supply carrier, and she figured she needed a paper sack, since the washcloth might still be damp.

In the laundry room, she rummaged through a stack of paper goods earmarked for the recycling bin until she found what she needed. She folded the medium-size sack into a small, flat square, then slipped it inside her apron pocket.

Midway up the stairs, she frowned. Why was the television set off? she wondered. Usually the infernal thing stayed on nonstop, day and night.

Outside Clarice's bedroom, she rapped lightly on the doorframe. "Miss Clarice," she called out, "I'm ready to clean your room now." She peeked around the open doorway. "May I come in?"

The old lady was perched on top of the bed and propped up by several pillows. In her hands was a book, of all things. Even more surprising was that she had changed from her nightgown into a cotton knit pantsuit. Her hair was brushed, and Charlotte was astonished to see that she had even applied a touch of rouge and lipstick.

Clarice glanced up over the top of her glasses. "You can stop your gawking and come in." She motioned impatiently for Charlotte to enter. "I do dress up once in a while, you know," she said defensively. "Wouldn't want to be an embarrassment to anyone."

And committing murder isn't an embarrassment? Charlotte had to bite her tongue to keep from blurting out the thought. Afraid that what she was thinking would show, she quickly lowered her gaze to stare at the floor. "Since you're reading," she said evenly, "maybe you'd like to sit out on the gallery while I change the sheets. That way I won't disturb you." Hoping the old lady would be cooperative for a change, she added, "It's a beautiful day this morning."

"One day's the same as another when you get to be my age," Clarice grumbled. "And the sheets are just fine. They don't need changing. Besides, I'm tired. I don't want to go outside. Just clean around me. But hurry up. My ten o'clock soap opera comes on soon."

By all means, we wouldn't want to miss our soap opera. To hide her contemptuous thoughts, Charlotte forced a smile through tight lips. "I'll start in the bathroom," she said politely.

Once inside the small room, she nudged the door closed behind her and set down her supply carrier. She figured her fingerprints were already on the suspect prescription bottle, since she'd handled it when she'd gotten a pill for Jeanne, but she donned a pair of thin disposable gloves, anyway, before she sorted through the prescription bottles. Thank goodness for Jeanne's absentmindedness, she thought when she found the phenobarbital bottle and saw that Jeanne had neglected to get the medication refilled.

Charlotte narrowed her gaze and peered at the date that the prescription was last filled. According to the number of tablets that were supposed to be in the bottle, minus the one she'd given Jeanne, she calculated that at least four were missing. Though Charlotte knew she was far from an expert on drugs, she figured that four would have been just enough to render a man Jackson's size unconscious without outright killing him.

She slipped the prescription bottle into the paper sack she'd brought with her, then turned to the dirty clothes hamper. The hamper was so full that clothes were spilling over the edges.

The flannel nightgown Clarice had just changed out of was on top. She removed the gown and several damp towels under it. Just beneath another crumpled nightgown, she spied what she hoped was the corner of the washcloth she was looking for.

"There you are," she whispered, half in anticipation, half in dread.

It's not too late. You can still walk away and forget about it.

Charlotte hesitated, her mind reeling with sudden misgivings despite her earlier conclusions. Part of her wanted to be wrong about everything, wanted it to all be just another example of her own imagination gone wild, while part of her railed against the idea that anyone could cold-bloodedly murder another human being and get away with it.

Knowing in her heart of hearts that there was only one way to find out for sure and that she couldn't live with herself until she did, Charlotte took a deep breath and braced herself for what had to be done.

She had figured that the washcloth might still be damp. But just in case it had dried out, she didn't want to risk losing even one grain of the powdery residue from the crushed tablets that might still be on it. Ever so carefully, she reached to remove the wadded-up nightgown first.

The moment she closed her fingers around the silky gown, something sharp pricked her finger. "Ouch!" she cried as she snatched back her hand.

"Charlotte?" Clarice called out from the bedroom. "What's all the ruckus in there? What on earth are you doing?"

Charlotte yanked off the plastic gloves. A small pearl of blood bubbled on the inside of her right forefinger. "Ah . . . I—I'm cleaning. I just jammed my finger," she lied, her gaze shifting to the closed door. What if the old woman decided to come check on her? Then what?

"Yeah, right," Charlotte muttered as she turned her attention back to her finger. Since when had Clarice worried about anyone but Clarice?

At first, Charlotte couldn't figure out what had stuck her, since nothing was in her finger. When she picked up the glove and carefully turned it inside out, she spotted a small sliver of glass.

Glass?

Using her fingernails, she removed the sliver and placed it on the countertop, then rinsed her hands beneath the faucet.

Why would a sliver of glass be embedded in a nightgown? she wondered as she retrieved a roll of paper towels from her supply carrier and tore off a sheet.

As she blotted her hands dry and applied pressure to her bleeding finger, she stared at the gown. One sliver of glass in and of itself wasn't that significant. But if there were more . . .

Reaching down, she cautiously tugged around the edges of the crumpled gown. She pulled back and straightened one of the sleeves but didn't see anything. Then she gingerly examined the other sleeve. Sure enough, caught in the row of tightly gathered ruffles near the wrist of the sleeve were several more tiny slivers of glass. Like minuscule diamonds, they sparkled in the glare of the overhead light fixture.

As Charlotte stared at the gown, the overwhelming significance of her discovery hit her like a bolt of lightning. She drew in a sharp breath and felt blood roaring in her ears.

She'd wanted proof, but she'd also held out the tiniest bit of hope that she was mistaken, that Jackson's murder was indeed a random act of burglary gone bad.

There was no mistake, though. Even without the prescription bottle and the washcloth, the nightgown, with its sleeve of glass slivers, would be all the proof that the police would need.

Charlotte's stomach turned queasy. At least one of Judith's theories was correct, she thought. The murder of Jackson Dubuisson was most definitely an inside job, an elaborate setup from the beginning.

From downstairs came the grating sound of the front-gate buzzer.

"Someone's at the gate, Charlotte," Clarice called out.

Charlotte glanced at her watch. Had to be the caterers, she thought. She took a steadying breath. *Just keep cool.* "I heard it," she finally answered. "I'm on my way. In just a minute," she added, pausing to glare at the nightgown.

Knowing that the consequences of what she was about to do would be staggering, once again indecision plagued her. Charlotte sighed wearily. Before she could change her mind, she pulled on a fresh pair of gloves and slipped the sliver of glass into the paper sack. Then she reached into the clothes hamper and carefully removed the gown. Once she'd placed it in the sack, too, she removed the gloves and stuffed them in her apron pocket. With the paper sack firmly in her grasp, she picked up her supply carrier and left the bathroom.

The short journey from the bathroom through Clarice's bedroom took ten seconds at the most, but Charlotte could feel Clarice's eyes on her, watching her every step of the way, as she briskly walked across the bedroom to the hallway door. Only when she reached the hallway, out of sight of the old lady's curious gaze, did Charlotte remember to breathe.

Downstairs, Charlotte peeked out the entrance-door side light. When she saw two uniformed delivery men standing at the gate, their arms loaded down with white boxes, she hit the RELEASE button for the gate, then opened the front door.

Once the men were inside, she led them back to the kitchen. After they had deposited the boxes on the countertops, the older of the two produced an itemized receipt, while the other man went back out for the rest of the delivery.

Charlotte hurriedly checked the items listed against the contents of the boxes. Once she was finally satisfied that everything that had been ordered had been delivered, she signed the receipt and handed it back to the man.

After the delivery men left, she made a quick trip to her van and loaded her cleaning supplies. It would soon be time for those who had attended the funeral to start arriving, so on her way back inside, she decided to leave the front gate ajar instead of locking it.

From that moment on, she was so caught up in hurrying to vacuum the parlor, then setting out and arranging the food in preparation for the influx of guests, that she didn't have time to dwell on anything else but the task at hand.

She'd just finished filling the ice bucket when the peal of the doorbell echoed throughout the house. Hands on her hips, Charlotte glanced around the kitchen, then nodded with satisfaction.

In the dining room, she paused and looked around. Everything was ready. The food was out and properly displayed, and the downstairs half of the house was clean and orderly.

Charlotte hurried through the dining room to the foyer.

At the entrance door, she took a moment to straighten her apron. Then, taking a deep breath, she opened the door.

Her eyes widened with shock, and she gasped.

Chapter
Nineteen

Standing in the doorway, his camera slung over his shoulder, was the newspaper reporter who had chased her down and harassed her.

Charlotte's hand tightened on the doorknob. "What are you doing here?"

"I'm here to interview Mrs. St. Martin."

"To what!"

"Mrs. St. Martin," he repeated. "I'm here to interview Mrs. Clarice St. Martin, the mother-in-law of the murder victim."

Charlotte shook her head. "No way!"

He shrugged. "Hey, lady, she called me."

"She called—" Suddenly it all made sense, a strange, weird kind of sense. When she'd first seen Clarice all dressed up, she'd assumed the old lady wanted to look her best because of the people coming over after the funeral. She should have known better. Clarice didn't give a hoot about what anyone who was supposedly mourning Jackson Dubuisson's death thought despite what she'd said to the contrary. The old lady had dressed up for an interview with the newspaper reporter.

But why? Why would Clarice want to be interviewed? What did she hope to accomplish?

The best defense is an offense. The moment the old saying popped into Charlotte's mind, she suddenly knew exactly what Clarice hoped to accomplish. The old lady was shrewd and a bit crazy, she decided. Crazy like a fox. Charlotte figured Clarice was going to spout the same song and dance she'd given her about Brian O'Connor, but even if this was another attempt to shift suspicion to Brian, there was still the question as to how she knew to call this particular man?

Charlotte raised one imperious eyebrow. "You're lying," she accused, "lying through your teeth. I don't believe for one second that Mrs. St. Martin called you."

The reporter rolled his eyes upward. "Okay, okay, you got me dead to rights. She didn't call me. I called her. But she agreed," he quickly added.

Charlotte drew herself up to her full height. Clarice might be clever, but there was more than one way to skin a rabbit. Or in this case, a fox, she thought as an idea began to form.

"Young man, do you know what day this is?"

He frowned in annoyance. "It's Friday. So what?"

"So what indeed! Today is the funeral of Jackson Dubuisson. Any minute now, his friends and family will be arriving."

The reporter's frown deepened. "That can't be," he said. "The old lady—Mrs. St. Martin— She said the funeral was tomorrow—on Saturday. She was very insistent that I was to come today. Not that it matters," he quickly injected. "One day is as good as another."

Charlotte gave him a look of disgust. "I guess I shouldn't be surprised that you don't have any manners or respect for the dead. It's people like you who give the news media a bad name." She paused, then, in her most pitying tone, said, "And I guess I shouldn't be surprised that Miss Clarice got the days mixed up. Senility is such a terrible disease. Poor thing. After all, she is getting on in years and tends to get confused now and then. If you know what I mean," she added for emphasis.

"She's senile?"

Charlotte simply shrugged, neither denying nor confirming the reporter's assumption.

The sound of car doors slamming behind him momentarily diverted his attention, and he glanced nervously over his shoulder.

"The funeral must be over," Charlotte said, getting a bit nervous herself as her gaze shifted to a small crowd of people gathering just outside the gate. She needed to get rid of this pesky man, she thought, but how, without making a scene?

Then Charlotte spotted her niece making her way through the group of people. Though she wasn't that surprised to see Judith, for it was a standard practice for the police to attend the funeral and the gathering after the funeral of a murder victim, she suddenly knew exactly how she could force the reporter to leave.

"Oh, there's Ms. Monroe," Charlotte said, careful to inject just the right amount of surprise in her voice. "She's one of the police detectives assigned to this case, you know."

The reporter turned around to stare. "Detective? Which one?" he asked, unable to contain his excitement. "Do you think she would answer a couple of questions for me?"

Not if I know my niece, Charlotte thought as a sly smile pulled at her lips. "Why don't we ask her and find out? Why, here she is now," Charlotte said as her niece approached the steps leading up to the gallery.

"Good morning."

Charlotte's smile grew wider. "Good morning yourself. Judith, dear, this young man is a reporter and wants to ask you a few questions about poor Jackson's murder."

"He what?" Judith stopped midway up the steps, just long enough to glare at the reporter. "Of all the nerve!" Her eyes blazing with daggers, she stomped up the remaining steps.

She pointed an accusing finger at him. "You're on private property, bub. Get lost now or I'll run you in for trespassing."

The look of defeat on the reporter's face was poignant. Realizing he'd been had, he turned and glared at Charlotte. "Clever. Very clever," he murmured.

With more guests arriving by the minute, Charlotte decided to station herself by the open door, just inside the foyer. As she greeted the guests and directed them to the dining room, Judith stood on the porch and made sure that the reporter left without harassing anyone.

"I can't believe he had the nerve to show up here after the funeral," she told Charlotte a few minutes later. "I've got a good mind to call the *Times-Picayune* and complain."

"I've already called," Charlotte said. "I spoke to Mary Johnson, and she—"

"Who's Mary Johnson?" Judith interrupted.

"She's the daughter of Claude and Lydia Johnson, who were longtime clients of mine before Claude retired. You know—the ones who own that old mansion near St. Charles and Louisiana Avenue. Mary is one of the *Picayune*'s managing editors. Anyway, when I described the man to Mary, she said my description fits a man they've had complaints about before. And get this. He's not even a regular employee. He's just a freelance reporter they buy stories from once in a while."

"Well, that's certainly good to know," Judith said. "From our past dealings with the paper, the staff reporters have always been both courteous and cooperative. None of them would ever have pulled a stunt like that guy did today."

Charlotte placed her hand on her niece's arm. "You don't know the half of it," she said, thinking about Clarice. "But Judith," she confided, "I need to talk to you about something urgent." She glanced over her shoulder to make sure the guests who had just arrived had moved into the dining room.

Satisfied that the last of the newest arrivals were gravitating toward the front parlor, she turned back to Judith. Out of the corner of her eye, just beyond her niece's shoulder, she saw Judith's partner coming up the sidewalk. Behind him were Jeanne and Anna-Maria, accompanied by James Doucet.

"Earth to Charlotte."

Charlotte blinked. "Not now, hon. We'll have to talk later—before you leave." Charlotte didn't want to give Jeanne or Anna-Maria any reason to become suspicious. Besides, telling Judith was one thing. Her niece would take her seriously. But even if Jeanne and Anna-Maria hadn't chosen that moment to arrive, just the thought of explaining everything in front of Louis Thibodeaux made Charlotte's nerves jump.

"It's important," Charlotte stressed, wondering what it was about the man that intimidated her so. "Extremely important," she added, "so don't leave without seeing me first."

"Aunt Charley—"

Charlotte firmly shook her head, then turned and fled toward the dining room.

Later, as Charlotte was gathering the dirty dishes out of the front parlor, Anna-Maria approached her. There were dark circles beneath her eyes, and there was a look of sadness about her that almost broke Charlotte's heart. Out of everyone concerned, Anna-Maria stood to lose the most when the truth came out.

"I know you're busy," the younger woman said, "but when I took a tray of food up to Grandmother, she asked me to tell you she needs to talk to you."

Charlotte had a pretty good idea what Clarice wanted to talk about. By now the old lady was probably beside herself, wondering what had happened to her interview with the reporter.

Well, too bad, she thought. Clarice could just keep wondering for the time being.

"I don't see how I can leave just now," she told Anna-Maria, "but I'll go up just as soon as I can."

Anna-Maria nodded, and when she turned to walk away, Charlotte caught her by the arm.

"How are you doing, hon?"

Tears glistened in the younger woman's eyes. "I guess okay," she said. "It's just—just hard."

Before the day was over, it was going to get even harder, thought Charlotte as she fought to control the swift shadow of anger that suddenly swept through her. Anna-Maria was a complete innocent. Yet of everyone involved, she would be the one who suffered the most.

For once, Charlotte was at a loss for words. There was nothing she could say to ease the younger woman's suffering now and no way of preparing her for the pain yet to come.

She pulled the younger woman into her arms and gave her a quick hug. "You hang in there," she told her. "Stay strong."

Chapter
Twenty

For the next hour, the low buzz of voices filled the foyer, the parlor, and the dining room as friends, acquaintances, and Jackson's business associates dropped by to pay their respects to Jeanne and Anna-Maria. Charlotte soon lost count as people came and went. Many of them she recognized, some she didn't, as she refilled the platters with sandwiches.

Several times as she picked up the dirty dishes left in the parlor, she overheard someone ask about Clarice. And each time Jeanne's response was the same. On each occasion, she spun the lie that Clarice had grieved herself sick because of Jackson's death.

Upon hearing Jeanne's response, it took every ounce of self-restraint that Charlotte could muster to keep a firm grip on her anger, mostly at herself for having been so blind to the truth all along.

Charlotte was replenishing a tray of sliced turkey sandwiches in the kitchen when the doorbell rang. At first, she ignored it, just as she'd ignored it for the past half hour. Since

Judith was there in her official capacity, she had stationed herself in the foyer and had taken over the job of letting visitors in while her partner hovered about in the parlor. It was the sudden break in the steady murmur of voices in the dining room and foyer that got Charlotte's attention. The quiet moment only lasted a heartbeat, but it was enough.

Unable to contain her curiosity, Charlotte left the half-full tray of sandwiches and walked through the dining room to the foyer. The moment she spotted Sydney and Tony Marriott near the parlor door, she immediately understood the reason for the brief silence.

Many of the same guests at Jackson's funeral had also attended the Zoo To Do event. Like Charlotte, they had seen Jackson and Sydney dancing and had also witnessed the volatile confrontation between Jackson and Tony.

Had the gossip about the altercation filtered back to Jeanne? she wondered as she discreetly followed the couple from the foyer into the parlor. Did Jeanne know about the incident, and if she did, how would she react to having the couple in her house?

A small group of people were clustered around Jeanne and Anna-Maria, so Sydney and Tony weren't able to talk to them right away. While the couple awaited their turn, Charlotte took her time gathering the few dirty dishes left by guests and tried to ignore the disturbing presence of Louis Thibodeaux, standing just behind the two women.

When the couple were finally face-to-face with Jeanne, as far as Charlotte could tell, there was no outward sign that their presence bothered her, at least not at first. Ever the gracious hostess, she greeted Sydney and Tony with a polite but sad little half-smile and thanked them for coming.

The first sign of emotion that Jeanne allowed to surface was when the couple started to leave. She warmly embraced Tony. But when Sydney reached out to her, Jeanne stepped back, just out of reach, and shook her head once, but succinctly, her expression cold and forbidding, an expression that spoke volumes about her feelings toward the other woman.

Since Sydney's back was to Charlotte, she couldn't see the other woman's initial reaction. But when Sydney finally turned and walked away from Jeanne, her face was flushed, and her eyes were cast downward, almost as if she were afraid to look at anyone.

At the Zoo To Do, Sydney's and Jackson's behavior had been suspect, and at the time, Charlotte had wondered if the couple might be having an affair. But she'd also considered that Tony could have simply been acting the part of the jealous husband.

After witnessing Jeanne's reaction to Sydney and Sydney's response, Charlotte decided that it was highly probable that the couple had indeed been involved in an affair. It also seemed highly certain that Jeanne knew that her husband had been cheating on her with Sydney.

Sydney and Tony stayed for only a few minutes more after the encounter, just long enough to be polite. During those few minutes, though, Charlotte couldn't help noticing that Tony did most of the socializing; Sydney stood by his side with a tight little polite smile on her lips.

Just moments after the Marriotts walked out the door, Charlotte saw Louis Thibodeaux whisper something to Judith; then he left, too.

It was drawing near two P.M. when Charlotte finally decided it was time to have her talk with Judith. The crush of people had thinned out; only a few diehards still lingered in the parlor.

She located Judith keeping vigil just inside the parlor door. Jeanne stood a few feet away, talking quietly to Anna-Maria.

"Ms. Monroe?" Charlotte placed her hand on Judith's

arm. "I wonder if I could have a word with you in private about that matter I mentioned earlier?"

Judith gave her an odd look but nodded and followed Charlotte back to the kitchen.

"What's with the 'Ms. Monroe' business?" she asked when they entered the kitchen.

"Just being discreet," Charlotte answered. "You did say you didn't want anyone to know that we're related."

Judith closed her eyes and sighed. Then she opened them. "Yes—yes I did, didn't I? Of course I did. Sorry, Aunt Charley, but it's this case. It's driving me crazy. Half the time I don't know if I'm coming or going. Now, what did you want to talk to me about?"

"I know who killed Jackson Dubuisson, and I have proof."

For several seconds, Judith simply stared at her aunt as if she were trying to make up her mind whether Charlotte was serious.

"Okay," she finally said. "Why don't you tell me what you think you know."

Charlotte began by explaining about the missing phenobarbital tablets and the crushed powder she'd found in Clarice's bathroom. Then she told Judith about the scuff marks made by Clarice's walker in the bathroom as well as on the stairs. She also revealed that Clarice was the one who had told her about the relationship between Brian O'Connor and Jeanne.

Suddenly, Judith tilted her head and gestured for Charlotte to be silent. She eased over to the dining-room door and peeked inside. With a shrug of her shoulders, she stepped back into the kitchen. "I thought I heard someone in the dining room," she said. "Just in case, though, talk a little softer, Auntie. We don't want to tip our hand."

"I can't explain right now, but tipping our hand is exactly what we want to do," Charlotte told her. "Just go with the flow for now."

Before Judith could question her or object and ignoring her niece's admonition to talk softer, Charlotte launched into an explanation. "I had my suspicions all along, but when I found the glass embedded in the nightgown this morning, I knew for sure."

Judith rolled her eyes toward the ceiling and sighed. "You should never have touched any of it, Auntie. You've probably contaminated the only decent evidence we have."

"I'll have you know I was extremely careful," Charlotte retorted. "Besides, with the medicine bottle it doesn't matter, anyway. My fingerprints were already on it. But I was still careful. I wore rubber gloves, and I used a paper sack for the gown and the bottle, which—by the way—is safely tucked away in the back of the pantry. I'll give it to you when you're ready to leave."

Judith stared at Charlotte, a thoughtful expression on her face. "It all makes sense, and it's what I've suspected all along, but I need to talk to Louis about—"

"Charlotte?"

Both Judith and Charlotte froze at the sound of Jeanne's voice. When they turned, she was standing in the doorway leading to the dining room. Though she looked a little pale, her face was composed, and nothing about her expression indicated that she'd overheard any of their discussion. Her gaze slid from Charlotte to Judith, then back again. "Is everything okay in here? Is there a problem?"

Charlotte shook her head. "No—"

Judith cut in. "No problem, Mrs. Dubuisson. I just had a few more questions I wanted to ask Charlotte."

Jeanne switched her attention to Judith. "Questions? About what?"

Judith made a dismissive gesture. "Nothing important."

Jeanne slowly nodded. "In that case—" She turned to Charlotte. "I wanted to let you know most everyone has left. If you will finish clearing out the dishes in the parlor and pick up the serving platters in the dining room, then you can go, too."

Again Judith interrupted. "Has Detective Thibodeaux returned yet?"

Jeanne shrugged. "I guess I didn't realize he'd left to begin with, but no, I haven't seen him lately."

Charlotte picked up an empty tray from the cabinet. "It shouldn't take me long to clear away what's left," she said. Then, with butterflies beating a nervous rhythm in her stomach, she purposely stood there and waited for Jeanne to make the first move.

Jeanne hesitated only a moment before she led the way back to the parlor. "How's Miss Anna-Maria holding out?" Charlotte asked in an attempt to maintain some sense of normalcy.

"Not too good, I'm afraid," Jeanne answered, an edge to her tone. "Which reminds me, in case anyone asks, she's gone to her room to rest, and I don't want her to be disturbed. Once everyone has left—if they ever do," she muttered, "I intend to do the same."

Charlotte took her time gathering up the few remaining dishes, and Judith stood near the window, her gaze following Jeanne as she escorted the last of the guests to the foyer.

Charlotte heard the front door close. When several moments passed and Jeanne still hadn't returned, Charlotte walked over to Judith. She held up her forefinger against her lips to indicate silence, then motioned for Judith to follow her.

Jeanne wasn't in the foyer, nor was she in the dining room. With Judith trailing close behind her, Charlotte entered the kitchen just in time to see Jeanne slip out the back door.

Charlotte made a beeline for the pantry. The sack she'd placed inside on the floor earlier was gone.

"She took the bait," Charlotte told her niece.

"Bait? You mean the evidence?"

Charlotte pulled Judith over to the window that overlooked the back deck. "Let's just watch and see what she does with it."

Outside, Jeanne set the sack she'd taken from the pantry down on the deck near the gas grill. She opened up the grill, turned on the gas, and lit it with a match. Then she snatched up the sack and dropped it on top of the burners. Within seconds, flames engulfed the sack.

"We've got to stop her!" Judith cried.

She started toward the door, but Charlotte grabbed her by the arm. "No," she told her. "It's okay. Just watch and listen."

"But Aunt Charley!" Judith tried to pull away, but Charlotte held firm and shook her head.

"I promise it will be okay."

"But she's burning the evidence."

Charlotte shook her head again. "No, she's not. She just thinks she is. And stop looking at me like I've suddenly gone senile. I know how Jeanne thinks, and I know what I'm doing. This is the only way we'll get the truth out of her."

Still looking a bit skeptical, after a moment Judith grudgingly gave in. "Okay, Auntie, you win for now, but I sure hope you know what you're doing. If you don't, we could both be in big trouble."

"It's going to be okay," Charlotte assured her niece as she finally released her hold on Judith's arm.

In no time at all, the hot flames of the grill reduced the sack and its contents to ashes. With Charlotte and Judith watching, Jeanne continued staring at the grill long after there was nothing left to burn. After what seemed like forever, she finally shut off the burners and then closed the lid.

When Jeanne reentered the kitchen, Charlotte and Judith were standing in the middle of the room, waiting for her. Sending up a silent prayer that she was doing the right thing, Charlotte confronted her. "You burned the wrong sack," she told her. "The real evidence is locked in my van."

Watching Jeanne's reaction was like witnessing a balloon slowly deflate. "Charlotte, I—I—" She glanced at Judith, then back again at Charlotte. Her eyes filled, and tears spilled over onto her cheeks. Her lips quivering, she whispered, "I didn't want to do it, b-but there was no other way." A haunted expression crossed her face. "Don't you see? I couldn't let Mother—"

"That's enough, Jeanne!"

At the sound of Clarice St. Martin's stern voice, all three women jerked their heads around. The old woman was standing in the dining-room doorway. She was leaning heavily on her walker, her face was flushed, and for a moment, she seemed to gasp for each breath she drew. Finally, her breathing slowed to normal. "I'd say you've said more than enough," she muttered, a warning look in her eyes.

"Mother, I—"

Clarice shook her head. "I said enough, and I meant it!"

Jeanne's lower lip quivered, but she finally gave in.

Clarice gave her a curt nod, then turned to glare at Judith. "Leave my daughter out of this," she warned in a harsh, raw voice. "It's no secret that I despised my son-in-law, so it won't be a stretch for you to believe that I killed him."

"Mrs. St. Martin—" Judith stepped toward the old lady. "Are you confessing to the murder of Jackson Dubuisson?"

"Didn't I just say that?"

"If that's the case, then I have to advise you that you have the right—"

Clarice sliced the air with her hand. "I know what my rights are, young lady, and I don't need you or anyone else telling me."

"That may be," Judith shot back, undaunted and not the least bit intimidated, "but by law I still have to do this, so just indulge me. Clarice St. Martin, you're under arrest for the murder of—"

"No! Stop it!" Jeanne demanded. "She's lying—just like

before." Her eyes fierce with defiance, she glared at her mother and shook her head. "Not this time, Mother."

"Shut up, Jeanne!"

"I won't shut up. I can't let you take the blame this time, not again." She whirled to face Charlotte. "But you already knew that, didn't you, Charlotte?"

Charlotte felt her throat grow tight with emotion as she nodded slowly. "I didn't want to believe it, Jeanne. I still don't want to believe it, but—"

"Wait a minute," Judith interrupted. "What's she talking about? What did you already know?"

With her eyes on Jeanne, Charlotte took a deep breath, then let it out in a defeated sigh. "Not only did Jeanne kill Jackson, but she killed her father, too."

Judith's eyes widened. "Her father?"

"That's a damned lie!" Clarice shouted. "We want a lawyer!"

Judith leveled a warning look at Clarice. "Be quiet, Mrs. St. Martin."

"You have to allow us to call our lawyer."

"I'm not denying you counsel," Judith retorted. She pointed her finger at the old lady. "But if you say another word, I'll confine you to another room."

Clarice opened her mouth.

"Just one word," Judith warned.

Her eyes shooting daggers, Clarice snapped her mouth shut again and pressed her lips into a tight line of anger.

Finally satisfied that Clarice wouldn't interrupt, Judith motioned for Charlotte to continue.

"Andrew St. Martin was Jeanne's father," Charlotte explained. "He was murdered about fifteen years ago. You remember me telling you about Brian O'Connor? Well, it was Miss Clarice who gave me that information—deliberately, I'm sure—in an attempt to shift suspicion away from Jeanne. I suspect that Miss Clarice somehow found out that you're my niece and hoped that I would leak the information about

Brian to you. Between her trying to throw suspicion on Brian O'Connor and some gossip I got from another client of mine, I was able to fill in the blanks, so to speak."

Judith narrowed her eyes skeptically. "So to speak?"

Undaunted, Charlotte continued. "Almost twenty years ago, Brian O'Connor, the son of a gardener, had a summer job working for the St. Martins." Charlotte motioned toward Jeanne. "He and Jeanne fell in love. Then Jeanne came up pregnant.

"Besides being a socially prominent attorney, according to rumors, Andrew St. Martin was also an abusive, controlling man. His future plans for his daughter didn't include having an uneducated gardener's son for a son-in-law. But St. Martin knew better than to simply forbid the union. He knew he had to get rid of Brian, so he set him up—had him arrested for stealing. And with the help of a judge, who just happened to be one of Andrew's old buddies, Brian was sent to prison.

"Andrew then arranged for Jeanne to marry a young protégé of his who worked for him. He promised Jackson Dubuisson a partnership in his law firm if he would marry Jeanne and claim her unborn baby as his own. Then he threatened to cut Jeanne off without a penny unless she agreed to the arrangement." Charlotte turned to Jeanne. "Am I right so far?"

Jeanne hung her head. "I didn't want to marry Jackson," she mumbled. "But what choice did I have? I was only eighteen. Without a college education or job skills and with Brian in prison, I couldn't support a baby . . ." Her voice trailed away.

"But Brian didn't stay in prison forever," Charlotte said, resuming her explanation. "Five years later, when he was released, I figure that Jeanne saw her chance to finally be with the man she loved. But she made a mistake—either that or she slipped up and somehow her father found out that she had plans to divorce Jackson. I have my suspicions about what he threatened her with that time." Again she turned to Jeanne. "Probably the disinheritance thing again—but it didn't work, did it, Jeanne? What else did he threaten you with?"

Jeanne lifted her head, and her gaze slid to Clarice. "I couldn't let him do it," she said, her voice rising with anger. "He said he would sign everything over to Jackson and leave my mother without a penny."

Clarice opened her mouth as if to protest, then closed it, but before she bowed her head, Charlotte saw the single tear that trailed down her pale cheek.

Charlotte swallowed hard against the ache in her own throat. "I figure he also made some kind of threat against Brian again, too," she said softly. "None of which Jeanne could allow to happen. Once again he'd cornered her, but Jeanne was no longer a schoolgirl he could intimidate. She was older and wiser. She figured that the only way out was to get rid of the threat once and for all. And Clarice—" Charlotte turned her gaze to the old lady. "After years of being subjected to an abusive, controlling husband, she covered for her daughter, as any mother would—provided her with an alibi. Just as she'd tried to cover for Jeanne this time when Jeanne murdered Jackson."

Suddenly, Clarice jerked herself upright and glared at Charlotte. "That's all a bunch of hogwash!" she shouted. She turned to Judith. "There's not a shred of proof of anything she's saying," she told her. "My husband was killed by a burglar, and the police never proved otherwise." She thumped herself on the chest. "And I killed that no-good, two-timing bastard Jackson." She shook her finger at Judith. "And it's your duty to take me in."

Charlotte shook her head, and in spite of herself, she felt sorry for the old lady. "It's no use, Miss Clarice," she said softly, in her most reasonable voice. "This time you didn't do as good a job of covering up for Jeanne as you did the first time. I found her nightgown in your dirty-clothes hamper—the one she wore the night she killed Jackson. It still had slivers of glass embedded in the sleeve. Those slivers could only have gotten there one way. Jeanne used the sleeve of the gown for protection against getting cut when she punched in the pane of the French doors."

"That's a lie," Clarice shouted. "You don't know what you're talking about. And who's going to believe you, anyway?" she sneered. "Why, you're a nobody—nothing but a maid. You—"

"That's enough!" Judith glared at the old lady. "She may be only a maid, but she's one of the most intelligent women I've ever known, so just watch your mouth. I told you once, and I won't tell you again. I don't want to hear another word out of you unless I ask you a question. Do I make myself clear?" When Clarice refused to reply, Judith made a menacing move toward her. "I said, Do I make myself clear?"

Even as Clarice nodded, she paled and swayed against the walker.

"Stop it!" Jeanne cried. She rushed over to Clarice. "Can't you see that she's not well?" She placed her arm around her mother's waist to steady her and urged her toward a nearby chair. "Here, Mother, sit down before you fall down."

Charlotte expected Clarice to give Jeanne an argument. The fact that the old lady obeyed her without a protest was a clear indication of how exhausted she was becoming.

"Maybe she should go to bed," Charlotte suggested.

"I think you're right," Jeanne agreed. "If you helped me, we could probably manage to get her up the stairs."

"Ah, excuse me!" Judith interrupted, sarcasm dripping with each word. "I'm trying to conduct a murder investigation here, and no one's going anywhere until I get some more answers."

"You have all the answers you need," Clarice said in a weak, raspy voice. "Arrest me and be done with it."

Judith rolled her eyes toward the ceiling and sighed wearily. "Give me patience," she whispered.

Charlotte patted Judith's arm. "What else do you need to know, hon?"

"For starters, I need a reason, Aunt Charley. Motive. Why'd she do it?" She glared at Jeanne. "If you killed your father to be with Brian, why didn't you go ahead and divorce Jackson then? Wasn't that the whole point?"

Jeanne shook her head. "You wouldn't understand."

"Try me," Judith challenged.

When long seconds passed and it became obvious that Jeanne wasn't going to answer, Charlotte intervened. "Jeanne's right," she told Judith. "You wouldn't understand, not unless you had a child. According to Miss Clarice, Jackson used Anna-Maria to hold Jeanne. He told Jeanne if she ever left him, he'd make sure that Anna-Maria found out all about how her real father was an ex-con; then he'd tell everyone else, too. Now you have to remember," Charlotte added, "that Anna-Maria was only about five and thought that Jackson was her real father."

Judith made a face and shook her head. "You're right. I don't understand. Be that as it may, I still don't consider any of that a real motive for killing Jackson, though Lord knows, people have been murdered for a lot less." She stared hard at Jeanne. "Why now? You've lived with the man for almost twenty years? Was it jealousy? Was your husband cheating on you? Was he?"

"To be jealous, you have to give a damn," Jeanne snapped.

"Aha, I see," Judith said sagely. "What happened, Mrs. Dubuisson? Did he cut your allowance?"

Jeanne's eyes suddenly blazed. "My-my allowance!" she sputtered.

Though Charlotte was careful to hide her thoughts, she silently applauded her niece's interrogation tactics. Judith had just pushed the right buttons.

"Of all the absurd—" Jeanne shook her head violently. "It was all mine to begin with!" she shouted. "He was stealing from *me!* After everything I've put up with—his affairs, his—his—after my father handed him the firm on a silver platter— But that wasn't good enough. Oh, no! He wanted it all so he and his tootsie could run off together. When Brian first told me, I didn't believe him. But I checked, anyway. I may not be a lawyer, but I've lived around them all of my life. He wasn't quite as clever as he thought he was, and I found out about his little account in the Cayman Islands. He was going to leave me—leave us—with nothing."

"So Brian O'Connor helped you?"

"No!" Jeanne cried. "Brian had nothing to do with any of it."

"Then how did he know Jackson was stealing your money?"

Jeanne glared at Judith. "I'm not saying another word without an attorney."

A cackle of laughter suddenly erupted from Clarice. "You've already said too much, you idiot!" She laughed again and glared at Charlotte and Judith. "And you're all a bunch of fools if you believe anything my daughter says. Can't you see that she's a fruitcake—a damn fruitcake. Why, if you put her brain in a mockingbird, he'd fly backwards."

"Mother! Stop it!"

"I won't stop it!"

"That's enough from the both of you!" Judith quickly closed the distance between herself and the two women. "And you—" She grabbed Jeanne by the arm and pushed her away from her mother. "Why are you trying to protect Brian O'Connor? Did he help you murder your husband? Maybe it was his idea to begin with."

Jeanne wrenched her arm free and shook her head violently. "I want an attorney."

"She's protecting him because she loves him," Charlotte said softly. "But Brian didn't kill Jackson. All Brian wanted was to be near his daughter. Isn't that right, Jeanne?"

Jeanne's eyes darkened with pain, then filled with tears again. "All he wanted was to see her . . ." Her voice erupted in a sob.

"At night he would sneak onto the gallery," Charlotte continued, "just outside the library. That's where he'd sit and wait for Anna-Maria to come home from one of her dates. I figure Jeanne's telling the truth at least about that part. All he wanted was to get a glimpse of the daughter he was cheated out of. On one of those nights, he could have very well over-heard Jackson talking on the phone inside the library to Sydney. Am I right, Jeanne?"

The younger woman covered her face with her hands, and her shoulders shook with sobs. "I—I should have listened to him from the beginning. He—he told me to get a lawyer. But by the time I finally started listening, it was too late. Jackson had already transferred almost everything—almost all of it."

"But if Jackson died, then you—as his widow—would get it all back, wouldn't you?" Charlotte asked.

Jeanne scrubbed at her eyes, then lifted her head. Ignoring Charlotte, she told Judith, "I want an attorney. You haven't arrested me or read me my rights, so none of what I've said or what my mother has said can be construed as any kind of admission of guilt."

Several tense moments passed before Judith finally nod-ded. "Jeanne Dubuisson, I'm placing you under arrest for the murder of your husband, Jackson Dubuisson. You have the right to remain silent—"

"No, no, no!" Clarice moaned. With a strength that took them all by surprise, she launched herself out of the chair and grabbed Judith around the neck. "Run, Jeanne!" she cried out. "Run!"

For the moment, Charlotte was too stunned to move. Jeanne hesitated, clearly torn between her concern for her mother and her chance to escape.

"No, Jeanne!" Charlotte tensed. "Don't do it!"

Chapter
Twenty-one

To the amazement of everyone, instead of bolting for the door, Jeanne marched over to where Judith was still struggling with Clarice.

"Mother, stop it!" Jeanne demanded. She grabbed the old lady's arms. "That's enough!" She forced her mother's arms loose. "I'm not running," she told her firmly, "so give it up."

Clarice took one look at Jeanne, then crumpled in her daughter's arms as great sobs shook her frail body. "Oh, Jeanne, girl," she whimpered, "what are we going to do now? What's to become of us?"

Rubbing her neck, Judith backed away from the two women. Though she was none the worse for wear after her wrestling match, Charlotte could tell that she was shaken.

"Oh, Mother, don't," Jeanne cried, tears streaming down her face as she held Clarice close. "It's going to be okay. I promise everything will be okay."

"Mother—Grandmother—"

Except for Clarice, all eyes turned to the doorway of the

foyer, where Anna-Maria stood with a bewildered look on her face that was intensified by the fear in her eyes.

"Ha-has something happened?" She rushed over to her mother and grandmother. "Mother, what's going on? Is Grandmother ill? Please," she pleaded, "say something. You're scaring me."

Jeanne swallowed hard. "It's okay, darling," she finally choked out. "We—we're okay. Here, help me—" She glanced over at Judith. "Could we move my mother to the sofa in the parlor . . . please?"

"Mother, I don't understand. What's wrong with Grandmother?"

"Not now, darling. Your grandmother will be just fine, and I'll explain it all, but first let's get her settled where she can rest." Again she looked at Judith, waiting for permission, and with a tight grimace, Judith finally nodded her consent.

While Jeanne and Anna-Maria struggled to get Clarice to the parlor, Judith reached into her jacket pocket and pulled out her cell phone as she followed close behind. Clarice began moaning, and Charlotte couldn't hear who Judith called or what was said.

By the time they had settled Clarice onto the largest of the parlor sofas, the old lady was alarmingly pale, and her breathing was shallow.

Judith took one look at her, then asked Jeanne, "Do you want me to call an ambulance?"

Jeanne hesitated, then shook her head as she covered her mother with an afghan. "No, I don't think so—not yet." She turned to Anna-Maria. "Get your grandmother a glass of orange juice from the kitchen and get me a wet washcloth."

Charlotte stepped forward. "I'll get the juice and washcloth."

"No, Charlotte." Jeanne gave her a pointed look. "I—I need you to do something else. Let Anna-Maria get it."

The moment that Anna-Maria disappeared through the

doorway, Jeanne said, "I didn't want her to hear, Charlotte." She turned to Judith. "I know I don't have any right to ask favors, but could you please let me have a few minutes alone with my daughter before you take me away? I—I'd like to try and explain things to her."

Judith frowned. "I—"

"If I was going to run, I would have done so earlier. Please . . . It's all going to be such a shock to her."

Still Judith hesitated, and at that moment, the peal of the doorbell sounded.

"I'll get the door," Charlotte offered, relieved to have something to do.

"I hope it's Louis," Judith muttered. "But if it's anyone else, get rid of them."

Charlotte nodded and rushed from the room.

The person at the door was Louis Thibodeaux. Standing just behind him were two uniformed police officers.

By way of greeting, he nodded curtly to Charlotte. "Where's Judith?" he asked gruffly.

Charlotte stood to the side and motioned toward the parlor. "In there," she said. "She's been looking for you."

"I know" was all he said before he turned to the two officers behind him. "Ted, you take the back door, and Barry, you stay here. No one comes in or out without my permission." Then, without a word to Charlotte, he brushed past her and strode down the foyer toward the parlor.

Charlotte closed the front door and turned to follow, but a movement to her left caught her eye.

Anna-Maria stood in the dining-room doorway, a glass of orange juice in one hand and a washcloth in the other. The look of confusion on her pale face turned quickly to fear as she followed the stocky detective with her eyes. Her hand that held the juice began to shake, and Charlotte quickly stepped closer and took the glass from her.

"What's happening?" the younger woman whispered. She

turned to Charlotte. "Please, won't someone tell me what's going on?"

"Just try and stay calm, hon. Right now your mother needs you to be strong."

"But why? I don't understand."

"Anna-Maria, your mother is in trouble. Just remember that no matter what happens, she loves you more than life itself."

"Why won't you just tell me what's happening?"

"Because it's not my place, hon. Your mother will explain everything. Now let's get this juice and washcloth in there to your grandmother." Charlotte nudged her toward the parlor with her free hand.

As if in a trance, Anna-Maria let Charlotte guide her. As soon as they entered the room, Jeanne grabbed the juice. Once she'd gotten Clarice to take several swallows, she directed Anna-Maria to place the washcloth over Clarice's brow. Then she leaned down and kissed the old lady on the cheek and whispered something in her ear. When she straightened, she looked at Judith.

"You've got thirty minutes," Judith told her. "Detective Thibodeaux will be right outside the door. Don't make me sorry that I'm allowing this," she warned.

"Thank you," Jeanne whispered. With a sideways glance at Louis Thibodeaux, she turned to her daughter and held out her hand. "Come along to the library with me, darling. We need to talk."

Judith nodded at her partner. "You go with them, Lou, and I'll tell Barry to station himself outside, on the porch in front of the French doors."

"Something tells me that this isn't a good idea," he muttered, but he did as Judith requested and followed Jeanne and Anna-Maria.

"I can stay with Miss Clarice," Charlotte offered.

"Thanks, Aunt Charley."

* * *

Time seemed to slow to a crawl as Charlotte waited alone with Clarice. The house was still and quiet, so quiet that she could hear the ticking of the grandfather clock in the foyer.

A part of her was glad that Judith had given Jeanne and Anna-Maria a few minutes alone. Her heart ached for Anna-Maria, but all she could do was pray that the girl would be strong enough to bear what was ahead. Even so, for once, Charlotte had to agree with Louis Thibodeaux. Something about the whole thing just didn't feel right.

She glanced at her watch and estimated that at least fifteen of the thirty allotted minutes had passed. So where was Judith? And why hadn't she returned yet?

Then she eyed Clarice, and the unease she'd felt grew. The old lady was staring straight up at the ceiling with unblinking eyes. She had a pasty pallor to her skin that didn't look right to Charlotte, and she'd yet to utter a sound since Jeanne had kissed her. The only way Charlotte knew for sure that she was still breathing was the faint movement of her chest.

She moved closer to the sofa. "Miss Clarice, how are you feeling?" When the old lady didn't answer or even acknowledge her in any way, warning spasms of alarm erupted within Charlotte. Clarice had already suffered one stroke. What if she was in the throes of another one?

Charlotte leaned over the old lady and gently shook her shoulder. "Miss Clarice, please say something?" Clarice rolled her eyes but offered no other response.

"Aunt Charley, is something wrong?"

Charlotte looked up. "Oh, Judith, thank goodness you're back. I think we'd better call an ambulance."

Clarice moaned, as if in protest, then tried to talk. But her words slurred together and came out garbled.

Judith glanced at Charlotte, and her eyes reflected Charlotte's own fear.

"Oh, God, I think you're right, Aunt Charley." Judith whipped out her cell phone and hit 911.

Chapter
Twenty-two

"Stay with her, Aunt Charley," Judith told her. "I need to let Louis know what's happening, and I need to tell Barry to show the paramedics in when they arrive."

From a first-aid class she'd taken once, Charlotte knew that the only thing she could do for the old lady was to watch her breathing and keep her quiet and warm. Kneeling beside the sofa, she tucked the afghan closer around Clarice's frail body.

"Just hang in there, Miss Clarice. Help is on the way." She removed the washcloth, refolded it, and placed it back on Clarice's forehead. How long? she wondered as minutes seemed to drag by. How long before the ambulance would come?

Raised voices in the hallway drew her attention. "Now what?" she murmured. The voices grew louder, and with a worried look at Clarice, she pushed herself up and hurried to the doorway.

Anna-Maria, flanked by Louis Thibodeaux, was standing in the foyer. She had tears streaming down her face and was sobbing incoherently while Judith was snapping out questions.

"Where's your mother?" she demanded.

"Sh-she's gone."

"What do you mean she's gone?"

Anna-Maria whimpered and shook her head as she covered her face with her hands.

When Judith realized she wasn't getting anywhere with the girl, she turned to Louis Thibodeaux. "What happened, Lou? How can she be gone? Barry swears she didn't come out his way."

"Well, don't look at me," he snapped. "I told you I had a bad feeling about this, and unless she's a damned ghost, she didn't come out my way, either." He glared at Anna-Maria. "You'd better start coming up with some answers, young lady. Now stop that blubbering and tell us where your mother went."

When Anna-Maria cowered away from him, all of Charlotte's maternal defenses went up. The man was nothing but a bully. With one last worried glance at Clarice, she rushed over to the group. "Both of you, stop badgering her," she demanded. She purposely stepped between Louis Thibodeaux and Anna-Maria, then gathered the younger woman into her arms.

"Oh, Charlotte," Anna-Maria cried, burying her head against Charlotte's shoulder. "What am I going to do?"

"Hush, now, hon." Charlotte smoothed the younger woman's hair. "The first thing you need to do is calm down," she told her gently. "There, there, that's better." After a moment more, she placed her hand beneath the younger woman's chin and tilted her head up. "Remember what I said about being strong?"

Anna-Maria blinked several times, then nodded.

"You can do it," Charlotte encouraged. "Just try to answer their questions the best you can."

With one last shaky sob, Anna-Maria scrubbed at her face, took a deep breath, and pulled away from Charlotte. "My-my mother left," she told Judith. "Sh-she left through the secret passage."

Judith eyed her skeptically. "Secret passage! What secret passage?"

Anna-Maria looked at Charlotte, and Charlotte nodded encouragement. "Tell her, hon."

"It-it's behind one of bookcases," Anna-Maria said, her answer directed at Judith. "It was once a part of an underground-railroad route used to help hide runaway slaves."

Louis Thibodeaux glared at Charlotte, and in a voice as cold as his eyes, he said, "Did you know about this so-called secret passage?"

Hands on her hips, Charlotte whirled to face him. She'd had just about enough of the insufferable man. "Just what are you suggesting, Detective Thibodeaux?" she challenged.

"Louis, don't," Judith warned. "My aunt is not a suspect here."

He gave Judith a level look. "Come on, Monroe. She's worked for them for several years. Don't you think it stands to reason that if she's cleaned their house for that long, she'd know the ins and outs of it?"

Though Charlotte knew the history of the secret passages and had heard that some of the old homes in the District still had them, no one was more surprised than she about the existence of one in the Dubuissons' library. And she strongly resented the detective's implication, especially after all she'd done to help prove Jeanne had murdered Jackson.

"What I think is that we're wasting time," Judith snapped. "We need to check out this so-called secret passage."

"You won't find her." Anna-Maria's voice shook with emotion. With a trembling hand, she held out a piece of paper, offering it to Judith.

"What's this?" Judith snatched it from the girl.

"A-a letter," Anna-Maria stammered. "My-my mother said to give it to you."

As Judith skimmed the letter quickly, her face grew dark with fury. "Well, isn't that just peachy?" she sneered. "Forget the secret passage. She's long gone." She held out the letter to her partner.

He took the paper, glanced over it, then handed it back. "I'll put out the APB," he told her. "They couldn't have gotten far."

They? Jeanne and who else? Though Charlotte had her suspicions and was dying to know what was in the letter, at that moment the distant sound of a siren drew her attention. "I hope that's the ambulance," she muttered.

Anna-Maria's eyes grew wide. "Ambulance?"

Charlotte thrust out her hand to the younger woman, and ignoring both Judith and Louis Thibodeaux, she said, "Come along with me, hon. Your grandmother is ill, and we need to check on her."

Back in the parlor, Charlotte was relieved to see that Clarice's condition seemed to be about the same. While Anna-Maria murmured encouragement and hovered over the old lady, Charlotte stood by and waited. Outside, the siren grew louder, and for the moment, both Judith and her partner had disappeared.

When the siren finally ceased its incessant wailing, within minutes two paramedics, followed by the officer named Barry, rushed into the room.

It didn't take long for the EMTs to determine that Clarice had indeed suffered another stroke. While they prepared the old lady for a transfer to St. Charles General Hospital, Charlotte kept a wary eye on Anna-Maria.

To her surprise, the girl held up like a trooper. She thoroughly questioned the medics about her grandmother's condition, then made a quick phone call to her fiancé. After a brief explanation, she asked him to meet her at the hospital.

For the first time that afternoon, Charlotte felt as if Anna-Maria were going to be okay. But she was worried about Clarice.

Just before they wheeled the old lady out on the stretcher, Anna-Maria leaned over and kissed her on her pale cheek. "They're going to take you to the hospital, Grandmother. They won't let me ride in the ambulance with you, but I'll be following in my car. You just hang in there and I'll see you at the hospital." Then she leaned down close to the old lady and whispered something in her ear.

Charlotte strongly suspected that Anna-Maria said something to her grandmother about Jeanne, but she couldn't be sure. Whatever she said caused Clarice to whimper and close her eyes. Then her lips thinned, and one side of her mouth turned up slightly at the corner. Charlotte could have sworn that the old lady was smiling as the paramedics took her away.

Anna-Maria watched from the doorway as they rolled her grandmother through the foyer, out the front door, and down the gallery steps. Once they were gone, she turned to face Charlotte. "Thank you for your help with Grandmother," she said stiffly. She paused for a moment, as if unsure what to say next. Then she grimaced. "To be honest, I don't know whether to hate you or hug you."

Charlotte felt her throat tighten and tears threaten. She blinked back the tears and swallowed to relieve the tightness in her throat. "If it's any help," she told her gently, "I understand. And I'm sorry—" She hesitated. To say she was sorry for blowing the whistle on Jeanne would be a lie. None of what Jeanne had been through was reason enough to murder her father or her husband in cold blood. "I'm sorry that you have to go through all of this," Charlotte finally said, her voice trailing away as she waited anxiously for Anna-Maria's response.

The younger woman's lower lip began quivering, and she blinked rapidly. Then she cleared her throat. "I need to get to the hospital, but I stayed behind on purpose because I have a message for you." She paused long enough to make sure that no one was within hearing range. Finally satisfied that they wouldn't be overheard, she looked Charlotte straight in the eyes and said, "I have a message for you from my mother."

Chapter
Twenty-three

Charlotte felt as if a heavy fist were squeezing her heart, but all she could do was wait, wait and wonder what Jeanne could have possibly wanted her to know. She didn't have to wait long.

"My mother asked me to tell you that she doesn't blame you for what you did. She said that she understands why you had to do it, and in spite of everything, you've been more of a friend to her than anyone she knows."

Charlotte felt a single tear slide down her cheek, but she was too choked up for words.

In a controlled voice that Charlotte barely recognized, Anna-Maria continued. "Now I must get to the hospital, and I'd like to lock up before I leave, so you'll have to go now."

Charlotte nodded. "I'll just get my purse," she murmured, stepping toward the doorway. When she drew even with Anna-Maria, she stopped and looked her in the eyes. "For what it's worth," she told her, "I wish you and your grandmother well. And if you ever need me—for anything—all you have to do is call."

* * *

Outside, the warm afternoon was fast turning into dusk. When Charlotte realized how late it was, a sudden weariness came over her, a weariness born of a sorrow that went bone-deep. It grieved her deeply that her association with the Dubuisson family had to end as it did.

It should have been gratifying to know that she'd helped solve Jackson's murder, but thoughts of Jeanne and what she had come to mean to her haunted and confused her. For the most part, she was horrified by what Jeanne had done, horrified and angry. When all was said and done, she'd grown to love Jeanne like the daughter she'd never had. Even so, Charlotte had learned over the years that loving someone could be a double-edged sword. It didn't mean you had to like what they did or even condone their actions.

Judith's car was still parked out front, and she was waiting for Charlotte by the van. Charlotte joined her, and they both stood and watched as Anna-Maria backed out of the driveway and drove down the street.

Though Charlotte was pretty sure that Judith had waited for her to see if Anna-Maria had divulged anything different from what she'd said earlier, she was also itching with curiosity about the letter Jeanne had left. Did she dare hope that Judith would let her read the letter? she wondered.

"Ah . . . where's your partner?" she asked as soon as Anna-Maria's car disappeared from sight.

Judith gave a one-shoulder shrug. "I'm not really sure, but he said something about following up on a lead."

"A lead about Jeanne?"

Judith shrugged again. "Maybe. Like I said, I'm not sure where he went. But if they're still in the city, we'll catch up to them sooner or later."

"They?"

Judith nodded. "Brian O'Connor is with her, wherever

she is." Her gaze slid away, and she stared at the ground. She shifted from one foot to the other, then fidgeted with the strap of her purse.

"Just say it," Charlotte told her, recognizing her niece's nervous gestures.

"I don't want to ask this, Aunt Charley." She glanced up, and her eyes reflected the strain she was under. "I have to, though. It's my job."

"Judith, honey, just do what you have to do. I'll love you, anyway."

A tiny smile pulled at Judith's lips. "And no matter what you tell me, I'll still love you, too."

Charlotte grinned. "Touché."

Judith suddenly grew serious again. "Did you know, Auntie? It doesn't stand to reason that you did, considering how you helped trap Jeanne in the first place. For the record, though, I have to ask. Did you know that there was a secret passage in the library?"

Unlike her reaction to her niece's partner when he'd as much as accused her of knowing, Charlotte felt sorry for Judith. She held up her right hand, palm out, fingers together straight up. "As God is my witness, I didn't know about it."

"I didn't really think so, but—"

"You had to ask." Charlotte finished the sentence, then smiled. "I understand, honey, so stop worrying about it."

Judith sighed. "Okay, but I'm afraid there's a couple of other things I need to clear up, too. First of all, do you have any idea whatsoever where Jeanne and Brian could have gone or where they might be heading?"

Charlotte frowned in thought. Something, some fleeting memory, nibbled at her subconscious, but the harder she tried to remember, the more vague it grew. "I honestly don't know," she finally said. "But if I think of anything, I'll get in touch."

"One last thing, Auntie. What did Anna-Maria have to say to you? Anything I should know about?"

For reasons she couldn't begin to fathom, Charlotte found herself reluctant to share the message from Jeanne. She slowly shook her head. "No, it was personal," she said. "Nothing you should be concerned about." Charlotte cleared her throat. "Now I'd like to ask you a question."

Judith nodded.

"What was in that letter that Jeanne left? In fact, I'd like to read it."

"I don't object to you reading it, but I don't have it. Lou took it with him. But I can tell you what was in it. Jeanne said that it wouldn't do any good for us to look for her or Brian. Evidently, she'd planned ahead in case something went wrong, because she said that she'd arranged for the two of them to disappear, but she needed a twenty-minute head start." Judith's face flushed. "And, like an idiot, I gave her the twenty minutes."

"Don't," Charlotte admonished. "Don't beat yourself up about that. There was no way you could have known, and you took every precaution possible."

Judith waved away Charlotte's reasoning. "Yeah, yeah, I know, but it still ticks me off, and you can bet I'll hear about it from the chief. I'll be lucky if they let me give out parking tickets. Anyway, the only other thing Jeanne said was that finally her inheritance would go to the person she'd always intended it to go to—her daughter. She inferred that a long time ago she'd set up a trust fund for her daughter that would pay out on the girl's twenty-first birthday. And that's just about it," she added.

Charlotte could tell that Judith was still worried. Knowing her niece, she figured she wouldn't rest easy until Jeanne was caught. She wished there was something she could say or do to make Judith feel better, but all she knew to do was be there for her when she needed her. She reached out and squeezed her niece's hand. "You're a good detective, hon, but even more than that, you're a decent, caring human being."

A sad little smile pulled at Judith's lips. "Thanks, Auntie. You're not so bad yourself."

Charlotte grinned. "I'm glad you think so. But seriously, hon, you know I love you, and if you ever need to just talk or if you ever need anything, if it's within my power, I'll be there for you."

Judith nodded. "I know. But enough of all this serious stuff. It's been a long day, and I'm tired of thinking about it all. How about a bite to eat or a cup of coffee somewhere? This time, my treat."

All Charlotte really wanted was to go home and soak in a warm tub of water, away from prying questions and from the reminders of her part in the whole affair. Still, it was getting close to suppertime, and after what she'd just said, there was no graceful way of refusing. She forced a smile and enthusiasm she didn't feel. "Sounds good to me. I could use a bite to eat, especially if you're treating."

"Oh, good. How about the Trolley Stop? It's not exactly Commander's Palace, but the food is excellent."

Charlotte had eaten at both places over the years, and she'd always enjoyed the food and the ambience. Most of the times she'd dined at Commander's Palace had been for special occasions, occasions of celebration. For tonight and considering the circumstances, the more casual atmosphere of the small café, built in the shape of the trolleys that still ran along St. Charles Avenue, would be a welcome relief. "Then the Trolley Stop it is," she said. "Do you want to ride along with me or take your car?"

"We'd better ride separately," Judith answered, "in case I get called out on a case."

"Since I'm parked in front of you, why don't you follow me, then?"

Finding a parking place along St. Charles Avenue was always a pain. Luckily for Charlotte, she spotted a car pulling away from the curb just before she reached the Trolley Stop. Once she'd maneuvered the van into the narrow space, she shoved the gearshift into park and shut off the engine.

Judith wasn't so lucky, she noted, as she watched her turn onto one of the side streets past the Pontchartrain Hotel.

Since traffic was heavy and she'd be risking her life as well as the door of her van if she got out on the driver's side, Charlotte figured that the safest exit would be from the passenger side.

But climbing over the hump between the front seats to the passenger side wasn't as easy as it seemed, and by the time she stepped out of the van and locked the door, she was out of breath. With her eyes searching up ahead for sight of Judith, she didn't see the man approach her from behind.

"Having problems?"

Charlotte jumped at the sound of the deep male voice that belonged to Louis Thibodeaux. She whirled around, her hands clenched into fists, and it took every bit of restraint that she could muster to keep from hauling off and slugging him. "That's the second time this week that you've scared the daylights out of me!" she snapped.

He held up his hands in a defensive motion. "Hey, I'm sorry." His craggy face wrinkled into a frown. "I didn't mean to scare you."

"Yeah, right," she muttered, not believing him for a second. "What are you doing here, anyway?"

A puzzled look crossed his face. "Last time I heard, it was still a free country. Besides, the Trolley Stop is sort of a watering hole for some of the detectives in this district. Fast service, good food at a decent price," he added. Then the infuriating man had the gall to grin. Charlotte couldn't remember ever seeing him even smile, and the transformation was astonishing.

"And what are you doing here?" he asked. "After all"—he winked—"turnabout's fair play."

She couldn't believe her eyes. If she didn't know better,

she would swear he was actually flirting with her. Something weird was going on, she decided. Either the man had a Dr. Jekyll-Mr. Hyde complex or he was drunk. The amiable, likable man standing before her couldn't be the same bully who, less than an hour earlier, had all but accused her of plotting to help a murderess escape.

"I'm here with Judith," she blurted out. "To eat." Charlotte glanced nervously up the street and was relieved to see her niece striding toward them.

"Hey, Lou," Judith called out. "I wondered where you got off to." She nodded toward the Trolley Stop. "I should have guessed, though," she quipped.

"I'll have you know, missy, that I just got here. I've been out tracking down Joseph O'Connor, for all the good that did," he added with a growl. "I remembered that I'd seen him working a couple of streets over from the Dubuissons' earlier this afternoon."

"So?" Judith prompted.

"Nothing, *nada*," he shot back. "Made out like he didn't know what I was talking about. Funny thing is, the old man seemed pretty upset about the whole thing."

"Maybe he really didn't know anything," Charlotte suggested defensively.

Louis Thibodeaux rolled his eyes, then shrugged. Not for the first time, Charlotte noticed how dark his eyes were—so brown they almost were black. And his eyelashes, long, equally dark lashes that any woman would covet.

"I guess it's possible," he admitted. "Anything is possible. But enough of that for now. I'm hungry, and I hate eating by myself. Could I persuade you ladies to join me?"

Charlotte was on the verge of automatically refusing when, to her horror, Judith nodded. "Only if you're paying," she quipped.

Louis Thibodeaux gave a curt little half-bow that somehow came across as elegant instead of silly. "It would be my honor and my pleasure."

Without warning, he stepped over and wrapped his arm around Charlotte's shoulder. Though there was nothing remotely sexual in the gesture, Charlotte felt a warm flush crawl up her neck. She was sure that she was turning six shades of red, but even worse, she was mortified that the heavy warmth of the detective's arm felt so good. Then he held out his other arm to Judith. With a giggle, Judith stepped close enough for him to sling his arm over her shoulder.

With a swinging gesture, he stepped back, then forward, pulling both women with him, and in a singsong baritone voice, he chanted, "All for one and one for all."

The café was crowded. Charlotte was sure that they would end up waiting forever for a table. The burly detective had been forced to release her and Judith once they got to the entrance door, but because of the crush of people jammed in the waiting area, Charlotte found herself forced to stand so close to him that she could smell his cologne, a sharp, spicy scent that suited the man perfectly.

Within moments of entering the café, one of the waitresses spotted Louis and Judith. With a smile and a wave, she signaled for them to come on through.

"Thanks, Betty," Judith told the woman once they had shoved their way through to the front of the crowd.

"Your table should be free in just a sec," the waitress replied.

Judith leaned toward Charlotte. "They try to keep a table open for us," she said by way of explanation. "Good public relations with the department and all of that."

Within minutes, the waitress was back again. "The table is ready now."

Ignoring the scowls of the other customers who had been waiting, Charlotte followed Judith and Louis to a small table in the corner by the front windows that looked out onto the avenue. Still playing the part of the gentleman, Louis held

Charlotte's chair for her, then did the same for Judith, before he seated himself.

Just as Charlotte reached for the menu, the distinctive trill of a telephone sounded. Judith and Louis automatically checked their phones.

When both of them shook their heads and stared at Charlotte, she smiled sheepishly. So much had happened, she'd completely forgotten that she'd programmed her calls earlier that morning to be forwarded to her cell phone.

"Guess it must be mine, then," she offered as she fumbled with the zipper of the compartment on the outside of her purse, which held the tiny telephone. Once she'd removed the phone and punched the TALK button, she said, "Maid-for-a-Day, Charlotte speaking."

"Charlotte, this is Jeanne Dubuisson."

Chapter
Twenty-four

For a moment, Charlotte was too stunned to speak. Her gaze flew first to Judith, then to Louis. Both detectives returned her look, their eyes gleaming with interest.

Her first thought was that she should she tell them that her caller was Jeanne, but Charlotte wavered. Even if she told them, what good would it do? There was no way they could possibly trace the call, she reasoned, not on the spur of the moment.

As much as she hated deceiving the two detectives, she decided against letting on that her caller was Jeanne. Instead, she turned away from the table, seeking a bit of privacy from their curious looks.

"Ah . . . yes," she stammered, not sure how else to respond.

"I didn't know who else to call," Jeanne said. "I'm worried sick about my mother. I've called several times, but no one's answering the phone at the house. Is she okay?"

"Ah . . . hold on just a minute." Charlotte shoved out of the chair. "I'm in a restaurant, and I'm having a hard time hearing you over the noise," she said for the benefit of the two detectives as she stepped away from the table. Without looking back, she headed straight for the door marked restrooms. Once inside, she locked the door behind her.

"Jeanne, my God, where are you?"

"Never mind that, Charlotte. It's better if you don't know. But please, I've been frantic with worry. What's happening? Why isn't anyone answering the phone at my house?"

Charlotte squeezed her eyes shut, then opened them. "I hate to tell you this, but Miss Clarice has had another stroke. An ambulance was called, and they took her to St. Charles General."

"Is she—do you know her condition?"

"Not yet," Charlotte admitted, suddenly ashamed that she hadn't bothered to even check on the old lady. "But Anna-Maria called James to meet her there, so Miss Clarice isn't alone."

"Oh, thank God." Jeanne paused. "I-I guess I could call the hospital."

Charlotte could hear the worry and tears in Jeanne's voice, but for once, she couldn't dredge up even an ounce of sympathy for her. Jeanne had no one to blame but herself for her circumstances. "You should turn yourself in," she blurted out. "The police are looking for you and Brian. They'll find you sooner or later. With a good lawyer, you . . ." Her voice trailed off, and she wondered if perhaps she'd said too much.

Jeanne sniffed, then cleared her throat. "You're probably right, but I can't turn myself in. I'd rather die first than go to jail, and I can't risk Brian having to spend more time in jail than he already has. One last thing, though, before I hang up. How—how is Anna-Maria? Is she okay?"

In her mind's eye, Charlotte could still picture the confusion and terror on Anna-Maria's face as she'd sobbed her heart out while being interrogated by Judith and Louis. Deep within Charlotte, a seed of anger took root, then suddenly erupted into full-blown fury. "How can you even ask such a question!" she demanded, her voice harsh with disbelief.

"Of course she's not *okay*. She's heartbroken and confused, and now, if her grandmother—God forbid—dies, she'll be left with no one—no family whatsoever. How could you do that to her? No amount of money is worth that kind of price."

For long moments, there was nothing but silence on the other end of the phone. "I'm sorry," Jeanne finally whispered brokenly. Then she disconnected the call.

Charlotte's knees suddenly went weak, and she sagged against the wall of the restroom. It took several minutes before she was finally able to stand without feeling as if she were going to pass out. She was horrified at what she saw in the mirror. She was almost as white as the walls of the tiny restroom.

For the first time in a long time, she suddenly felt old and very weary. How on earth had she gotten into this predicament? she wondered. How had she allowed herself to become so involved with these people?

Whether she wanted to admit it or not, Hank was right. He was always telling her that business was business, that the people she worked for were her clients, not her friends. Good advice, she decided. Too bad she hadn't listened to him.

Well, never again, she silently vowed. From now on she'd keep things strictly business where clients were concerned. If she would have done so to begin with, she wouldn't be in this predicament.

Just who did she think she was, anyway, for Pete's sake, scurrying around, gathering clues, trying to catch a murderer? And now this latest twist with Jeanne, a fugitive and murderer, calling her.

Charlotte sighed. Wouldn't Louis Thibodeaux just love to pounce on that little tidbit? He already had his doubts about her part in Jeanne's escape, and withholding vital information from the police could get her into even more trouble . . . if they found out.

A sharp rap on the door made her jump. "Ah . . . just—

just a minute," she stammered. Oh, Lord, she thought. How was she ever going to face Judith and Louis now?

"Aunt Charley, it's Judith." The muffled sound of her niece's voice came from the other side of the door. "Are you okay in there?"

Charlotte swallowed hard. "No," she whispered. "I'm anything but okay."

"Aunt Charley?"

Now what was she supposed to do? Charlotte wondered, her mind searching frantically for an answer. But no answer presented itself. With a bone-weary sigh, she turned, un-locked the door, and opened it.

"Oh, Auntie, what's wrong?"

Unable to look her niece in the eyes, Charlotte cast her gaze downward. "Actually I don't feel so well," she mum-bled. At least she wasn't lying, she thought. She was sick, sick at heart. "I think I need to go home."

"That phone call—did that upset you? Was it bad news? Is Hank—"

"No, no." Charlotte shook her head. "Nothing like that. The call was business. I-I guess I'm coming down with something." She was coming down with something, all right, coming down with a huge case of the guilts.

"Maybe you just need to eat something."

Charlotte shook her head. "No, hon." Just the thought of food made her want to gag. "I'm tired, and I just want to go home." There was no way on God's green earth that she could sit across the table from Judith and Louis and choke down food as if nothing had happened.

"I'd better drive you, then."

"No," Charlotte immediately protested. "It's not that far, and I—I'll be just fine. Please give my regrets to Detective Thibodeaux."

Judith eyed her with worry. "Call me when you get home so I'll know you're okay."

Charlotte nodded. "I'll talk to you later, then."

* * *

Charlotte phoned Judith as soon as she got home. After reassuring her niece that she would be just fine, she made a second phone call to St. Charles General Hospital. She was told that she could speak to the patient's family in the waiting room, but just the thought of talking to Anna-Marie made her nervous, so she asked to speak to someone in ICU instead.

From a nurse in ICU she learned that Clarice was still critical, and as she hung up the receiver, she whispered a prayer for the old lady.

After checking to make sure that Sweety Boy had plenty of food and water, she glanced at the clock. It was only half past six, but since she didn't plan on going out again and didn't expect visitors, she decided to go ahead and change into her pajamas.

In the bedroom, she eyed the bed longingly as she pulled off her uniform. She was tempted to simply crawl into bed and be done with this awful day once and for all, but common sense prevailed, and she knew she should eat something first.

None of the leftovers in the refrigerator appealed to her, so she opted for her old standby, a can of chicken-noodle soup out of the pantry. She opened the can, and while the soup was heating in the microwave, she poured herself a glass of milk.

Maybe she'd call Hank after she'd eaten, she thought as she unwrapped a package of crackers to go with the soup. It had been several days since she'd talked to him, and she knew that just the sound of her son's voice would be reassuring.

No, she decided. Given her present state of mind, calling Hank probably wasn't such a good idea, after all. Knowing her son, he would immediately sense that something was wrong, and he wouldn't be satisfied until he found out exactly what it was that was bothering her. Not only would she have to listen to a lecture on keeping her emotions separate from business, but this latest dilemma she'd gotten herself into would only add more fuel to his arguments for her to retire.

The microwave timer beeped just about the same time that her doorbell chimed. Charlotte decided to ignore the doorbell in the hope that whoever was outside would simply give up and go away.

But her visitor proved to be persistent and kept ringing the bell. Then Sweety Boy began squawking.

"Oh, for pity's sake," she muttered as she rushed into the bedroom to grab her robe. Throwing on the robe, she hurried to the door. She flipped on the porch light. "Who's there?" she demanded, irritation lacing her words.

"It's Louis Thibodeaux," a deep male voice answered.

Charlotte groaned. Louis Thibodeaux was the last person she wanted to see tonight. What on earth was *he* doing there? Then a frightening thought hit her. Had he found out about Jeanne's phone call?

"No way," she muttered, dismissing the thought. There was no way he could possibly know that her caller was Jeanne unless he'd been eavesdropping at the restroom door, and somehow she couldn't picture his doing such a thing.

So what did he want?

"Charlotte, are you okay in there?"

"Ah . . . yes, I'm fine. Just a minute, please." Her hand shook as she threw the deadbolt, and with a firm grip on the doorknob, she swung the door just wide enough to stick her head through the opening.

He was standing close to the door. Too close for comfort. "Judith was worried about you," he said, eyeing her with a calculating expression that made her want to squirm. "She had some paperwork to finish up at the office," he explained, "so I told her I would check on you on my way home. Here—" He held out a small styrofoam container. "It's an order of fried shrimp and a salad. We figured you might get hungry later."

We? He'd said we. Not just Judith. Charlotte took the container and tried to ignore the tingle of pleasure in the pit of her stomach. "That was very thoughtful," she offered. "Thank you."

He nodded, but instead of leaving, he crossed his arms over his chest and tilted his head. "Could I come inside for a minute? There's something I'd like to talk to you about. I won't stay long," he hastened to add.

Charlotte figured that other than being downright rude, she didn't have much of a choice, especially after he'd been nice enough to check on her and bring her food. Still, she couldn't imagine what he'd want to talk about other than the Dubuissons, and she was truly sick of even thinking about the whole affair.

"I'm really tired," she told him. "And I'm not feeling well."

She expected him to give her an argument. What she didn't expect was the look of sympathy and genuine concern that crossed his face. "Hey, no problem. It's nothing urgent, anyway." He backed away. "We can talk another time. I'll call you." With one last worried look, he turned and crossed the porch to the steps.

Charlotte shut the door and locked it again. She placed the container of food on the small table by the door, then stepped over to the window. As she pulled the curtain back just enough to peek out, her stomach did a funny flip-flop as she watched Louis Thibodeaux get into his car, and for a moment, she regretted that she'd sent him away. Even after the blue Taurus disappeared from sight, she continued to stare out into the night.

What had he wanted to talk to her about? she wondered. Jeanne? Maybe, but she didn't think so. If he'd wanted to question her about Jeanne, he would have done so in spite of her excuse of being tired and not feeling well . . . wouldn't he? If not Jeanne, then what?

Chapter
Twenty-five

Over a week had passed since the day of Jackson's funeral and Jeanne's escape. Charlotte had asked Hank to inquire about Clarice for her. According to what he'd learned, the old lady had survived her stroke, but her prognosis wasn't good. There was little hope that she would be much more than a vegetable for what remaining time she had left.

Because of her medical condition, it was doubtful that any criminal charges would be brought against her for her part in covering up Jeanne's crimes. Clarice was already in prison, serving a sentence that was far more harsh than any court could ever impose. She'd been sentenced to what little life she had left in a body that no longer did her bidding.

Louis Thibodeaux had yet to call, and Charlotte still wondered what he'd wanted to talk with her about.

Judith had stayed in touch, though. According to the information Charlotte got from her niece, in spite of an all-out manhunt, the police had yet to uncover even a clue as to Jeanne's whereabouts. It was as if Jeanne and Brian had vanished off the face of the earth.

But life goes on, Charlotte reflected as she finished packing her supply carrier and went in search of her newest client.

Marian Hebert had been one of the two prospective clients who had called Charlotte on the day of the Zoo To Do festivities. A trim, dark-haired woman in her late thirties, Marian was recently widowed. She and her husband had owned one of the largest real-estate agencies in the city before a freak gas-leak explosion had claimed his life four months earlier.

Left with two young sons to raise and a business that had taken an abrupt nosedive after her husband's death, Marian had hired Charlotte to come in three mornings a week to give her more time to salvage what she could of the failing real-estate company.

With the gaping hole left in her schedule by the Dubuissons, it had been easy to plug Marian into the Monday, Wednesday, and Friday slot.

Like the majority of the houses in the Garden District, the Heberts' home was well over a century old; the raised cottage type was also a valuable piece of real estate. The original floor plan was simple and consisted of four rooms, evenly arranged and separated by a wide center hall. Raised six to eight feet off the ground, the main living area was on the second level, with a staircase in front leading to the entrance.

Broad galleries had once flanked the front and back of the house. Though the front gallery still remained intact, the back gallery had been replaced by two large rooms, equal in size; one was a modern kitchen-living combination, and the other was used as a home office. The rooms had been added by the Heberts when they bought the old home.

Charlotte located Marian, who was pecking away at the computer keyboard in the office.

Marian glanced up the moment Charlotte entered the room. "Is it one o'clock already?"

When Charlotte smiled and nodded, Marian shook her

head. "My goodness, there never seems to be enough hours in the day." She motioned toward the large wooden desk that dominated the back wall. "Your check is over there, on top of that stack of papers in the middle. See you Wednesday morning?"

"I'll be here," Charlotte assured her.

With a satisfied smile, Marian turned back to concentrate on the computer screen, and Charlotte walked over to the desk. She spotted the check immediately. As she picked up the check, the papers beneath it caught her eye.

Charlotte went stone-still as she stared at the legal-sized document on top of the stack. A prickly feeling of déjà vu came over her, and a vague memory fought its way to the surface of her mind.

Like a bolt of lightning, it suddenly hit her, and Charlotte felt her knees go weak. The paper was a mortgage contract, the same type of legal document that she'd seen on Jeanne's desk the Friday before Jackson was murdered. In her mind's eye, she could still picture the exact location and description of the property described in the contract. At the time, she'd assumed that the Colorado real estate was simply one of the Dubuissons' many investments. But now ... What if ...

She should call Judith right away. If what she suspected was true, then Judith needed to know about it as soon as possible.

Charlotte slid the check into her apron pocket as she turned and hurried from the room. She grabbed her purse and the supply carrier on her way out and made a beeline for her van. As soon as she was inside the van, she pulled her cell phone out of her purse and punched in Judith's number. With her forefinger poised over the SEND button, she suddenly froze.

"What on earth do you think you're doing?" she muttered as she squeezed her eyes closed, then groaned. Hadn't she promised herself that she would never get personally involved with a client again? Only days ago, she'd been in a tailspin over her relationship with the Dubuissons; yet here she was, about to stick her nose in the big middle of it again.

Not again, she vowed.

Before she could change her mind, Charlotte switched off the phone and shoved it back into her purse. Before she went off half-cocked, she would think things through this time.

Though Charlotte tried her best to ignore her conscience as well as the revelation concerning the Dubuissons' Colorado property, the drive home was pure torture. Like an itch that begged to be scratched, thoughts of the mortgage contract she'd seen on Jeanne's desk consumed her.

She'd never been to Colorado herself, but the husband of one of her former clients had made annual trips there each year to hunt elk. Even now she could still remember how the poor woman had worried about her husband the entire time he was gone. Her client had been born and raised in the city, and though she'd appreciated the beauty of the mountains and the forests, she'd once described the place where her husband hunted as being one of the loneliest, most god-forsaken places on earth.

What better place as a hideaway for two fugitives . . . a place away from civilization . . . a place away from prying eyes and curious neighbors? If Jeanne and Brian were holed up somewhere like that, it was no wonder that the police couldn't find them.

Charlotte tried telling herself that Jeanne and Brian's whereabouts was none of her concern, that she should mind her own business. But her conscience kept insisting that she had a moral obligation to report the information to the police, that right was right and wrong was wrong. No one should get away with murder.

In the fifteen minutes it took to reach her house, Charlotte continued wavering over her decision, so much so that by the time she turned onto her street, she was ready to scream.

When she spotted the blue Ford parked at the curb in front of her house, she could hardly believe her eyes. With sudden pulse-pounding certainty, it was at that moment that she knew the decision had been taken out of her hands. It was an omen. Fate, it seemed, had stepped in and made the decision for her.

Why else would Louis Thibodeaux show up on her doorstep at this precise time after an entire week of silence? Why else, unless the information she possessed had been meant to be shared with the police?

Indecision was the root of all worry, Charlotte decided as she guided the van into her driveway and parked it beneath the shed. Strange, she thought, how once a decision was made, the initial worry seemed to disappear. Even more strange was the fact that she was actually relieved, even glad, to see Louis Thibodeaux.

By the time she reached the front porch, he was waiting for her near the steps.

It was odd to see the detective dressed in snug-fitting jeans instead of his usual khaki pants. But the more casual look suited him, she decided, and made him look younger and somewhat less intimidating.

"I hope you don't mind me showing up without calling first," he said.

"Actually I'm glad you did show up," she told him, and for once she truly meant it. The surprised expression on his face was priceless, and though just the thought of catching *him* off guard for a change made her want to smile, what she needed to tell him was no laughing matter. Motioning for him to follow, she turned and climbed the steps. "Come inside. There's something we need to talk about."

Chapter
Twenty-six

Sweety Boy began his usual antics of prancing, preening, and squawking the moment Charlotte stepped inside the living room. She set her purse down on the table by the doorway.

The detective followed her in and glanced over at the birdcage. "I think he's glad to see you," he said with a chuckle.

At the sound of the detective's voice, the little bird suddenly ceased his squawking and went still so abruptly that he almost fell off his perch. If his actions hadn't been so bizarre, they would have been comical.

"What's your bird's name?" the detective asked.

"Sweety Boy," Charlotte answered, still watching the parakeet to see what he would do next. When his feathers suddenly began quivering, she narrowed her eyes.

"Well, I'll be a son of a gun." The detective stepped closer to the cage. "Look at that. Poor little fellow. He looks like he's scared to death. Hey, boy, it's okay. I'm not going to hurt you." The detective eased his forefinger through the cage wires.

Suddenly, with what sounded like a screech of terror, the little bird flew at the offending finger. His wings flapping, feathers flying, he attacked it with claws and beak.

"Hey, watch it! Ouch!" The detective jerked his finger back.

"Sweety Boy!" Charlotte cried.

While the detective rubbed his injured finger with his thumb, Sweety Boy squawked again, then quickly retreated to the opposite side of his cage.

"Guess he doesn't like strangers much, does he?"

Charlotte was mortified. "He's usually pretty friendly," she said apologetically. "Did he break the skin?"

"Naw, no harm done." Louis Thibodeaux held out his finger for her inspection.

There had never been a reason for Charlotte to even notice his hands or fingers before, but she liked what she saw. Though long and slender, his fingers looked strong and capable, and his bluntly trimmed nails were clean. Other than a small red welt near the first knuckle, his forefinger looked none the worse for the bird's assault.

"Sorry about that," she offered. "With the exception of my sister, he's usually pretty friendly to everyone."

"Does he attack her, too?"

Charlotte shook her head. "No." Then she laughed. "She knows better than to get that close. But just last week she swears he called her crazy."

The detective chuckled. "Hmm, a discriminating parakeet. Interesting company you keep, Charlotte."

"Like I said, I'm sorry he was so rude."

"Don't worry about it. He probably just needs a little time to get used to me."

The detective's statement struck her as a bit odd. He didn't seem the type to throw out an offhanded remark unless he meant it, so exactly what did he mean? she wondered.

"You said there was something we needed to talk about," he reminded her.

"Ah . . . yes, yes there is. Won't you sit down?" She motioned toward the sofa. Once he was seated, she asked, "Would you like something to drink? Iced tea? Coffee?"

"No, thanks. I'm fine for now. Maybe later."

Though Charlotte was far too jittery to sit, she felt it would be awkward to remain standing, so she chose a chair opposite the sofa. Perched on the edge of the cushion, her hands clasped tightly together, she didn't know any other way to say it but straight out. "I—I think I know where you might find Jeanne and Brian," she told him. "I'm not positive, mind you, but I just remembered something I saw on Jeanne's desk the Friday before Jackson was murdered."

As she explained about the mortgage contract on the property in Gould, Colorado, it was hard to gauge the detective's reaction from the deadpan look on his face. Even when she'd finished her explanation, his expression didn't change. She wasn't sure exactly how she'd expected him to react, but the longer the silence grew between them, the more nervous she became.

"I was going to call Judith," she said, hating the defensive tone in her voice, "but since you were already here—" Charlotte suddenly frowned. "Why are you here, by the way? Why were you waiting for me?"

"That's not important at the moment," he said, quickly dismissing her question with a succinct shake of his head. "Right now I'm just trying to figure out why it's taken you over a week to remember about this property in Colorado."

All of Charlotte's defenses instantly went on red alert. "Just what are you implying, Detective?"

"I'm not *implying* anything, but I'm wondering if there's a part of you that wanted Jeanne to escape, so much so that you conveniently forgot about this property until now."

Charlotte's tenuous hold on her temper slipped a notch. "If that were true," she shot back, "then why would I even bother telling you now?"

He shrugged. "I don't pretend to be privy to the inner

workings of the female mind. Who knows why women do half the stuff they do?"

"Because most men are male-chauvinist pigs." The second she blurted out the words, she wished she hadn't. After all, he was a police detective, for Pete's sake, and the last thing she needed or wanted was to antagonize the police.

For a moment, he simply stared at her. Then, suddenly, he threw back his head and roared with laughter. "I wondered what it would take to get your dander up," he finally said, still chuckling. "Well, now I know, but I had you going for a while there, didn't I?"

Charlotte didn't know whether to laugh along with him or throw something at him.

As it turned out, she did neither, because he abruptly rose to his feet. "We'll check out the information," he said, "and I'm willing to bet that you're right on about it. So far, it's the best lead we have. Humph! Who am I kidding? It's the only lead we have."

He turned toward the door, and Charlotte pushed out of the chair. He'd only taken a couple of steps when he suddenly stopped and faced her again. "By the way," he said gruffly, his dark eyes boring into hers in a way that made her pulse race. "Thanks for the tip. I realize that telling me—or anyone—wasn't an easy decision for you to make, considering your relationship with that family. If it's any comfort, it was the right decision."

His insight broadsided her and caught her completely off guard. Something deep within her, some long, forgotten emotion twisted hard, and Charlotte almost melted on the spot. That he'd even recognized that she'd had a dilemma was totally unexpected. But given the circumstances, his attempt to comfort her and reassure her was truly amazing.

The firm click of the door closing behind him was what finally shook her out of her daze. Charlotte closed her eyes and sighed. "Just goes to show," she muttered. "You shouldn't judge a book by the cover."

She blinked several times, then marched over to the door. Once she'd snapped the deadbolt into place, she turned toward the birdcage. "And you—" She shook her finger at the little bird inside. "You should be ashamed of yourself, attacking a policeman like that. Silly bird, don't you know that he's one of the good guys."

It was true, she realized with sudden clarity. He was one of the good guys. And given her past experiences dealing with men, good guys weren't that easy to come by anymore.

Or could it be that you like him a little too much?

Was Judith right, after all? she wondered.

"Crazy," Sweety Boy squawked. "Crazy, crazy."

Charlotte glared at the little bird, then burst out laughing. "Maybe so," she said. Maybe it was crazy to be considering a relationship with Louis Thibodeaux. "And just maybe you're jumping the gun a bit," she muttered. Just because the man had teased her a little didn't mean he'd been flirting. And just because he'd been understanding and showed her a bit of compassion didn't mean he was interested in her as a woman or in a relationship . . . Or did it?

Charlotte suddenly frowned. He never had told her why he'd stopped by in the first place or what it was that he'd wanted to talk to her about.

She was still frowning when she noticed that she had a message on her answering machine. She tapped the PLAY button.

"Hi, Mom. Sorry I didn't catch you at home, but I thought you would want to know that I checked on Mrs. St. Martin for you this morning." There was a momentary pause. "I hate telling you this, but the old lady has taken a turn for the worse. She's developed pneumonia, and her kidneys are shutting down. It doesn't look good for her." After another pause, he said, "Call me if you want to talk. I love you."

Chapter Twenty-seven

On Thursday morning, Charlotte chose a light breakfast of cereal and juice before she struck out for her daily walk. According to the early-morning weather forecast, the day promised to be full of sunshine, with a moderate high of around seventy degrees.

After her walk, she placed a call to Hank. He was in between patients, so his receptionist put her call through.

"Hi, honey. I know you're busy, but I won't keep you but a minute. I was wondering if you'd checked on Miss Clarice this morning yet?"

"Yes, ma'am, I checked. I was going to call you later. She made it through the night, but she's going downhill fast. It's just a matter of time now. Sorry, Mom."

"Me, too," Charlotte murmured as her thoughts strayed to Anna-Maria. She wondered how the young woman was holding up with so much tragedy happening in her life in such a short time.

"Are you going to try to see her?"

"I would really like to—but no. Under the circumstances, I don't think they would want me there."

"Are you going to be okay, Mom?"

"Yeah, honey. I'll be okay. Talk to you later."

As Charlotte hung up the receiver, she thought about their conversation. That Hank hadn't questioned why the Dubuissons wouldn't want her to visit Clarice at the hospital came as no surprise. Though she'd chosen not to tell him about her part in the whole affair, Charlotte knew that he and Judith often talked and kept each other apprised of the happenings in their mothers' lives. Knowing her son, he wouldn't let on that his cousin had spilled the beans.

After she'd talked to Hank, Charlotte had showered and dressed, but the news about Clarice had cast a pall on the day for her.

When she returned to the living room, she paused to stare out the front window. She longed to be outside, to feel the sun on her back, anything to keep from dwelling on the tragic circumstances surrounding the Dubuisson women.

But life went on, she reminded herself as she turned away from the window. And there was work to be done.

Recording the expenses and receipts she accrued each month was one of her least favorite tasks of running her own business, and she tended to procrastinate.

With a resigned sigh, Charlotte walked over to her desk and sat down. Out of the top right-hand drawer, she pulled out her expense ledger. Then, out of the top left-hand drawer, she removed a bundle of receipts that were secured by a rubber band. It had been a month since she'd bothered to update the ledger, and she groaned when she saw how many she'd accumulated during just a few short weeks.

Charlotte was almost halfway through the stack of receipts when the doorbell rang. Glad for the interruption, she hurried to the front window and peeped out. When she saw that her visitor was Cheré Warner, she quickly opened the door.

"Hey, Cheré. This is a surprise. What are you doing here this time of day?"

Cheré grinned. "Hey, yourself. Sorry for dropping by without calling first, but I came straight from school. I had my last final this morning and finished early."

Charlotte waved away the girl's apology. "No problem. Come on in." She stepped aside, and Cheré walked past her into the living room. "You saved me from a morning of boredom," Charlotte said as she closed the door and locked it. "Just doing a little bookkeeping." She motioned for Cheré to be seated. "How about something to drink? Coffee? Iced tea?"

Cheré shook her head. "No, thanks. Any more caffeine after last night and I'm liable to jump right out of my skin."

"Now what have I told you about pulling those all-nighters?"

Cheré rolled her eyes. "Yeah, yeah, I know, but like I said, the test I took this morning was a final, and my grades in that class haven't been that great this semester."

"So how did you do?"

The girl shrugged. "I think pretty good. Who knows, though? But hey, listen, I stopped by to tell you the latest on that Devillier job. Unfortunately, Roussel Construction has had a teeny tiny setback."

Cheré's bit of sarcasm wasn't lost on Charlotte. "Uh-oh," she murmured. "What happened?"

Cheré grimaced. "Seems that the city inspectors didn't like the wiring job. And among a number of other smaller problems, they also found a couple of substantial cracks in the foundation that have to be fixed."

It was Charlotte's turn to grimace. "Sounds like some major stuff."

"Yeah, tell me about it. Todd was in charge of the electrician crew, and his old man is pretty hot. Todd figures that one of the crew must have cut corners and pocketed the money, but when he tried to talk to his dad about it, they got into a big fight. Now they aren't speaking to each other."

Charlotte shook her head. "That's a shame."

"I'll say. Most of the wiring has to be pulled, and we're talking big bucks."

"Yes, of course—" Charlotte interrupted. "That, too—but what I meant was that it's a shame that Todd and his father aren't speaking."

"Yeah, Todd's pretty bummed out about it," Cheré agreed. "But hey—" She shrugged. "They'll get over it. Anyway, the bottom line is that the wiring, along with all the other changes, will probably delay the whole project a good three to six months."

Charlotte winced. "Guess that means the bidding for the cleanup will be delayed, too." Which also meant that for the time being, she could kiss the chance to make some extra money for her retirement account good-bye.

Cheré nodded. "I'm really sorry."

"Me, too, hon, but it's not your fault. Stuff happens."

Again Cheré nodded, then stood. "I hate to drop the bad news on you and then leave, but I'm scheduled to clean the Parkers' house at two this afternoon." Cheré headed for the door. "I'm meeting Todd for lunch first, and I have to pick up some clothes at the dry cleaner after that."

By the time Charlotte closed the door behind Cheré, she felt as if she'd just survived a whirlwind. The energy level of the girl was unreal, and it made Charlotte tired just thinking about the hectic schedule Cheré kept.

"Time for another cup of coffee," she muttered, heading for the kitchen. But the coffeepot was empty, and as Charlotte was debating on whether to brew another pot, the phone rang.

The caller was Judith.

"Hi, Auntie. I don't have but a minute to talk, but I thought you'd like to know what we found when we checked out that information you gave Lou. Seems you were right on the money," she continued. "I was able to verify that the Dubuissons did—in fact—buy a piece of property just outside Gould, Colorado, just about a month ago."

"That would be just about the time that Brian moved back to New Orleans," Charlotte said.

"Exactly, Auntie. And by checking the phone records of all the calls placed from the Dubuissons' house, I hit pay dirt. There was one call made to the residence of a Mr. and Mrs. Earl Langly, an elderly couple who live just outside of Gould. I talked to Mr. Langly, and he told me that right after Jackson bought the property, he'd hired the Langlys to keep a check on things. When I asked about the recent phone call, he claims it came from a woman who said she was Jackson's secretary. She told him to lay in some supplies and ready the place for some friends of Jackson who wanted to borrow the place for a while."

Judith paused for a moment. "But this is the kicker, Auntie. Not only does Jackson's secretary deny making such a call, but that call was placed the day *after* Jackson was murdered. And since the call was made from the house, we can pretty well assume it was made by Jeanne."

Mixed emotions churned within Charlotte, and she didn't know quite how to feel about her niece's news. "So what happens now?" she asked.

"Even as we speak, the feds are on their way to Gould. And with any luck, Jeanne Dubuisson and Brian O'Connor will be in custody before the sun sets."

After Charlotte hung up the phone, she had to keep reminding herself of all of the reasons that Jeanne and Brian should be caught and punished.

Jeanne had committed murder. She'd murdered both her father and her husband. She'd also caused her daughter heartache that not even time would mend.

Then there was Brian. Regardless of how much Jeanne had protested Brian's involvement, he had to have known what was going on. Charlotte was no lawyer, but she was pretty sure that by knowing and doing nothing to prevent it, he'd made himself an accessory to Jackson's murder.

But there was a part of Charlotte, a tiny part, she finally admitted, albeit reluctantly, that was glad the couple hadn't been caught right away. Jeanne would get her punishment soon enough. Of that, Charlotte was more sure now than ever before. But at least she'd had a week to finally be with the man she had loved for almost a lifetime.

Was it worth it? Charlotte wondered. When Jeanne and Brian were brought back in handcuffs and put on trial, when they were found guilty, then sentenced to either life imprisonment or death, would Jeanne think it had been worth it all?

Only Jeanne could answer that question, she decided.

Chapter
Twenty-eight

By the hardest, Charlotte was able to finish recording her business receipts and expenses by noon. She'd even managed to choke down a sandwich for lunch.

After lunch, she decided that if she didn't get out of the house, she was going to start climbing the walls.

It took a while, but she finally located her gardening gloves in the back corner of the shed. Within twenty minutes, sweat was dribbling down her back as she yanked on the stubborn crabgrass that had encroached upon her flower bed near the porch steps. Yet, in spite of the heat and physical exertion, her thoughts kept returning to Jeanne and Brian.

Had the feds caught up with them yet?

I'd rather die first than go to jail.

Had Jeanne meant what she'd said, or had she just been spouting off a bunch of nonsense? Would Jeanne and Brian put up a fight? she wondered. She couldn't imagine Jeanne in a shoot-out with the police. But she'd never imagined that Jeanne was the type who would kill anyone, either.

Then a horrible thought came over her. What if Jeanne and Brian had planned some type of suicide pact?

Behind her, a car door slammed. Grateful for any kind of distraction from the awful stuff she was imagining, Charlotte glanced over her shoulder.

"Making any headway?"

Charlotte swallowed hard at the sight and sound of Louis Thibodeaux. Grabbing hold of the rail of the porch steps for support, she got to her feet. "Not a lot," she answered as she pulled off her gloves and tried to brush away the grass and dirt that stubbornly clung to the knees of her pants.

The detective approached her. "I hope you don't mind, but I was in the neighborhood and thought I'd take a chance that you might be home. There's something I've been meaning to talk to you about."

She gave a one-shoulder shrug. "It's no problem. I usually keep Thursdays free to run errands and catch up on stuff," she explained. "But I do have a phone, you know. You could have called at any time," she added.

"I could have, I suppose, but I like to see what I'm getting."

At first, Charlotte thought she'd heard him wrong. "Pardon me?"

"Oops! That didn't exactly come out right, did it?"

Raising one imperious eyebrow, she said, "I guess that depends on what you think you're getting."

"Yeah . . . well, what I'm trying to say is that I'm interested in renting the other half of your house—if it's available. Judith told me she thought it was empty and that you sometimes rent it out."

Even as Charlotte began shaking her head, disappointment washed through her. In spite of the heat, she felt her face grow even warmer. Up until that very moment, she hadn't realized how much she'd hoped that whatever he'd wanted to talk about was a bit more personal. So much for silly daydreams, she thought. "I haven't really considered renting it again anytime soon," she finally said.

He nodded. "Yeah, she told me about your last renters, how they tore up the place, then skipped out on the rent. You wouldn't have to worry about that with me, though. Think of the advantages of having a cop living next door."

She could think of plenty of advantages of having *him* living next door even if he wasn't a cop. Then a picture of the messy desk where she'd sat at the police station came to mind. "I don't know," she hedged.

"I just need somewhere to stay for a few months," he explained. "I'm building a camp on some property I own on Lake Maurepas. At the end of the year, after I retire, I plan on moving out there permanently. I'd also planned on staying in my house till the camp was finished, but I got an offer—one of those kind that are too good to refuse." He shrugged. "So, how about it?"

At the mention of his retirement, she was reminded of her own retirement looming in the near future. The extra money from his rent would be a nice addition to her account. "When would you want to move in?"

Pure devilment danced in his dark eyes. "Like I said before, I like to see what I'm getting."

"Well, you know the old saying," she quipped. "What you see is what you get. And right now I have to get the key." She started up the steps. "Be right back," she said over her shoulder, and as she stepped inside the door, she heard the trill of his cell phone ringing.

Once she'd located the key, she took a minute to glance in the mirror on the wall near the front door. Only a complete overhaul would help, she decided with a frown as she wiped a smudge of dirt off her cheek, then did a quick finger-comb through her hair. "Oh, well," she muttered. "Too bad."

Charlotte turned away from the mirror. When she stepped outside, he was waiting for her on the porch, his cell phone still in his hand. From the look on his face, she figured that the call must have been bad news.

She was curious about who had called him, but for once, she was determined to mind her own business. "Here's the key," she said, holding it up for him to see. "I just aired the place out last week, but it needs a good cleaning." She stepped toward the door of the vacant half of the double.

"Charlotte—wait." He slipped the cell phone into his pocket. "That was Judith on the phone."

A feeling of foreboding came over her. "Wh—what did she want?"

"She was calling to let me know that the feds came up empty at the house in Colorado."

"Empty?"

"Yeah, as in no one at home. They found evidence that someone had been there, though—been there probably as recently as last night."

"So close yet so far away," she murmured.

"Yeah, but close only counts in horseshoes."

"Hmm, maybe . . . maybe not—not if Jeanne got worried enough about her mother to check on her in person." As soon as the words came out of her mouth, she immediately realized her mistake.

"Why would she do that?" Louis narrowed his gaze and stared hard at Charlotte. "We've kept the old lady's condition out of the news. We've also got a tap on all the phones. So far, Jeanne hasn't tried to contact anyone, so there's no reason to think that she even knows about her mother's collapse."

Charlotte's stomach turned sour. She was trapped, trapped by her own duplicity. And now there was no way out, no way she could tell him that Jeanne did know about her mother, not without admitting she'd talked to her. And admitting she had talked to her would make it look as if she'd been helping Jeanne all along.

"Charlotte? Is there something you're not telling me? Something I should know?"

She never had been good at lying, and she never had been good at poker. But for once she was going to have to lie through her teeth and bluff her butt off.

"Uh-oh, you caught me." Charlotte forced a laugh. "I hate to admit it, but lately I've been having a lot of what they call 'senior moments.' I'd forgotten that Jeanne escaped *before* Clarice was taken to the hospital."

From the expression on the detective's face, there was no way to tell if he'd bought her excuse. Until he said otherwise, Charlotte decided to pretend he had. "Ready to look around next door?" She held out the key again.

While Louis Thibodeaux inspected the other side of the double, Charlotte waited in agony on the porch swing. She figured that Jeanne was smart enough to realize that the phones would be tapped. Considering the relationship between mother and daughter all these years, Charlotte also figured that Jeanne wouldn't be able to stand not knowing her mother's condition, even at the risk of being caught.

The more Charlotte thought about it, the more it made perfect sense that Jeanne just might show up at the hospital, especially if she'd somehow found out that Clarice was probably dying.

Somehow, someway, the police needed to know, needed to be watching for her to show up. Charlotte sighed. But how? How could she tip them off without admitting to the phone call, without incriminating herself?

When the solution came to her, her stomach began churning with anxiety and indecision. She pushed out of the swing and began pacing. Knowing a way out was one thing. Actually doing something about it was an entirely different matter.

Chapter
Twenty-nine

Charlotte hated hospitals. It had been two years since she'd last been in one to have her gall bladder removed. Despite the newer laser technology that had been used on her, she could still remember how sore she'd been after the surgery.

As she passed up the main information desk and headed straight for the elevators, she kept a sharp eye out for anyone who looked even vaguely familiar. She wasn't that worried about being recognized. With the help of an old, loose-fitting dress that hid her shape, a black wig, and heavy makeup, a shade darker than she normally wore, she'd hardly recognized herself once she'd finished donning the disguise. But she was hoping to recognize Jeanne if, in fact, Jeanne did show.

At the elevator, Charlotte punched the ARROW button that pointed up and waited. It had been a couple of hours since Louis Thibodeaux had left. Once he'd inspected the other side of the double, it hadn't taken him long to decide that he wanted to rent from her. He'd hastily written out a deposit check, then hurried out the door with the excuse that he had some work to catch up on.

The elevator bell dinged. When the door slid open, Charlotte stepped inside. Scanning the floor numbers on the panel, she selected the fourth floor, where the ICU was located. The elevator doors closed, but Charlotte couldn't stop thinking about the way the detective had rushed off. Right up until he'd received the phone call from Judith, he'd acted as if he had all the time in the world.

The elevator was slow. When it finally reached the fourth floor and stopped, it seemed to take forever for the doors to open. Charlotte reached up to adjust her purse strap. Like her dress, the purse was old. But it was the only one she owned that was big enough to tote around the hardcover book she was reading. She'd figured it was going to be a long night, so she might as well catch up on her reading while she waited.

Once the doors opened, Charlotte took a deep breath and stepped out into a wide hallway.

Her plan had been a simple one in theory. She would disguise herself and stake out the ICU area. When and if Jeanne did show up, Charlotte would make an anonymous call to the police, then leave before they got there.

If anyone questioned her about her presence on the floor, she'd decided to pretend she was there sitting with a neighbor who had a relative in ICU.

As Charlotte quickly glanced around to size up the place, a set of wide double doors across the hallway suddenly swung open. A nurse, accompanied by a doctor, walked through. Something about the way the doctor walked seemed vaguely familiar, but Charlotte couldn't get a good look at him, because he still had on the mask and cap of surgery scrubs.

But she did get a good look at the ICU area beyond the doors before they closed. Somewhere on the other side of the doors was poor Clarice.

Would Jeanne show up? she wondered yet again. And if she did, would she get there in time, before her mother died?

The doctor and nurse who had come out of the ICU were slowly walking away from her down the hallway. Behind Charlotte, the elevator doors slid open. Her back was to the elevator, but she automatically stepped to the side to make way for anyone getting off.

"Grandmother's internist said he thought she was a little better when he did his rounds at noon."

Charlotte's pulse jumped. Even without turning around, she immediately recognized Anna-Maria's voice. Praying that her disguise would be enough, she stood frozen to the spot until Anna-Maria, accompanied by James, walked past her toward the double doors across the hallway. James reached out and tapped a square metal plate on the wall, and the doors immediately swung open.

For long seconds after the doors closed behind the couple, Charlotte still couldn't move.

They always get better before they die.

Charlotte shivered as the old saying came to mind. How many times had she heard of a terminally ill patient who would rally around and appear to be improving just before they died?

She was still lost in her reverie when a sudden prickly uneasiness came over her. It was the same feeling she'd experienced the day she'd been walking and Louis Thibodeaux had followed her in his car.

Someone was watching her.

As casually as she could, she glanced to her right, then to her left. The doctor and nurse she'd seen earlier were still standing in the hallway. Both were staring at her.

Charlotte stared back. When she nodded and smiled, the nurse broke away and walked toward her.

"Can I help you?" she called out.

"I certainly hope so," Charlotte said, pitching her voice a

bit lower than normal. "I'm looking for the ICU waiting room."

The nurse nodded. "Do you have a relative in ICU?"

"No, but my neighbor does. I'm just here to keep her company."

The nurse pointed to Charlotte's right. "Go down to the end of the hall. It's on your left. You can't miss it."

Charlotte nodded, and as she followed the nurse's instructions, she could feel the woman's eyes watching her as she walked away.

The nurse had been right. The ICU waiting room was plainly labeled. The outside wall of the room was mostly glass. Except for a teenager sprawled out asleep on one of the small sofas, the room was empty. Charlotte chose to settle in a chair near the glass wall. Seated in the chair, she had an excellent view of the rest of the room as well as a view of the main elevators.

Except for a quick trip to the hospital cafeteria for a bite of supper and the three times Charlotte had gone to the restroom, she'd kept her vigil of watching and waiting.

Charlotte glanced up at the large round clock on the wall. Both hands were almost straight-up midnight. So far, none of the women or the men she'd seen going in and out had even come close to resembling Jeanne.

Other than Anna-Maria and her fiancé, the only person she'd recognized so far was the nurse who had approached her earlier. A couple of times, Charlotte had seen her pass by in the hallway, but other than glancing inside the waiting room, to Charlotte's relief, the woman had ignored her.

Anna-Maria and her fiancé had only left the ICU once as far as Charlotte could tell. An hour after they'd left, they had returned, and she hadn't seen them since. From one of the women in the waiting room, Charlotte learned that it wasn't that uncommon for the nursing staff to allow close family members to stay in the room with a loved one who was dying.

Charlotte's heart ached for Anna-Maria, and she was at the point where she was beginning to question why she was even there in the first place. She was exhausted, so exhausted that she'd fallen asleep a couple of times despite the fact that she was sitting in a chair that only a sadist could have designed. The book she'd brought along had turned out to be boring, and not even the numerous cups of coffee she'd consumed had helped.

"Enough's enough," she grumbled. Charlotte stuffed her book back into her purse and headed for the elevator. It was time to call it quits and go home.

The elevator doors were already standing open, so Charlotte walked right in. She'd just stepped closer to the selection panel when she heard footsteps slapping against the tiled floor in the hallway . . . someone running. When Charlotte turned her head to see what was going on, a tall, dark-haired woman charged into the elevator.

"Move!" the woman yelled as she shoved Charlotte away from the floor-selection panel.

"Hey!" Charlotte grabbed the wall rail to keep her balance.

The woman ignored her as she frantically slapped at the button that closed the doors.

Unease crawled through Charlotte as she stared at the woman, and she backed away from her. The doors began sliding closed. Charlotte eyed the opening, wondering if she should make a run for it.

Suddenly, a doctor burst through the double doors of the ICU. "Stop her!" he shouted, bolting for the elevator.

The elevator doors slammed closed. Only a second passed before it registered who the doctor really was, but by the time Charlotte realized he was Louis Thibodeaux, it was already too late.

The woman whirled to face Charlotte and drew back her arm. In her hand was a scalpel.

In spite of the thick-rimmed glasses and the dyed black hair that had been cut in a shorter style, Charlotte knew the woman was Jeanne. Somehow she'd missed her. Either Jeanne had already been there, she decided, or she'd come in when Charlotte had gone to the cafeteria or the restroom.

"Don't make any sudden moves and you won't get hurt." Jeanne reached back and punched the emergency STOP button. The elevator bumped to a stop, and an alarm went off.

Charlotte's hand tightened on the rail. According to the number showing, they were stopped somewhere between the third and second floor. She figured she only had two choices. It was obvious that Jeanne hadn't recognized her, so she could keep her mouth shut and wait to see what she was going to do next. Or she could reveal who she was and try talking her into giving up.

But Jeanne was a desperate woman with nothing to lose, Charlotte reminded herself. She'd already killed two men, and she'd told Charlotte that she'd rather die than go to jail. So what was one more murder, especially the murder of the woman who had gathered the evidence against her to begin with?

Charlotte quickly decided on the first choice. She would wait Jeanne out, wait and pray that either Louis Thibodeaux or some other policeman would be there when the elevator doors opened again.

As if she'd read her mind, Jeanne glared at her. "When this elevator stops the next time," she said, "you're going to be my ticket out. I won't kill you because I need you as a hostage." She waved the scalpel. "But this little knife can cause a lot of pain. Understand?"

Charlotte nodded that she understood.

"Now—" Jeanne motioned at Charlotte. "Very slowly, move over here in front of me." Jeanne raised the scalpel threateningly.

Charlotte's thoughts were racing almost as fast as her pulse. Like a flash, in her mind's eye she saw into the future of the next few minutes. It was a long walk to the entrance of the hospital and an even longer one to the parking facilities at the back of the hospital. The police would be waiting for them when the elevator doors opened.

Once again in her life, Jeanne was desperate and cornered, and she wasn't thinking things through. Despite her hastily conceived hostage plan, the NOPD had sharpshooters who wouldn't hesitate to take a shot if one came open. One or both of them was going to end up dead . . . unless . . .

Jeanne waved the scalpel again. "I said get over here!"

Charlotte nodded even as she took a firmer grip on her purse. Only about three good steps separated them. Charlotte made the first step slowly. When she stepped out again, she brought up her purse and smacked it hard against the hand holding the scalpel.

The purse hit its mark, and the scalpel flew out of Jeanne's hand. Before Jeanne could recover, Charlotte lowered her shoulder. Using her elbow like a battering ram, she slammed it into Jeanne's stomach.

When Jeanne clutched her stomach and doubled over, Charlotte jumped back and searched frantically for the scalpel. She spotted it on the floor in the opposite corner and quickly scooped it up.

With wary eyes on Charlotte, Jeanne struggled to get to her feet. "Please," she gasped. "Don't hurt me. I—I wasn't going to hurt *you*."

Charlotte wasn't exactly sure why, but something told her to keep quiet and not give herself away. Charlotte drew back her arm, and using the scalpel in the same threatening manner that Jeanne had used it, she motioned for her to move away from the elevator's control panel.

Jeanne backed away toward the opposite corner. "I have money," she cried. "If you help me, I'll pay you. Please!" she begged. "Please help me."

Charlotte only hesitated a moment. Then she firmly shook her head and reached for the emergency STOP button. Once she'd pulled it, she hit the first-floor button. When the elevator began moving again, Jeanne burst into sobs. Covering her face with her hands, she crumpled to the floor.

Within seconds, the elevator stopped again, and the doors slid open. The first person Charlotte saw was Louis Thibodeaux. He was half-hidden, crouched behind the edge of the doorway leading into the hospital gift shop.

"NOPD!" he yelled. "Drop the scalpel, lady. Drop it now!"

Charlotte was so relieved to see him that if it hadn't been for the gun he was pointing at her, she would have hugged him. Then, suddenly, it seemed as if there were police everywhere, all pointing their guns at her.

Only then did Charlotte remember that she was in disguise, that neither Louis nor anyone else knew who she was. She dropped the scalpel, and it clattered to the floor.

"Now kick it out here," he demanded.

Charlotte did as he asked. As soon as the scalpel cleared the door of the elevator, an officer darted over and grabbed it.

"Now come on out of there." Louis motioned at her with his gun. "And you—on the floor—you get out here, too."

The moment Charlotte stepped out of the elevator, she was seized by an officer who was waiting, out of sight, on the side of the elevator doors. He yanked her purse off her shoulder, then grabbed her by the arm and twisted it up behind her back. Charlotte winced with pain when she felt the handcuffs tighten around her wrist. Then he yanked her other arm behind her back and cuffed that wrist, too.

Still sobbing, Jeanne stumbled out and stopped just behind Charlotte. Another officer seized her and performed the same ritual.

Once they were both handcuffed, Louis holstered his gun and approached them. Pointing at Jeanne, he told the officer standing beside her, "Read her her rights, then take her to lockup. She's the one wanted for murder."

The officer nodded, and as he pulled her toward the front hospital entrance, he began reading Jeanne her rights.

"What about this one?" the officer beside Charlotte asked.

Louis shook his head. "I'll take care of her." With a shrug, the officer handed over Charlotte's purse and walked away.

Louis tucked the purse beneath his arm, then turned and watched until Jeanne was well out of earshot. When he faced Charlotte again, the angry look on his face made her flinch. He narrowed his eyes. "I'm taking *you* in personally."

With his free hand, he reached out and grabbed hold of her arm. Left with little choice but to stumble along beside him, Charlotte panicked. "Louis—wait." She tried to shrug loose, but with her hands handcuffed behind her back, there was no way to dislodge his grip. "Don't you recognize me?" she cried. "Please!"

Suddenly, he stopped. Yanking her to a standstill, he rounded on her. "You bet I recognize you, Ms. Charlotte LaRue. And I was right all along. You've been involved in this mess from the beginning, haven't you? You've been helping her every step of the way."

Sudden bone-chilling fear seized Charlotte. "No!" she cried. "No—you've got it all wrong."

"Oh, have I, now?" he drawled nastily. "If I've got it all wrong, just how did you know Jeanne would show up at the hospital tonight? Just what in blue blazes did you think you were doing?" His dark eyes were full of contempt as they swept over her from head to toe. "Of all the harebrained, idiotic stunts you've pulled so far, this one takes the cake. Maybe this will teach you to stay out of police business from now on."

Charlotte was taken aback by his vehemence. She'd seen him angry before, but this was different. This was overkill. But why?

Maybe this will teach you . . . Out of the blue, it suddenly dawned on Charlotte what he was doing. If he had meant to arrest her, he would have already done so. Plain and simple, he was trying to throw a scare into her. Yet again, she had to wonder why.

No pat answer presented itself, but Charlotte's insides churned with a bevy of warring emotions. She was confused as well as annoyed with him. But she was angry, too, angry enough to chew nails.

Just who did he think he was, anyway, trying to teach her a lesson as if she didn't have good sense? No one had ever dared talk to her as he had and got away with it. And no one, but no one, had ever accused her of being harebrained or idiotic.

Charlotte doubled her hands into tight fists. Enough was enough. More than enough. Her temper seething, she glared up at him. "Are you arresting me, Detective?"

"I ought to."

"On what charges?" she demanded.

"Aiding and abetting a murderer, for starters," he snapped.

"Ah, pu-lease," she said, sarcasm dripping, "give me some credit. I wasn't born yesterday. Either do it or take these handcuffs off."

For what seemed like an eternity, he did nothing but glare right back at her. But Charlotte was in no mood to play his stupid game.

"Take them off now!" she demanded. With one last scathing look, she deliberately turned her back to him and waited.

Several tense moments passed before he finally grabbed her hands and unlocked the cuffs. The moment he pulled them off, she jerked her hands free and whirled to face him.

"My purse." She stuck out her hand, palm up, and tapped her foot impatiently.

"Charlotte, I—"

"Give me my purse!" she yelled.

"Okay, okay. Here!" He handed over the purse.

She should have left well enough alone. After all, she'd called his bluff and won. But everything about the man personified the prejudices she'd been up against most of her life, and it was high time that someone put *him* in his place.

She lifted her chin and looked him straight in the eyes. "Just in case no one has informed you, *Detective*," she sneered, "this is the twenty-first century. Women not only have the right to vote now, but most of us have even learned how to get along in this world without a great big macho man to take care of us."

With one final, contemptuous glare, she whirled around and stomped off toward the entrance doors of the hospital.

Chapter Thirty

The moment Charlotte climbed inside her van, she jerked off the wig and tossed it on the floor. Switching on the dome light, she leaned forward and peered into the rearview mirror. The reflection she saw made her groan. She looked awful, with her flattened-out hair and too-dark makeup. Wishing she'd brought along a brush, she tried finger-combing her hair, but finally gave up. What difference did it make, anyway? she thought. There was no one to see her, no one to impress with how she looked . . . not anymore.

With one last glare at the wig on the floor, she switched off the dome light and cranked the van. If she never saw the thing again, it would be too soon. Not only had the wig made her head itch, but it was a stark reminder of how Louis Thibodeaux had tried to humiliate her. The minute she got home, she intended to stuff it in the garbage.

The drive home didn't take long, but as she wound her way through the dimly lit narrow streets that were all but deserted, she kept seeing the astonished look on the detective's face when she'd told him off.

There was something to be said for getting in the last

word. So why did she feel so rotten? she wondered. But Charlotte knew why. She knew exactly why.

Although his initial response had been enormously gratifying at the time, she'd violated two of her most sacred codes for living. She'd always tried her best to honor the Golden Rule. And for the most part, she'd always tried to turn the other cheek.

In Charlotte's opinion, though, living by those codes wasn't synonymous with being a doormat for anyone and everyone to walk on. If Louis Thibodeaux—or any other man, for that matter—thought they could bully her, then they had another think coming. Charlotte LaRue was no one's doormat.

Charlotte was able to hold on to her righteous indignation until she finally reached home. But doing so required energy, and Charlotte was running on empty.

By the time she walked through her front door, all she felt was hollow inside. When all was said and done, her would-be relationship with the detective was a drop in the bucket compared to the ruined lives of the Dubuisson family. Jackson was dead, Clarice was dying, Jeanne was in jail, and Anna-Maria . . . poor Anna-Maria was left to deal with all the ramifications.

After a quick check on Sweety Boy, Charlotte switched off the living-room lights and headed straight for her bedroom. What she needed was a good night's sleep. As she passed by her desk, the blinking light of her answering machine flashed like a tiny beacon in the semidarkened room.

All she could think about was how tired she was, and she was sorely tempted to ignore the infernal thing. But according to the digital number count, she'd had six phone calls.

Unease crawled up her spine. To have that many calls in the course of one evening could mean that something was wrong.

Charlotte shook her head. "And it could mean nothing," she muttered. But there was only one way to find out.

Charlotte switched on the desk lamp. When she finally

located a notepad and pen beneath a stack of mail, she hit the answering machine's PLAY button.

The first call was from Judith.

"Aunt Charley, when you get home, give me a call."

The machine beeped, and the next message played.

"Where are you, Auntie? It's after nine. Why haven't you called me?"

Again the machine beeped.

"Mom, Judith phoned me, and she's worried because you're not home. It's ten-thirty, and I'm beginning to get worried, too. Call me as soon as you get home."

"Oh, great," Charlotte murmured as the machine beeped. "Next thing I know they'll put out an APB on me."

The last three calls were hang-ups, but the digital voice of the answering machine revealed that they had come in at eleven and eleven-thirty. The last call had been made at twelve, just about the time that she'd been wrestling with Jeanne in the hospital elevator.

Charlotte shuddered, remembering the maniacal look in Jeanne's eyes as she'd held the scalpel. Hoping she wouldn't have nightmares about it, she glanced up at the cuckoo. It was almost one A.M.

Now what? she wondered. No matter which call she returned, she'd have to explain about the whole humiliating mess at the hospital. Hank would have a fit. Then she'd have to listen to a lecture from him. And Judith . . . Charlotte frowned. Since Judith was Louis Thibodeaux's partner, shouldn't she have been there tonight? So why wasn't she at the hospital, too? she wondered.

Charlotte tapped her fingers impatiently on the desktop. She'd think about all of that tomorrow, but right now, she needed to decide what to do about the phone messages. If she didn't call at least one of them, she would run the risk of both of them showing up on her doorstep.

Outside, a car door slammed shut, and Charlotte frowned. Then she heard another door slam shut.

Speak of the devil and he appears.

"No," she moaned the minute the old saying popped into her head. "Please say it ain't so."

Even expecting it, Charlotte jumped when the doorbell buzzed. Before she had time to push herself out of the chair, she heard her niece's muffled voice.

"Use the key, Hank."

The key jiggled in the lock, then the door swung open. Hank, with Judith close on his heels, burst into the room.

He flipped on the overhead light. "Mother! Didn't you hear us? Are you okay?"

Charlotte raised both hands. "I'm okay, I'm okay."

"My, God, Mother, what happened to you?"

"Auntie, what's wrong?"

"Don't use the Lord's name like that, Hank."

"Mother!"

Both of them kept staring at her strangely, and the longer they stared, the more uncomfortable Charlotte became. It was when she reached up and self-consciously smoothed back her hair that she recalled the earlier image of herself in the rearview mirror. No wonder they were staring as if she were some kind of weirdo.

Charlotte suddenly giggled. The more she thought about it, the funnier it became, and she began to laugh. When Hank and Judith frowned at the same time, it was almost as if they had coordinated their responses. Their worried looks only made matters worse, and Charlotte laughed even harder.

She was laughing so hard that her sides were beginning to hurt. Within reason she knew that her uncontrolled response was hysterical laughter, simply a release from all the tension of the evening, combined with exhaustion, but she couldn't seem to help herself.

Hank and Judith both rushed over to her. With Judith hovering close by, Hank felt her forehead. When he grabbed her wrist and tried to take her pulse, Charlotte was laughing so hard that tears streamed down her cheeks.

"I'm okay, son," she sputtered. "I promise that I'm okay." She waved him away. "Just give me a minute and I'll explain.

"I'll get her some water," Judith offered.

When Hank nodded, Judith rushed off toward the kitchen.

As Hank continued staring at her, Charlotte tried to get control of herself, but the serious expression on his face brought on a new burst of laughter.

He knelt down beside the chair and took her hands in his. "Mom, you need to calm down," he said gently.

It was the genuine concern in his tone as well as the tender way he held her hands that finally sobered her.

Judith returned with the water and handed it to Hank. "Here, Mom, drink this," he told her.

To humor him, she took the glass and drank a sip. Surprisingly, the water tasted good to her, and realizing just how thirsty she was, she drank it all.

"Better now?" he asked.

Charlotte nodded. "Let's sit over there." She motioned toward the sofa and chairs in the living room. Hank and Judith sat on the sofa, and Charlotte sat across from them in a chair.

"I'm sorry you were worried tonight," she said. "Now don't get me wrong. I appreciate your concern—I think it's really sweet." She centered her gaze on her son. "But I'm not an old woman who needs to be constantly checked on. Not yet, anyway."

Hank's mouth was already tight and grim, and she knew her mild reproof had hit its mark when his mouth tightened even more.

"I've still got a few good years left," she added.

"Auntie, I know it's really none of our business, but where were you tonight? And why are you dressed like that."

"You're right, hon. It is none of your business." Charlotte

smiled to soften her rebuke. "The truth is, I'm a bit reluctant to tell you. And I'm a little embarrassed. I guess you'll find out soon enough, though, and better it comes from me than someone else." She could just imagine the kind of spin that Louis Thibodeaux would put on the story. "But let me start from the beginning. Do you remember the night that we were going to eat at the Trolley Stop with your partner?"

Judith nodded. "The day that Jeanne escaped."

"Yes, and if you remember, I received a phone call at the restaurant just after we were seated."

Again Judith nodded. Taking a deep breath for courage, Charlotte told her niece and her son about the call from Jeanne. She also told them about her visit from Louis Thibodeaux earlier that day. "I already knew that Clarice wasn't expected to live much longer, but it was right after Louis got the call from you, Judith, that I began to realize that Jeanne might somehow know about her mother, too. It just made sense to me that she would try to see Clarice before she died."

"But you couldn't tell Louis because of the phone call."

"No—no, I couldn't, especially after he as much accused me of helping her escape to begin with."

Judith narrowed her eyes shrewdly. "So let me guess here. I'm guessing that you decided to disguise yourself and stake out the hospital."

Charlotte lowered her gaze and stared at her hands, clenched tightly in her lap. "Yes—yes I did."

"And Louis busted you and gave you a hard time."

Charlotte raised her head. "Not before I busted Jeanne, but how did you know?"

"I know because I know how Louis operates. I thought it was kind of strange that he insisted I needed a night off. He even offered to take any calls that came in. Now I know why. But get back to the part about busting Jeanne. I take it she showed up."

"Oh, she showed up, all right." And as Charlotte told about her harrowing experience in the elevator, Hank's face twisted into a horrified expression of disbelief and rage.

"You did what?" He jumped to his feet. "God Almighty, you could have been killed!" He advanced toward her. "What on earth possessed you to do such a thing? Why—"

"Don't—" Charlotte abruptly rose to face him. "Don't say another word. I've already heard it once tonight, and I'm in no mood to hear it again."

A muscle in his jaw twitched, and his mouth thinned into a line of disapproval as he glared at her. Charlotte lifted her chin and glared right back.

"Sit down, Cuz," Judith told him firmly. "Your mom is here, and obviously she wasn't hurt, so just sit down and let her finish."

Charlotte could almost see the wheels turning in her son's head. To his credit, he finally backed down, albeit reluctantly. But from the expression on his face, Charlotte figured she hadn't heard the last of it from him.

"There's really not much else to tell," she continued as Hank walked over to stare out the window. "Jeanne was arrested, but I don't know if they've caught Brian yet. One thing I do know, though. I'm very, very tired."

Judith pushed herself up off the sofa. "I think that's our cue." She walked over to Charlotte. "I'm glad you're okay, Auntie." She reached out and gave Charlotte a hug. "But next time—"

Charlotte shook her head and laughed. "There's not going to be a next time."

"Well, I certainly hope not," Hank said from across the room.

"Oh, put a sock in it," Judith told him. She turned and walked toward the front door. "Now give your mom a hug," she said when she passed him, "and let her get some sleep." She turned her head and winked at Charlotte. "Catching the bad guys is tough work."

Hank snorted his disapproval, but he retraced his steps back to Charlotte, and wrapping his arms around her, he hugged her. "I love you, Mom," he told her against her hair. After a moment, he released her. "Now get some rest." Then he grinned. "Doctor's orders."

Charlotte's heart melted. "I love you, too, sweetheart," she whispered.

Charlotte watched from the door until they got into their cars. Closing the door, she locked it, switched off the overhead lights and the desk light, and then made a beeline for the bedroom.

In the bathroom, she scrubbed off the makeup, undressed, and slipped into her pajamas. She'd just turned off the lamp and laid her head down on her pillow when the phone beside her bed rang.

"Now what?" she groaned. Figuring it had to be either a wrong number or a crank call, she decided to let the answering machine take the call.

"Aunt Charley, I know you're probably already in bed, but I thought you might like to know that I called Lou when I left. He said they caught Brian O'Connor. O'Connor was spotted cruising back and forth in front of the hospital right after they arrested Jeanne." There was a pause. "And by the way, I gave Lou a piece of my mind for keeping me out of the loop on this thing. Sweet dreams, Auntie."

Charlotte sighed and snuggled deeper beneath the covers. "That'll teach him to mess with the women in this family," she muttered with a smile.

Within minutes, she felt herself contentedly drifting off to sleep.

Please turn the page for an exciting sneak peek
of Barbara Colley's newest Charlotte LaRue mystery

DEATH TIDIES UP

coming soon in hardcover!

Charlotte had almost finished cleaning the last window in the living room when there was a sudden, earsplitting shriek from upstairs.

"Charrrrlotte!"

For a moment, she was too stunned to move as the sound echoed throughout the empty house.

Not a cry of pain, her mind registered, but terror. It was a cry of sheer terror.

"Charrrrlotte!"

Janet, Charlotte thought, her heart pounding. Janet was the one screaming out her name.

It was the thump-thump of running footsteps above her that finally jerked her into action. Was someone chasing Janet and Cheré? Were they in danger?

A weapon. She needed a weapon of some sort. Charlotte glanced frantically around the room. Nothing. There was nothing she could use except . . . her fingers tightened on the spray bottle of ammonia in her hand. *Better than nothing.*

Vaguely aware that Emily had bolted from the bathroom,

Charlotte dashed out into the hallway and sprinted for the stairs. "You stay down here," she shouted at Emily.

Halfway up the staircase, she met the other two women scrambling down.

"What on earth?" Charlotte cried. "What's going on?"

Janet was shivering so hard she could barely talk. Crowded close behind her, Cheré's face was drained of color, and her dark eyes were wide with horror.

"D-dead," Janet stuttered, her voice cracking. "I—I turned on th-the light, and th-there's a dead man in-in the closet.

A dead man . . . dead . . . Charlotte's stomach turned queasy, and she heard Emily utter a startled cry from the foot of the stairs.

"Okay, okay, hon." Charlotte squeezed Janet's arm. "Now just calm down. Are-are you sure—sure he's dead?"

"Well he's not moving," Janet cried. "An-and I don't th-think he's breathing."

Charlotte squeezed her arm again. "But you don't know for sure." Janet shook her head with short, jerky motions.

Cheré shuddered. "He-he looked dead to me," she whispered.

"But neither of you felt for a pulse?" One look at the horrified expressions on their faces told her they hadn't. "No, of course you didn't." She took a deep breath, and though she was already pretty sure what the answer would be, she asked anyway. "Which apartment—which one were you cleaning?"

"The one to the left of the landing," Cheré told her.

Charlotte swallowed hard. It was the same one, the one she'd found the food sacks in during her walk-through, the one that had the toothpaste smeared in the bathroom sink. "Which room?"

"The m-master bedroom," Janet whispered. "He-he's in the walk-in closet."

Charlotte knew what she had to do. Whether she wanted

to or not—and she most definitely did not want to—she was going to have to check it out for herself. What if the man wasn't really dead? What if he was just unconscious and needed help?

"Okay, here's what we're going to do," she told them. "You two join Emily downstairs while I go check. And here—" She handed Janet the bottle of ammonia. "Take this with you." Then she pulled her cell phone from her pocket and thrust it at Cheré. "You take this and call the police. Be sure and ask for my niece."

Cheré took the phone. "But Charlotte!"

Charlotte shook her head. "It'll be okay. Just go." Willing her legs to move, she squeezed past the two women and hurried up the remaining stairs.

Once she was inside the apartment though, she hesitated at the door to the master bedroom to catch her breath.

A sleeping bag was spread out in the middle of the room on the floor. Near the foot of the sleeping bag was an open duffel with clothes spilling out of it, and in the midst of the clothes was a small camera, one of the disposable kinds, she noted. And beside the camera were several pictures scattered about.

"Weird," she murmured. For one thing, the sleeping bag and the duffel bag both looked almost brand new. And expensive. *And don't forget the toothpaste in the sink.*

It was just as she'd suspected, she thought, eyeing the dark green sleeping bag. Someone, probably the man in the closet, *had* been camping out in the empty house after all.

With a heavy feeling of dread Charlotte moved farther into the room. Maybe she'd been wrong about the homeless angle after all. But if the man in the closet wasn't a homeless person, then who was he? And why had he been camping out in the old house?

The walk-in closet door was open. A wave of apprehension swept through her as she edged nearer the opening. Any minute she expected to see a hand or foot or some evidence of a body. But there was nothing yet, nothing but an odd-looking, half-smoked cigar that had been ground out into the floor.

Charlotte took the last two steps that would bring her to the closet door. Swallowing hard, she leaned forward and peeked around the door.

"Oh, dear Lord," she whispered, as she reached out and grabbed the door frame to steady herself. The man was in the back corner of the closet, half-sitting, half-slumped sideways against the wall.

The Amanda Hazard Series
By Connie Feddersen